MW01140902

To Ashley
I love you.

Jeannette K. Leigh

2015

PAST
AND
FUTURE

PAST
AND
FUTURE

Jeannette K. Leigh

Library of Congress Control Number:		2015913024
ISBN:	Hardcover	978-1-5035-9459-3
	Softcover	978-1-5035-9458-6
	eBook	978-1-5035-9457-9

Print information available on the last page.

Rev. date: 08/18/2015

To order additional copies of this book, contact:
Xlibris
1-888-795-4274
www.Xlibris.com
Orders@Xlibris.com
719441

CHAPTER 1

Adri was impatient with the idea that she had been called to jury duty. That didn't mean she wasn't willing to serve if picked. She was willing but had so many negative opinions about men, and the defendant in the case was a man. Besides, it was such a beautiful spring day, and she would rather be working on new arrangements in her business. She sighed in resignation as she parked her car and got out.

The light breeze was a little cool now but would feel really nice as the temperature warmed up. The breeze gently ruffled the ends of her hair that hung midway down her back and the bottom of her long old-fashioned skirt as she walked toward the main sidewalk leading up to the courthouse. As she was looking around to spot the signs of spring, she noticed a sporty silver convertible pull up to the curb a short distance away. There was a man with chocolate brown hair parking and was in the process of raising the roof as she turned to approach the court house door.

As she opened the large glass door, she turned to take one last breath of fresh air and admire the spring blossoms around the courthouse lawn. She noticed the man had gotten out of the convertible and noticed he was tall and well built and had just enough length to his hair to have to smooth it into place after driving with the top down.

Adri didn't usually take any real notice of men in general, except to turn away and ignore them. In her experience, she had found men to be annoyingly full of themselves or real jerks toward women in general. She had a father of the first type and a brother of the second type. She had been relieved when they had decided to remove their unpleasant selves to the West Coast, three thousand miles away from West Virginia. The one man she had dated turned out to be a jerk of a different kind.

Funny how strange thoughts came and went today. Adri thought she was content in her life, but all the distasteful things kind of took her off guard all of a sudden on this perfect spring day.

Adri found herself on the third floor of the courthouse where the court rooms were. She slowly walked toward the window where the clerk was checking off the list of people who were checking in for jury duty selection. There were three ahead of her. As she stepped forward for her turn, she felt a presence behind her.

Adri smiled and gave her name. "Good morning, Adrianne M. Winfield."

The clerk didn't look up but asked. "Is that 1911 Dover Lane?"

"No, sir, I am at 1119 Dover Lane."

Now he looked up and grinned. "We have another Adriaan M. Winfield on the list and must live next door to you."

There was movement behind Adri as the man raised his hand and said in an amazingly deep voice. "That would be me at 1911 Dover Lane."

Adri felt shivers run up her spin as she turned, and even though she was tall, she had to look up slightly to meet his eyes. Her light blue eyes collided with shockingly dark brown smiling eyes.

Adri now felt a pleasant shiver go down her spine, and she quickly turned back as the clerk spoke. "I need to see identification." Adri reached in her shoulder bag and pulled out her wallet and showed her driver's license. The clerk nodded and asked her to step aside.

Adriaan, the man, stepped up and presented his driver's license; and as the clerk nodded, he followed Adri to a far wall. He stepped in too close, he guessed, as Adri moved away from him a couple of steps. He smiled, and an eyebrow went up as he spoke. "Let me guess. You go by Adri, and you have Adri's Attic Antiques."

She smiled shyly. "Yes, that's right."

Adriaan saw that she relaxed slightly, so he said, "My middle initial is *M* for Maxwell, and I don't go by Adriaan but go by Max."

Adri smiled, ducked her head a little, and then looked up with a blush of pink in her cheeks as she held out her hand. "Pleased to meet you, Max." They shook hands, and Adri wished she could stop the flush of warmth that went radiating up to her arm, to her neck, coloring her cheeks, pinker still. She quickly withdrew her hand and clasped both her hands in front of her. "How strange is this? Two Adrian Winfields with the same middle initial called to jury duty and next-door neighbors on the same road."

"I was thinking the same thing. What does your *M* stand for?" Max asked softly.

"Margaret."

"There are a few minutes yet before they'll call us in. I have a question about your business." Adri nodded and again smiled shyly. "Does Adri's Attic Antiques have larger furniture or just smaller items that would truly come out of attics?"

Adri laughed happily, her enthusiasm building on her favorite subject. "I love the surprised look on people's faces when they walk in and see all the big pieces! I have a marvelously large building, and I pick up a lot at auctions. So the answer is yes, I have furnishings and so much more."

Max was delighted with her laugh as it gave him a breathless feeling. When he felt he had his breath back, he smiled as he asked, "Do you do antique furniture restoration also?"

"I used to, but it took up too much time and energy to do it all myself. I try to get only antiques in good condition, but when there is a really magnificent piece, I might still get it and pay to have it restored. I have an aunt who lives nearby that still does restoration. She taught me how to do it." Adri's enthusiasm bubbled over. Then she felt embarrassed and looked down self-consciously and then up shyly as her cheeks took on the pink blush. "Probably more than you wanted to know."

Max gave her a gentle smile. His sense of her told him he needed to be gentle. "Your passion for the antique world is fascinating. I have always appreciated the continuance of family possessions being passed down from generation to generation. That is the true attraction of antiques, I think, and if they could talk, the stories they could tell!"

"Yes! I look up family histories when I know where the antiques come from, and it really is interesting to find out the connections!" Adri responded excitedly.

Max laughed softly just as the clerk called for attention. Max whispered, "I'd love to hear more."

The clerk instructed the group of people about the approaching jury selection process.

As the forty or so people began to file into the court room, Adri joined in the line, and Max stood back to let a small group of women proceed ahead of him. When seated in the galley, Adri was seated at the isle on the right, three rows back, and Max was at the isle on the left, two rows back.

Even though Adri had never been a part of the jury selection process, she was having a hard time keeping her full attention on the proceedings. Every time Max was in her line of vision, her thoughts had a tendency to stray.

He has such a rugged profile, but his face is very pleasant. Wonder if his name is of Dutch origin? Probably. Why am I even thinking this way? Men are not something I am interested in! But Max . . . he seemed to be really interested in what I had to say. I need to be careful—I know how bad it hurts to be misused by men.

Her attention came back to the court room when Max was in the next group to go for selection. *Wonder what number they're on. How many have they chosen?*

She did her best to pay attention. Max was the second to the last of this group of twelve questioned. Adri gave her full attention to the questions and the answers Max gave and continued to be fascinated by the depth of his voice. When he answered that he read a lot of newspapers and certainly had an idea of what the media was saying about this case, or certainly any case, the defense attorney rejected him as a potential juror. She still didn't know how many jurors had been chosen, so she was starting to get nervous that she might have to serve.

Adri continued to pay close attention as the next person was questioned. Both attorneys agreed on this individual. The judge thanked everyone for their presence and dismissed all but the twelve jurors that were picked and the one alternate. When Adri realized she wouldn't be called up, she sighed, and her shoulders relaxed. *Knowing the defendant is a man, I would not have been an impartial juror. And I really couldn't close the showroom all week or however long this trial would last. I've really left it too long, hiring more help. I'm glad this is over.*

Max saw Adri's reaction as he was standing to leave. *She was nervous about this. Wonder why?* Max lengthened his stride to make sure he didn't lose sight of Adri. *Of course, with that beautiful long blond hair, she should be easy to spot anywhere. And she's tall for a woman. That's nice.* He was free all afternoon and wondered if he could talk her into lunch and a tour of her antique shop.

There were two other ladies going down the indoor steps to the entrance floor behind Adri. Max was a flight behind. When Adri reached the end of the steps, Max called out to her quietly.

"Adri."

There was no mistaking who called her name, and she stopped and turned, then stepped aside as the two behind her proceeded to the front entrance. As Max reached the bottom step, she gave a puzzled smile. "Yes?"

He smiled and asked, "Is there a chance you would be free to join me for lunch? I would really enjoy hearing more about your antiques."

Adri's smile faded, and a guarded look came across her face.

Max was puzzled by her hesitation.

She spoke hesitantly. "I'm not sure . . ." She let the sentence trail off.

There were more people coming down the stairs now, so Max gently took her elbow and urged her toward the door. "Let's talk outside."

Adri's elbow tingled where Max touched, and she nodded. She went through the door as Max released her elbow to hold the door open. Adri went down the front steps and led the way to a corner of the wide sidewalk. She stopped, turned to Max, and waited for him to speak.

Max studied her for a moment. She was still guarded.

"Perhaps we should skip lunch, and I'll just come look at you antiques about two o'clock this afternoon. I live in a big house, and I moved from a condo, so there are a lot of rooms begging for classic furnishings."

Adri's face lost the guarded look. She smiled hesitantly and answered, "That would be fine. You could bring your wife and pick out some things."

Max felt relief slide through him. *She thinks I'm married!* He smiled and said gently. "No wife, no kids. There is just me and my housekeeper." He saw her shoulders relax, so he continued. "My primary interest at the moment is the master's bedroom. There was no way I would put condo furniture in such a large and elegant room."

Adri didn't understand the giddy feelings she experienced when he said there was no wife. She wished her past experiences weren't so tainted. He seemed to be a very nice and proper person, but she didn't know him and certainly didn't think she trusted any of his motives, as the ghosts from the past made her cautious, even as nice as he seemed. But in her place of business, she could handle it, she thought, she hoped.

She finally answered, "I have several different sets, American and European styles that would go well into a large and elegant room." Now she smiled a genuine smile.

Max caught his breath. Her smile extended to her eyes, and one eyebrow lifted slightly with the smile. "I look forward to seeing what you have. Be aware, though, I know what I like. I just don't know what goes together."

Adri laughed happily again. "I won't let you make any really bad mistakes!" Max enjoyed the musical sound of her laugh and again felt breathless.

Max pulled a small puff of air into his lungs and laughed too. The laugh rumbled deep in his chest. Adri shivered slightly at the sound.

"I'm glad. I plan to make this my home for a long time, and I'd like it to be right!"

Adri turned to go. "I'll see you at two."

Max said to her back. "Thank you." And he turned too but held back. She didn't seem to want him to walk with her, and he didn't want to seem too familiar, in case it scared her.

Adri was glad that she was so organized in her style arrangements. It would be a simple task to help Max pick out what he would need for a master's bedroom. She had a feeling she didn't want to spend too much time with Max. Remembering how distracted she had been in the court room and the train of thought she had, well, she was pretty sure that spending time with Max would be very distracting. She remembered too the tingles and blushes when he touched her. She recognized the turmoil roiling in her stomach as she thought about letting a man close.

It was bad enough that they were next-door neighbors. She didn't know if that meant she would see a lot of him, and she just wasn't sure she was ready for that.

Adri accomplished an errand in town and grabbed a quick sandwich at home before she went out to her antique world. She walked around and moved a few smaller pieces in with the bedroom sets and placed some oil paintings with the arrangements to give decorative accents. She looked at her watch. One forty-five. Max would be here shortly. She went to her office near the entrance to wait for her customer.

CHAPTER 2

Max went straight home and checked in with his housekeeper, Betty Ozlow. She hadn't expected him for lunch, but she would have something ready in thirty minutes.

Max went to the library of the large house. One end was his office where he did his writing. The rest of the library was just a big empty space. He looked at the whole room and decided he really needed to get something in here as well. He appreciated that the previous owners had left the window dressings, so furniture and wall décor was what he really needed.

These were things he was pretty sure Adri would gladly help him with. *Adri seemed so different after the jury selection was over. It was like she wanted to run but instead put up a guard wall to block me out. She was so friendly and enthusiastic when talking about her antiques and her work. But she put up the guard on a more personal level. Has she had bad experiences with men in the past? I know she fascinates me, and I am attracted to her. I would like to find out who she is deep down. She is beautiful! I am so tired of being alone. Eight years is a lot of alone.*

It had been a little past eight years since the love of his life lost her life to cancer. At that time, he thought he would probably spend the rest of his life alone, but he had bought this house and made this move because of a deep restlessness and loneliness. He hoped he could find something to occupy some of his time. Grinding out one novel after another wasn't enough anymore.

Max shook his head to clear it. He was still standing in the center of the library and needed to rearrange his desk and put research files away. He had all but a pile of files finished when Betty brought his tray with lunch.

He put the tray on his desk, this one piece of furniture that was truly a part of his own heritage as it was passed to him by his dad who had received it from his dad. On thinking about the desk, Max wondered if Adri could tell him some more about it, as he did not know where it was made or who made it. After looking at the tray to see what he would be eating, he turned to his computer. He was going to do some research on Adri. *Wonder how many ways you can spell Adriaan? Her spelling should be different than mine. Maybe she has a web page in Antiques. That may be a simpler way.*

Max set his search engine in motion. Sure enough. Adrianne Winfield of Adri's Attic Antiques came up. He read her history. She had been on this web page almost five years. Her business had always been at this address. He guessed she would be twenty-six maybe, four years younger than he was. With the correct name spelling, he looked for her under her name.

It was sketchy at best. She graduated from high school in a small town nearby. So she isn't living in her family home. That struck Max as sad, since she was so immersed in antiques and the history of the pieces she acquired.

Adri graduated college with a business administration degree at Northwest University. West Virginia was her place of birth and residence. Only three address changes: her family home, the home of Dixie Winfield, and her current address.

He almost missed an attachment. When he went to it, it was a newspaper article. The photo in the article was an astonishing likeness of Adri. He found the headline shocking.

DAVIES OIL EMPIRE HEIRESS COMMITS SUICIDE
Margaret Agnes (Davies) Winfield died at the age of twenty-nine by her own hand at Winfield Manor in Davenport, West Virginia, on the twenty-third of May 1993. She was the only child of Jonathan Davies, Oil Barron, and his wife Agnes (Williams) Davies of Dallas, Texas. Both parents preceded her in death. Margaret was born May 23, 1964, in Dallas.

Her sister-in-law, Constance, and husband, Carlton Basser, discovered the body in the master's bedroom of Winfield Manor at about 9:00 a.m. on Wednesday, May 23.

Chester E. Winfield, husband of the deceased, was on an extended fishing trip in the Caribbean. The deceased's children: Charles S., age 12; and Adrianne M., age 10, were away at boarding school in Charleston.

One other living relative is Dixie Winfield of West Virginia.

Max was stunned. *At ten years of age, Adri lost her mother in a tragic way. She spoke of her aunt that lived nearby. That would be Dixie. Dixie had probably played a big part in her growing-up years. How does a ten-year-old deal with that kind of event? It couldn't have been easy.*

Max shook his head. Even for a writer, he was having a hard time dealing with the information he had gained. He almost wished he didn't know all this. Upon finishing his lunch, he picked up the tray and carried it to the kitchen and told Betty his plans for the afternoon. Then he went back to the library and finished his filing.

Max leaned back in his office chair and looked up. His desk now faced the window at this end of the room. Without the trees, he guessed that he would be able to see Adri's place, as his house was on a slight incline. Even though his career was writing books, he loved the great outdoors. Being in the country now gave him lots of space to spend outdoors. He had already discovered the overgrown path that went down the hill toward Adri's place. He had discovered the cutout in the hedge dividing the properties but had not looked through.

Max checked the clock. One thirty. Should he walk or drive? He decided to walk. He would enjoy the exercise, and maybe it would clear his head of the sadness that had settled over him. Before he left the library, he whispered a quick prayer. *God, you have been my strength for a lot of years now, and I believe I may have an influence on Adri. Give me your wisdom. I believe you brought her into my life. Help me to be sensitive to where she's at in her emotional and spiritual life. You are a mighty God, and I trust your direction in my life and in Adri's life. Amen.*

Max went to change into jeans and a casual knit shirt. He took his time going down the path that led to Adri's place. Some of the overgrowth was a little difficult to maneuver through, so he was glad he didn't have to hurry. He decided that as soon as his most recent novel was finished, he would clear this path for easier access.

When Max came to the opening in the hedge, he hesitated. Would Adri consider this an invasion of her privacy? When he had discovered the opening, he had not looked through, so he did not know where it would come out on the other side. Should he go back and take the road? Or get his car? He looked at his watch. If he changed his mind now, he would be late. He decided to take the chance. He had to bend over to get through the hedge.

As he came out on Adri's property, what he saw took him by surprise. About thirty yards from the hedge, he saw the back side of a prefabricated house. It was one story, and it couldn't be more than three thousand six hundred square feet. By house standards around here, that was small.

There was a privacy fence that winged out both directions from the front of the house. The fence to his left went all the way to a curve in the hedge. The closer fence curved slightly and stopped at a blue spruce tree. There was a wide opening between the tree and another curve in the hedge. Max stepped around the tree and was pleasantly surprised at the view. There was a green lawn that stretched to the drive. There were small trees scattered across the lawn space.

As he moved toward the front of the house, he found another surprise. From the front, the house had an antique look. Not overstated but pleasing, supposedly to add to the general look of antiquity to the place in general.

As Max looked toward the road, he saw the entrance gate that he drove past whenever he went anywhere and the sign announcing the business. Looking the other direction, he saw a short drive that led to a double-car garage. Past the garage, a shed was partially visible. The building occupying the rest of the clearing across the drive was very large and again faced with the antique look the way the house was. Above the centered middle doors was the sign announcing, Adri's Attic Antiques. There was a good-sized parking area in front of the building.

As Max went down the slopped lawn toward the drive, he thought about how impressive this looked. It pretty much announced antiquity and simplicity. Just the setting gave Max insight into Adri.

When Max opened one of the solid wood antique doors to the building, a soft bell announced his arrival. He paused to let his eyes adjust to the dimness of the building and then called out.

"Adri, it's Max."

Adri observed Max as he stepped in and again saw the rugged profile but also noticed his broad shoulders and how the shirt he wore stretched slightly over the muscled shoulders and arms. There was a soft laugh to Max's right. He turned. Adri was standing in the doorway of what appeared to be an office. She spoke. "I know." She moved toward him. "I saw you come in, but I didn't hear your car." She was smiling.

Max smiled. "I walked. Weather is too nice to waste."

Adri continued to smile, but a puzzled look crossed her face. "If you came by the road, I still would have known you were here."

Max looked puzzled now. "How would you have known?"

"The front gate has a motion sensor. Any movement through the gate is announced with a buzzer." Adri had a puzzled frown now.

Max said softly. "Smart lady." He sobered. "Now I have a confession. I walked down the hill on a path that comes to your back hedge, where there is a cutout space in the hedge."

Adri's puzzled look became a look of surprise. "There's a path from your place?" Max nodded. "I had forgotten about the hole in the hedge." The look of surprise was replaced by the guarded look. *Who is this guy? He assumes I will accept that kind of intrusion?* Adri took a deep breath and turned partially away from Max. She took another deep breath before she turned back. She didn't meet his gaze but said, "Okay. You came in the back way. Now that you are here, you are welcome to browse, or I can give you a guided tour, whichever you prefer."

Max realized his mistake. He had intruded on her personal space. He spoke softly. "Adri, I apologize for using the back way. I wasn't thinking. I am so sorry." He paused. The guarded look was still there. He sighed inwardly and tried again. "I'll leave by the front gate."

Adri just turned away and suggested, "How about a guided tour of the bedroom sets?"

Max agreed, "That would be nice. Thank you."

Max followed Adri through a small aisle between every kind of occasional table a person could imagine. He wasn't really looking at the furniture, as his thoughts occupied him. *Tread softly. I have to remember that. What I read about her still didn't tell me why she is so guarded around me. Lord, give me insight into how I need to behave around Adri. I don't want to keep messing up.*

Adri stopped as she passed into a space that was obviously a bedroom arrangement. "These are the largest pieces and bulky in size, colonial in style. Even though the bed frame is not a match with the chests and accessories, it is certainly appropriate in this setting." Adri moved to the next arrangement but stood still and quiet as Max circled through the first set.

As Max moved to join her in the next set, Adri continued, "These are French in origin, and this is a complete set. The next arrangement is also French mix and match."

Adri stopped and watched as Max moved around the French setting, walking from piece to piece and looking at them. He moved more slowly through both of the French sets.

Max asked, "What else do you have?"

Adri led the way to a new setting. "This and the next are British in origin. The last is Italian."

Again, she stopped and watched. Max again moved through, more quickly in the British sets. These were more ornate, and he didn't like the look. The Italian set was very different, light in color and seemingly smaller, and he really wasn't sure how he felt about this last one. Max turned to Adri and smiled. "Definitely not the British and probably not this one. May I just browse back through the others?"

She nodded. "Just call out if you have questions." Adri turned and worked her way back to her office.

As she sat down slowly in her office chair, she wondered what she was going to do. *He feels comfortable enough to come in the back way, or is he just enough of a jerk to assume any intrusion is acceptable? Hopefully it is the first. He did apologize, and I could see by his expression he regretted his choice and was truly sorry. If I blocked the hedge, it would be an obvious snub, and I sure don't want to do that to a potential customer. He seems nice and decent! And why do I even care? My experience with men is that they just think of themselves and will walk away when their use of me doesn't matter anymore.* Adri sighed and rubbed her forehead.

But I am twenty-seven years old, and I just realized recently that my closest friends are my yard lady and the guys that make my deliveries for me. They try so hard to be my friends, but I really don't let them in. All right, Adri, admit it. You are lonely. God, why are you changing my life now? I thought I had moved past all the junk. Yet just this morning, I was thinking about my father and brother AND all the negatives. Of course, you know I really don't have any positive memories of either one of them. Well, I'm not sure I am open to a change, so, God, you will have to help me work this out. I really haven't trusted you about much since—well, you know how long it's been.

Adri was suddenly aware that Max had called out her name. She got up quickly and stepped out just as he came out of the colonial arrangement. She took a deep breath to evacuate the remainder of her thoughts and smiled as she walked toward Max.

"Did you have questions?"

Max was glad to see her smile, and he smiled in return. "Yes. I am having a hard time deciding. Maybe if I give you some information, you could give me your opinion."

Adri shrugged. "I am very conservative in giving my opinion. But go ahead."

Max's smile broadened. "Have you been inside my house, by any chance?" Adri shook her head no. "Okay. The master's bedroom has two large windows facing east. There would be room for two wardrobe chests or the bed between them with space to spare. The drapes in that room are medium-colored beige with a design that I can't describe. The walls are egg shell—at least I think that is the color with a wine-colored paper trim near the ceiling." Max took a breath. "Can you picture any of this?"

Adri laughed. "You are going to ask me what would look best in that room, except I don't know what you prefer, and you are leaving out too much detail." She smiled softly and then asked, "Which arrangement are you leaning toward?"

"I really like the colonial, but I think the bulkiness would overwhelm the room. My next choice is the French, but I'm not sure all the dark color would go with the décor, and I have no intention of changing that. Oh, and that bedroom is carpeted and has a fireplace. I guess I could go take some pictures . . ." Max was frowning by the time he got to the end of his thinking.

Adri could see that he was really at a loss. *Can I offer—but what would that mean—well, it's not like I haven't done it for others.* She smiled shyly and sighed. "Pictures would not do the room justice. I will offer my opinion on one condition."

Max's face brightened. "What's the condition?"

"That you don't blame me if you end up not liking it. Of course, I am a dealer and will take returns, but that will cost you." There was mischief in her smile at the end.

Max laughed softly. "I can handle that."

Adri laughed too. "Okay." *Well, here I go, and please don't let it be a mistake.* She ducked her head and then looked up, and there was color in her cheeks as she said shyly, "The best solution would be for me to come to your house and see the master's bedroom in person. I do that from time to time for my good clients."

The surprise on Max's face showed that this was the last thing in the world he expected. Her offer to come over to his house surely was outside her comfort zone.

There was a slight pause, and then he asked, "You would be willing to come take a look?"

Adri was aware of his surprise, and she was touched that he would be sensitive enough to be surprised after her past behavior. She was able to respond with a friendly reserve.

"Yes. I guess your housekeeper is there? And my best opinion could only be given if I see it."

Max exhaled slowly and then drew in a breath. "Yes, my housekeeper is there and would be very happy to know that I am getting help in this department." Max paused, and then with hesitation, he added, "I have one more room you could look at while you are there, if you are willing."

Adri smiled shyly and shrugged. "Why not? I have time right now."

Max felt his heart beat increase. He wondered if she had decided to trust him. *God, please help me not offend her in any way.* "I have time today too."

"Okay. Let me lock this place up, and we'll take my car to your house." Adri's stomach churned at this suggestion. This was a huge step out of her comfort zone. *Riding with a stranger in my car and trusting him to be telling the truth about someone else being there at his house.*

Max hesitated and then asked softly, "You don't mind giving me a ride?"

Adri blinked quickly and then looked directly into his beautiful dark brown eyes. She saw the gentle question there too. She pulled in a deep breath and felt the color creeping up her neck as she hesitated and then whispered, "I think it will be okay." Then she ducked her head and turned toward her office to close up and darken the showroom.

CHAPTER 3

$\mathbf{A}$s Adri pulled her car around the circle drive at Max's house, she asked as she slowed at the front door. "Is it okay for me to park here?"

"Yes. This is good."

As Max and Adri exited the car, Adri concentrated on the exterior of the house. It was beautiful! It had two-story columns along the entire front of the house. The veranda ran the whole length as well. Adri smiled.

"This is beautiful! I hadn't seen this house up close."

Max smiled. "I like it. Kind of gives the impression of gentle southern living."

They moved up the three shallow steps to the veranda.

Max said softly, "I have a question."

Adri ducked her head and then looked up at him, the pink blush appearing before she asked.

"You want to know why I offered to come here." Again, she surprised him, and he couldn't hide it. *His face is so honest. I think I can tell him.* She told him, "Your apology. You made an honest mistake and made an honest apology. It was something that a good person would do." She ducked her head again, and the blush deepened as she said shyly, "I would like to have your business and maybe get to know you as my neighbor." *Wow! I didn't know I was going to say that!*

Max felt like the wind had been knocked out of him by a linebacker. Not only had she opened up, but she had also introduced a wish for some kind of neighborly relationship. He walked up to the front door before he spoke.

"Adri, I recognize that I, for some reason, make you uncomfortable, but I am trying to tread softly. I recognize that you must have your reasons, and I respect that. So I ask that you tell me when I am about to step into quicksand. We really don't know each other."

Max opened the door, and Adri moved a step closer to Max and looked directly into his eyes as she solemnly answered, "I'll try to not overreact, but sometimes *I* am surprised by what bothers me. I have had some really bad experiences with men." *Please—I hope I didn't say too much this time!*

Max swallowed and murmured softly, "I'm sorry." Adri just ducked her head and stepped into the house.

As she stepped away from Max, she scolded herself. *Get your mind off those wonderful eyes and pay attention to business!* Adri looked around the large entry.

"What a peaceful entry. With a few additions, it would be very welcoming."

Max smiled as he sensed Adri relax a little. "Additions? Like what?"

Adri laughed, a little nervously. "This is just my opinion, okay?" Max nodded. "An old-fashioned boot bench there and a long, slender table with a mirror mounted here. An umbrella stand and a coat hook frame here. And maybe a large potted plant—real or fake, over there."

Max had pulled out a small spiral notebook from his jeans pocket and was writing quickly. When he stopped writing, he asked, "I guess you have all of that at your place?"

"Um-hum—except the plant. One more thing, a small round or square occasional table by the bench to set things on if you walk in with dirty boots and your hands are full."

Max laughed. "I can't just dump everything on the bench?"

"No. How will you put your dirty boots away?" This time there was mischief in her smile.

Max stopped laughing. "Oh. I didn't think of that."

Now Adri laughed. Max asked, "Is that all for this space?"

"I think so. Lead on to the master's bedroom." As Adri gave the command, Max's housekeeper came out from the kitchen.

Betty exclaimed, "We do have company! I was sure I heard voices out here, and I knew Max didn't talk to himself *that* loud!"

Adri smiled at Max. "You talk to yourself?"

Max grinned, almost boyish. "I do. Don't you?"

Adri just laughed. Max introduced them.

"Betty, this is Adri, from Adri's Attic Antiques. Adri, this is Betty Ozlow, my domestic engineer."

Betty laughed. "Pleased to meet you, Adri. And I'm his housekeeper and cook."

Adri smiled and said, "I am pleased to meet you. May I call you Betty?" Betty nodded. "And my birth certificate says I am Adrianne Margaret Winfield."

Betty covered her mouth with her hand as she gasped. She looked from Adri to Max and said in a muffled voice, "Two Adriaan M. Winfields?"

Max laughed. "We were amazed too. And we live next door to each other!"

Betty laughed now. "I guess you can expect your mail to get mixed up. What a deal!"

They all laughed. Betty spoke. "It is about time Max gets some decent furniture. At least, I guess you are here to tell him what he needs, and it'll be from your wonderful antiques!"

Max sighed and raised an eyebrow as he looked at Adri and spoke. "See, she confirms that I am hopeless with these kinds of choices. She has hated my 'condo furniture' from the moment she first saw it. Told me I had no taste."

Betty confirmed that. "He has no sense of good furniture and quality. Since you work with antiques, I'd say you have enough good sense to get him set up with real quality."

Adri blushed and laughed. "I am here to give my opinion. He still has to decide if he will follow my lead."

Betty shook a finger at Max. "You listen to Adri. Such a pretty name to use! And you, young lady"—she briefly touched Adri's arm—"don't hesitate to give him what-for. He needs all the help he can get!" She brushed her hands together and then added, "Go on now. I have work to do." And she hurried back into the kitchen.

There was longing on her face when she gave a shy smile as she spoke. "She's like family to you, isn't she?"

Max saw the longing, and he responded quietly, "Yes. We bonded the first time we met. Betty is a widow with grown children and grandchildren, and she is completely content to be busy. She says it keeps her from getting old."

Max turned them toward the staircase and pointed. As they started up the staircase, Adri asked, a little self-consciously, "Do you know her family?"

"Oh yes. Her yearly bonus is to have all her family come to visit, and I pick up the tab. She loves it, and so do they. So I get included a lot."

There was hesitancy and longing in her voice. "That sounds great!" They reached the top of the steps, and Max led the way to the master's bedroom just across the hall from the top of the stairs. He opened the door and let Adri go in ahead of him.

Adri turned around twice, getting the feel of the room. "With the light-colored walls and the medium color of the drapes, you need the dark French furniture. The colonial would shrink the room and make it seem crowded and overfilled. The dark color of the French would bring out the wine color at the top of the walls and in the drapes. The light rose-colored carpet is excellent!"

"In my own defense, I think I mentioned the colonial would overwhelm."

"You did. And you were right. The colonial style is wrong for the overall peacefulness of the room as well."

"What about arrangement? Where would you put the bed?"

"Between the windows." She walked around the edge. "Are you thinking the French set of furniture?" Max hesitated and then nodded. "You'll need two wardrobes to balance the room. That means I need to find you a second one." Adri gave her suggestions of how it could be arranged and what additional furniture he would need to give it the complete and cozy atmosphere desired in a bedroom. She informed him that the fireplace needed seating, two chairs and two tables.

Max wondered how wise it was but decided to ask. "Why two chairs and two side tables? There's only one of me."

Adri didn't laugh like he thought she would. Instead, she ducked her head, and there was a light blush on her cheeks when she raised her eyes and looked directly into his with a serious expression.

"For one thing, when you get married, your wife might enjoy sitting by the fire with you."

Max tilted his head and commented, "Well, then, it should be a love seat, not chairs. And what makes you think I'm going to get married?"

Adri blushed really pink, ducked her head, and fumbled with her blouse buttons. Max recognized how uncomfortable that question made her and was about to back up and apologize when she looked up, the challenge still in her eyes.

"A man like you should not be alone. Don't you want to be married?"

Max felt his heart skip a beat and then pick up to double time. He wanted to ask her if she was volunteering, but his instinct told him that would put him in the quicksand. Instead, he said quietly, "Thank you. And yes, I would like to marry again."

Adri's cheeks got pinker. She felt the need to escape, so she moved toward the door. *What was I thinking? Why would I say something like that to a man I hardly know? He could have thought I was hinting something. I wasn't. I'm through with men! Or am I? I am starting to like Max. He seems so different from other men I've encountered. I need to watch what I say.*

By the time her thoughts ended, she was at the top of the staircase.

Max recognized she needed a little space, so he let her go into the hall before he moved. As he came into the hall, he wondered if she would like to see more of the house.

"Adri, wait."

Adri turned from the steps, her face still flushed, her expression questioning. Max asked, "Would you like to see the rest of the upstairs? You really seem to be enjoying the parts you've already seen."

Adri smiled shyly. "Yes, I would like to see more."

Max used his head to point. "Most of it is back this way." Adri moved back toward him, and as she drew even, he moved to walk beside her. "I would like you to give your opinion on how these other rooms may have been used, if you don't mind."

Adri nodded and asked, "How they were used more recently, or how they may have been used in the distant past?"

Max laughed. "You really like to stump me. That may be one and the same, since it's been kept historically accurate, but I think I want to know about the past." He opened the next door down the hall but blocked it. "Please excuse the mess. This is where all my condo furniture was dumped that I am not using at the moment."

Adri smiled, and there was a teasing lilt to her voice. "So I'll get to see your taste in furniture too."

Max wasn't too enthused when he answered. "Yeah." Then he stepped aside.

Adri was still smiling as she swung around. "This isn't so bad. It's expensive and a very modern style. It's definitely not typical antique material."

Max laughed. "I think that was a backhanded compliment. After being in your showroom, I really don't like it much now."

Adri looked past the furniture at the room itself. "This was probably a young person's room. Someone past nursery stage and into the teens. That is, if the walls and drapes haven't been changed much."

"I know the drapes are less than a year old, but the realtor said that they were historically correct with what they replaced."

"In the whole house?"

"Yes."

"I think this would have been a girl's room." Adri moved to the door. "Next?"

Max closed the door behind him and moved across the hall. As Adri walked into this room, she knew immediately.

"This was the nursery." She walked over and opened a connecting door. "This is the nanny's quarters. There is another connecting door across the room, so that probably goes to the toddler room." She moved across the nanny quarters and opened the other door. "Yes, the toddler room."

Max moved up behind her and looked in. "Since you have identified these rooms, I can see it now."

"Didn't the realtor tell you all this?"

"No. He just told me the number of rooms and bathrooms on the second floor." Max pointed. "Let's go out that door."

Adri nodded and moved through the room toward the hall door. They moved to the next room beside the toddler room.

Max told her. "This is the room I am currently sleeping in." He opened the door.

Adri laughed merrily. "You are sleeping in the play room!"

Max grinned sheepishly. "I am?"

"Why?" Adri was still laughing.

"Because it was the room the most distance away from the rooms I thought I would fill first. And I thought since it was back in the corner, it would be the last room that would need to be emptied out."

Adri was just smiling now. "Okay, that makes sense. But there's no bathroom in here."

Max grinned. "There's one across the hall, and I have the upstairs to myself."

Adri blushed and changed the subject. "Since there are no closets, you kind of have a clothes storage problem." There were chairs lining one wall where different types of apparel were sorted and draped over the chair backs on hangers. There were a couple of chest of drawers also.

"Yeah. Betty is starting to complain. Guess I need to move in a wardrobe, quickly."

"Have you decided on the French set for sure, and when do you want it delivered?"

"Wow!" Max took a deep breath. "Yes, the matching French set. Delivery may need to wait until the weekend."

Adri smiled. "We'll work it out." Then she ducked her head and mumbled something that Max didn't catch. He wondered if he should ask and then decided to just carry on with the conversation.

"So you deliver?" Max grinned as Adri lifted her head and had a sweet, happy face.

"Yes, I have four guys that do shift work, and on their days off, they are more than happy to help with deliveries. I have my own truck too."

Max smiled softly. "That is service with a smile, I think!"

And maybe a surprise! Adri thought and then giggled.

Max asked, "What?" He was thrilled to see her enjoying herself, and the interaction was relaxed, much different than earlier today.

Adri just giggled again and shook her head. *Can't tell him I want to surprise him. I have never wanted to surprise anyone this way before!*

Max looked at his watch. "I am expecting a phone call in about fifteen minutes, so we need to finish up here."

Adri looked startled and asked, "What rooms are left here on the second floor?"

"The room across the hall and two rooms at the other end."

Her shoulders stiffened when she asked, "Would it be better if I leave now and finish the tour some other time?"

Max smiled and shook his head. "You need to finish the tour, unless you have to leave. I think Betty is probably planning on you staying for dinner."

Adri colored a little and remained tense. "Oh, she doesn't need to do that."

Max laughed. "She would be glad to have someone new sample her cooking. You would really disappoint her if you didn't stay." *Not to mention that I would be very disappointed.*

Adri's color was still high, but she sighed and said softly, "Okay. I'll stay. I think I would like that." Adri turned abruptly. "I want to look in this room." She moved across the hall and opened the door. After just looking in, she commented, "Yes, just as I thought, this would have been a boy's room." She closed the door and turned. "Let's see those last two rooms up here. Then you can get ready for your phone call."

Adri moved quickly down the hall. Max smiled and followed at a slower pace. *I think she was pleased to be invited for dinner. I know she was happy about finishing the tour. She is beautiful and so sweet and has such a childlike joy here in this house. God, you know my heart. I really like this woman, and I really hope this can be special.*

Adri had already looked at one room and was coming back down the hall to see the other. She told Max, "These rooms are just a little smaller, and I'm sure they are guest rooms. I know you're not crazy about the Italian style, but it would go perfect in that other room. And a smaller colonial set or a light-colored French set would go great in here with the dark walls." Adri was bubbling with her excitement. "This is a wonderful house! I am impressed with the subtle way the bathrooms were installed so as not to take away from the rooms at all!" She stopped abruptly in front of Max and asked, "Do you know when that remodeling was done?"

Max smiled. "The realtor did tell me that. The bathrooms were installed in the late thirties, and all the plumbing was updated ten years ago, keeping the décor and feel of the old-fashioned fixtures and squeezing in modern where possible."

"Well, I had located where the bathrooms were but hadn't actually looked in them." She laughed happily. "I'll see them next time!"

Max nodded slowly. *She said next time! She wants to come back.* He worked at keeping his voice even. "While I am in the library on the phone, you are welcome to roam through the rest of the house."

Adri gave him a shy, sweet smile. "Thank you. I don't have much opportunity to see the old houses from the inside. This is a special treat! What was the other room you wanted me to look at and help with?"

"The library. I have one corner occupied with my office area, but the rest is empty and feels forlorn." They had reached the bottom of the steps. "The library is back this way. That's where I'll be. I'll be talking to my publisher. He will probably put the pressure on for me to complete my current project this week, which means I couldn't move any furniture in until the weekend."

Adri's eyes widened. "You write?" Max nodded. "What do you write?"

Max grinned. "I write historical novels. Some adventure, some romance, some tragedy. I spend at least the first two weeks of my time doing research. I try to be historically accurate."

Adri's eyes grew wider. "Historically accurate? That's great!"

"It's one of the reasons I bought this house. I am so into history and wanted something that would fit me better." Max shrugged. "I was getting tired of being in the city too."

Adri smiled shyly. "We certainly have something besides our names in common. We live in the past, so to speak."

Max laughed softly. "That is why I was so fascinated this morning when you talked about researching the antiques. I certainly want to hear more about that sometime."

Adri blushed and then gave a shining smile. "We can talk about all that later. I want to see the rest of this marvelous house!"

Max laughed again. "Go for it! I may be a while." Max turned toward the library door, and Adri went the other direction.

CHAPTER 4

Max was smiling to himself as he walked into the library. *Adri is exactly right. We do have things in common. I hope at some point, she will trust me enough to talk about her personal past. If she could talk about her past, I may find the key to open her heart to me. God, I know you are working here. Help me to trust in your timing.*

Max's phone rang. It was his publisher.

Adri started toward the front of the house and then changed her mind and went toward the kitchen to find Betty. When she got to the kitchen, Betty was bent over the oven, pulling out a pan of dinner rolls. Adri spoke quietly as Betty set the pan on the counter.

"Hello."

Betty turned. "Hello, Adri. Were you looking for me?"

"Yes."

"Would you like a cup of coffee?"

"That would be nice. Do you have time to sit down and talk for a few minutes?"

Betty smiled. "You have perfect timing. I was going to sit down and have coffee myself anyway." Betty waved toward the table. "Have a seat. I'll join you shortly." Betty covered the pan of rolls, poured two cups of coffee, and came and sat down.

Adri took a sip of coffee and asked shyly, "May I ask you something?"

"Sure, honey, what do you want to know?" Betty smiled.

"Max is on the phone with his publisher, and he is talking like he is going to be very busy for the rest of the week." Adri hesitated. "Do I have that figured out right?"

Betty laughed. "Yes, you do have it right. Since Max doesn't have jury duty, his publisher will want him to finish his current book and get it to him before the weekend."

Adri nodded. "How well does Max deal with surprises?"

"Do you have a surprise in mind?"

Adri hesitated. Betty encouraged her. "Honey, go ahead and tell me what you are thinking, and I will tell you if it's something we can handle."

I love the way she said "we." They really are like family! Something I wish I had. But I'm happy right this minute. No negative thoughts!

"Max really needs the master bedroom set up, and the sooner, the better. If it would work for you, I would like to have my guys deliver Wednesday morning. I would be here to supervise the setup, and we would help move his things in while we're here. But I want to make sure I—we wouldn't be invading his personal space." The end of her sentence trailed off to a whisper.

Betty laughed happily. "Max would adore a surprise like that, and he'll have his attention so wrapped up in his work he won't even be aware of anything else going on! The roof could fall in, and he would just brush the dust away and keep working."

Adri smiled. "You really think it will be okay?"

"It will be very okay. I will work ahead, so the room will be ready, and you need to plan on you and your crew staying for lunch. How many are in your crew?" Betty was pretty excited.

"Oh, Betty, lunch is too much work for you!"

"Not a bit, honey. Like I said, I'll work ahead."

"Well, okay. I am going to bring four guys. The furniture is heavy, and those stairs will be a challenge. Are you sure it won't be too much trouble?" Adri was still doubtful.

"I would tell you to ask Max about that, but this is his surprise. Believe me, honey, I will love doing it. And Max doesn't get surprised very often, but I know he'll be pleased." Betty reached over and squeezed Adri's hand. "You are staying for dinner. I'm planning on you."

Adri smiled and answered shyly, "Max said I would disappoint you if I didn't stay."

"That's right."

Adri stood. "I want to see the rest of the house! Oh, Betty, do you live in the house?"

"Yes, honey, I do." She pointed to a door at the far end of the kitchen. "I have small suite of rooms right that way. You are welcome to look there too."

"Are you sure?" There was a light blush in her cheeks when she asked.

Betty laughed softly. "I am sure. Go on, take a peek!"

"Thank you," Adri said softly. "I'll look there first, and I'll walk around the rest of the downstairs, if that's okay." Betty nodded with a smile. Adri turned toward the door but then turned back. "Is nine o'clock on Wednesday morning okay?"

"Sounds good. You just run along now and make yourself at home. Enjoy yourself." Betty got up too and went in search of a recipe for Wednesday's lunch.

Adri was pleased to see Betty's space. It was all tastefully setup with smaller odds and ends of antiques and had a real homey feeling. Adri discovered a set of patio doors that went out onto a large covered porch that was set up with tasteful wicker furniture that made the space look cozy and welcoming. This porch would be Betty's own private space outdoors. Adri continued her tour and had found and looked at all the downstairs rooms, all empty at this point. She was standing in the arched doorway of the formal sitting room that had three shallow steps down. The room was painted a brilliant white, and the drapes covering the three large windows were a softer eggshell color. She was excited at all the possibilities for this space.

When Max finally came out of the library, he joined her in the doorway. He had been on the phone for forty-five minutes.

Max came over and stood beside Adri. "Have you figured out how the entire house should be filled?"

Adri laughed. "I have an opinion on all the options. That's all." She ducked her head and then looked up with color in her cheeks. "You don't really need me. Betty let me look in her rooms, and she could certainly decorate your whole house!"

Max grinned. "She won't do it though. Her things are collected over thirty-three years of marriage, and she couldn't part with them, so she made it work. Really well too, I think."

Adri stepped in front of Max and asked, "So is it crunch time for you?"

Max groaned. "Yes. I will probably put in eighteen or twenty hour days between now and Friday. I couldn't get Robert, my publisher, to extend the deadline. I had already pushed it off a week when I moved. But I did talk him into a sabbatical. After I get this book to him, he'll give me six months before the next one is due."

"Does that mean you don't have any new ideas?"

Max gave her a startled look. Then he pulled out his little spiral notebook, flipped the pages, and then held it out and fanned at least a dozen pages. "Each page is an idea for a new book."

Now Adri was startled. "You have that many ideas? Those would take you several years to write!"

"Yes, depending on the research, maybe even longer. I get my ideas from everyday happenings or from some research that took me on a rabbit trail or from people I meet and talk with." Max gave her a warm smile. "Meeting and talking with you gave me two new ideas, so now you know how inspiring you are."

Adri looked away for a long moment and then looked up at Max. Tears shimmered in her eyes as she looked up at him. "No man has ever thought I was worth anything, let alone inspiring. Are you sure you meant to say that?"

Max acted on instinct. He smiled gently, reached out, and cupped her cheek in his hand and said softly, "Adri, your work and fascination with antiques inspired me enough that I already know that my next book will be about furniture makers and transporters, and the one after that may be a sequel following furniture across America. Until I met you, those ideas never occurred to me." The tears left her eyes, and her expression relaxed. "Yes, I meant to say it." Max was about to remove his hand when her hand came up and covered it.

Adri had to clear her throat in order to speak. "Thank you" was all she could manage.

Max so badly wanted to pull her into his arms but sensed she wouldn't be ready for that, so he turned his hand over and gently squeezed her hand before he let go. "Now you know more than my publisher. I don't share about my ideas normally. But I would have had to share that much with you soon anyway as I am hoping you will consent to being one of my resources."

The tears came back to Adri's eyes. "You want me—you want—you want to use my knowledge . . ."

Max finished the sentence. "About antiques and some of your stories about the pieces as a resource, if you will consent to share with me."

A tear escaped Adri's right eye, and she quickly swiped it away. She whispered, "You have no idea how deeply I—I feel about—about your request." She ducked her head and wiped both eyes, then looked up and blushed softly. "I would be honored to share with you and be a resource."

Max felt a lump in his throat. He had to swallow before he could speak. "But first, I have to get through this week." He sighed and then asked, "Are you ready to see the library?"

Adri nodded. "Yes, please."

They walked side by side to the library. Adri gave her ideas on period and style of furniture and how it should be arranged, saving the fireplace setting as the last to describe. Max was smiling and nodding a lot. Adri turned to Max and asked, "What do you think?"

"It all sounds wonderful, but I won't be able to come back with you and pick out anything tonight. I will need to be working after dinner."

"Tell you what. I'll have time, so I'll set up something in my showroom like the bedroom sets were done so you can have a better idea before you decide for sure."

Betty appeared at the library door. "Dinner is ready. Come on you two, before it gets cold."

Max turned. "Thank you, Betty." He turned back to Adri. "Your idea is wonderful! May I escort you to the kitchen?" Max held out his arm.

Adri laughed, laid her hand lightly on Max's arm, and said, "Thank you, kind sir." Then her cheeks blushed. Max smiled, and Betty laughed as she turned back into the hall.

Dinner was delicious, and Adri felt so comfortable with these two people it almost felt like a family should feel. She just soaked it all up and talked freely with them, following their lead in keeping things light and pleasant.

After dinner, Adri shyly thanked Betty and excused herself, saying she should really get home. Max offered to walk her out to her car, and she accepted his offer.

As they reached the driver's side door, Adri turned to Max. "Thank you so much. This has been a wonderful afternoon, and dinner was great!" Max was beginning to recognize when Adri was stepping beyond her comfort zone. She would duck her head down and then look up with a light blush in her cheeks. She did that now as she finished talking about dinner.

"May I—I want—" She stopped and started again. "I want to give you a hug—as a—a friend. Is that—that okay?"

Max smiled gently, came a half a step closer, and raised his arms up slightly. Adri took the other step closer and wrapped her arms around his chest. Max's arms crossed her back in a loose hug. Adri rested her cheek on his shoulder briefly and then backed away. Her cheeks were a deeper shade of pink as she looked up, her eyes sparkling with something Max couldn't read. She smiled softly and whispered, "Thank you."

Max smiled and spoke just as softly, "Thank you, for trusting me."

Adri nodded and turned toward her car door. Max reached around and opened it for her. After she was seated, Max asked, "Will you wait just a minute? I wanted to give you two of my books, and I forgot until just this moment."

"Yes, I'll wait."

Max turned quickly and went back inside. He reappeared a half minute later and handed Adri two paperback books. She took them and laid them on the passenger seat. "That is so nice of you. Thank you."

Max smiled and nodded. "Good night, Adri. I'll talk to you on the weekend."

"Okay. Good night, Max."

She started the engine. Max stepped back and watched as she pulled out onto the road. He stood and listened. He faintly heard the garage door go up and the car motor stopped, and he heard the door go down. Then he walked slowly back into the house and secured the front door. He just stood there, waiting for his heart and his head to slow down. *Adri is almost childlike in reaching out. I can see that she's almost frightened in her effort to trust. And she said no man had ever thought she was worth anything. God, what has she been through that she would think that way? Does she know you? She needs to know her worth in your heart too.*

Max struggled to clear his head of Adri. He knew what it would take to get his current novel ready for the publisher and knew he would have a struggle keeping his mind on the novel. Her friendship hug had left him tingling with hope, but his logical mind told him that it would take time for anything close to that hope to be realized.

Dear Lord, help me to truly get back into my work. I trust Adri to you in the coming days. You are omnipresent, and she needs you. Give her your peace and show her your love.

Max went to the library to get to work.

CHAPTER 5

Adri went into her cozy little house. Even though she had lived here for a little over five years, she still felt like it was a place she just stayed. It had never become home to her. Her showroom felt more like home than her house did.

She was carrying Max's books in her left hand, next to her heart. She was still touched, deeply, by his gift to her in giving her these books. She was eager to read them but knew she was too restless tonight to even try to start one. She went into her bedroom and laid them on her bedside table.

I actually felt more at home at Max's place then I have felt anywhere. It's a wonderful house, and it was so nice of Max to let me see it all! If I had known that house was for sale, I would have bought it—but then I never would have met Max—or Betty. What a sweet lady! Max? Why am I so eager to do nice things for him? Because from the moment we met, I felt comfortable and—and accepted in his presence—or at least mostly comfortable. He is so gentle, so carefully caring.

I really had to struggle with some things though. Trust? Do I really trust Max? I think so. Adri discovered she was pacing in time with her thoughts. *This is ridiculous! I am restless, but it has been such a good day! I know. I'll go down to the showroom and move things around!*

She went and changed into jeans and a long-sleeved T-shirt and then jogged out to the showroom. First, she scooted Max's bedroom set out of the showroom to the loading dock area. Everything was on roller pads, so it took little effort for Adri to move things.

Adri rearranged the bedroom sets. Then in the back corner of the showroom, she shuffled things around. She needed to make room for two things. First of all, the display racks for the shipment of area rugs she had received, and second, for the library setup she had promised Max.

She discovered that while thinking about the house next door and the occupants of that house, she was every bit as content as she had been while at that house. The time flew, and when she finished the library setup, she looked at the clock. She was amazed to discover it was past midnight.

Adri laughed to herself and said out loud, "Time flies when I'm having fun!" Then she laughed again, remembering the conversation about talking to self. She looked at the library set one more time and was pleased with what she had put together. She made her way to the front of the building and shut it down and then went to the house and went to bed.

On waking the next morning, the thought that went through her mind was about the path that connected the two properties. She checked her calendar and discovered that today was the day for her yard keeper to be here. She made a quick decision. She would pay Amanda and her crew extra to clear that path and enlarge the space in the hedge. Maybe Max would realize that she was okay with him using that path.

Before getting out of bed, she picked up Max's books and read the titles and the back covers. She decided she would start with the one titled *Trail to Life*, but that would have to wait until this evening because it was time to get her day started.

Adri was busy the next few days. With the help of two of her crew, she got the rug stands up and the rugs installed on the far wall of her showroom on Tuesday evening. On Wednesday, all four were there at 7:30 a.m. to load the delivery truck, and they were headed over to Max's house by 8:50 a.m.

While moving things around the evening before, Adri had found two smaller Armoires that were an exact match to the bedroom set and would balance the room nicely. They were still in storage, so she had forgotten about them. They went to the dock to be loaded on the truck.

Some other things she decided to include were the entry pieces that she thought would work really nice in the front hall and a good table for the kitchen. She wished she had chairs to include, but she couldn't find any that she thought would work.

When Adri made out the sales invoice for Max, she didn't write up the extra things she included by her own decision. He could decide if he liked them first. And she gave him the standard discount for volume customers. She had a feeling she was going to be selling Max a lot of furniture.

The delivery went smoothly. Adri had the chance to get to know Betty a little more. She asked shyly at one point. "Have you seen much of Max?"

Betty laughed. "Just when I take food to him and go pick up the tray. I'm used to it."

Betty was thrilled with the double clover leaf-shaped table they moved into the kitchen. "So much better than that glass and metal condo table!" She also approved of the entry furniture. She was sure Max would like it as well.

Adri and her crew enjoyed the salad and casserole that Betty had made for them. There was even apple strudel for dessert.

Wednesday afternoon, while her crew was delivering two smaller orders from earlier in the week, Adri made another large sale that would be loaded Thursday morning and delivered Thursday afternoon. Adri would not need to go, as this was a repeat customer, and she always knew what she wanted. With that much of a turnover, she knew she would be digging things out of storage to get things set up again. She checked her calendar and realized that there were two huge auctions she planned to attend on Tuesday and Friday of the coming week. She was sure she would have things from those auctions to help fill the empty spaces in the showroom. She was dismayed that those auctions were coming up so soon but was excited about what she thought she might be able to get for Max's house. That thought brought her up short.

Why am I so interested in pleasing Max? When his house is done, will I just be tossed away again? NO! He wants me to be a resource, and that would go on for a while. He's not just interested in me for my furniture abilities but for my knowledge as well. Relax, girl, and just enjoy the work and see if Max is the man you think and sense he is.

With her thoughts about Max settled, she began pondering the needs of the business, wishing she wasn't so uptight about hiring more people. She recognized the need for more help. For quite a while now, when she went to auctions, she just closed up shop, but there had been some complaints from recent customers and realized that the best business practice would be to hire someone to be there or someone who could go to the auctions. Business in general was picking up, and someone needed to be there during business hours.

Adri made the decision. Hire an assistant and a part-time sales person. Just the idea that she would have to train new people made her stomach churn with uncertainty. She also realized that with the auctions coming up, she had left this task way too late. She may still need to close on Tuesday and Friday if she was going to make the auctions. Maybe she could talk to her crew about this. Seek the help of people she already trusted.

She was just about ready to head out to her showroom Thursday morning when her phone rang. She answered, "Hello."

"Good morning, Adri!" It was Max, and her heart beat increased. "I wanted to call and thank you for all these wonderful surprises you arranged for me." There was a big, warm smile in his voice.

Adri laughed happily, feeling the thud of her heart in her chest at the sound of Max's approval. "What surprises? What are you talking about?"

Max laughed with the sound rumbling over the phone. "Stop teasing. Betty told me."

Adri couldn't hold in her excitement now. "Do you like the bedroom? I thought it turned out great!"

Max's voice was soft, almost like a caress. "The bedroom is wonderful! The entry hall is wonderful! The table in the kitchen needs chairs."

Adri blushed and felt the thrill of his approval all the way to her toes. There was no question he liked everything she had done. She stammered a little. "I'm glad-glad you like-like it. And I know the-the table needs chairs." She took a deep breath and rushed to finish the explanation. "My inventory of chairs is low, and I couldn't find anything that would go with the table. I'll have to find some for you."

Max laughed softly, the rumble still coming across the phone. "No rush. Betty is thrilled with the table, so we are good for now." He paused, cleared his throat, and continued. "I had quite an adventure at two this morning. I went upstairs to fall into bed. When I got to the top of the stairs, the light was brightly shining out of the master's bedroom, and the door was wide open. I went to investigate and found the room completely set up and my . . . uh . . . things in place. I was groggy enough I thought for a moment I was hallucinating, until I touched the furniture. Then I knew it was real. It was wonderful, down to the bedside lamp!"

Adri laughed merrily. "At least Betty didn't make you look for your bed."

Max laughed again, the deep sound rumbling in his chest. "Thank God for Betty's foresight. I might have just curled up on the floor in the playroom instead of looking for my bed!"

Adri asked shyly, "How is the book coming? Are you going to get done on time?"

Max heard the shyness in Adri's voice and was touched that she had the courage to ask about the book. "Yes, I am. I read it today and change anything I'm not comfortable with. If—and I really mean *if* I have done as good a job as I think I have, it should be on the way to my publisher by noon tomorrow."

Adri's voice relaxed when she heard Max's conversational tone. "I'm glad. Does it always come down to a crunch like this?"

"No. At least not a week of crunch. When I am reading it, I like to do it in one sitting, so that is usually a long day. I try to set my own deadlines each week to avoid weeks like this."

"I need to let you get to it then. I am looking forward to showing you what I put together for the library."

"I am looking forward to seeing it. Again, Adri, I thank you for working ahead on things. This is wonderful!"

Adri answered softly, "You are so welcome. Have a good day!"

"You too."

Max hung up from talking to Adri Thursday morning. He allowed his thoughts to stay on her. *She was so pleased that I enjoyed the surprise. I sure didn't expect this kind of spontaneity from her. She is so reserved. I would love to see her in action with her customers. Wonder if she ever finds them difficult.* Max took a deep breath. *She was so bright and cheery on the phone. She is enjoying herself, I think. God, I ask that you continue to be with Adri today. Help me to have a clear head and get this book finished. Amen.*

CHAPTER 6

When Adri's crew came back to check out Thursday in the late afternoon, Adri asked that they have a meeting before they took off. This was new to Adri because even in boss mode, she felt uncertain about speaking with men, feeling uncertain about her value as a person in their eyes in this kind of situation. Max's treatment of her on Monday had given her the courage she needed to speak to her crew—she hoped.

Dan Folger was the first delivery man she had hired five years earlier when the business opened, and just two weeks later, Brad Waters and Kim O'Neil were hired. Dan had recommended them, and all three had worked well with her over the years. When large heavy orders needed to be delivered, it soon became necessary to hire a fourth person. After six different individuals in four years' time, Dan brought Jocko Martinez with him one day, and Jocko has been the fourth for the past year. Dan had come to Adri recommended by Amanda Cox, her landscaping and yard lady.

Adri had learned over time to trust her crew and respect their input from time to time with deliveries and room arrangements, but now, she was nervous about asking for their help in finding additional employees.

Adri invited them into her office. Jocko and Dan sat in the chairs across the desk from her. Kim leaned against the door frame, and Brad squatted at the corner of the desk. With all four men in such a small space, Adri had expected to feel intimidated and was surprised that all she felt was nervous. Adri looked from one to the next, ending with Dan, and he gave a thumbs-up motion. Adri nodded slightly before she spoke.

"I have known for some time that I am overextending myself. I-I have eight auctions in the next six weeks, two-two of them are next week." She huffed a big sigh before she continued. "I ne-need help in the showroom and an assistant. I-I am asking you to help me find some help." Her cheeks were bright red, an indication of how uncomfortable she was in voicing her concerns.

Dan leaned forward and spoke softly, "You came to the right people. Jocko may be part of the answer."

Adri looked startled. Then she looked at Jocko. "Wh-what do you mean?"

Dan sat back and stretched his legs in front of him. "Jocko, tell Adri your situation and explain your credentials."

Jocko turned red in the face but sat up straight and looked Adri in the eye. "Yes, ma'am, I am very interested in applying for the job as your assistant. I have a degree in business administration, and since I've been working for you, my wife and I have spent endless hours on the Internet researching antiques of every kind. We are both really fascinated by the antique world and have become well acquainted with the information. Gina is better at spotting a fake, but I am still working on it." He stopped and looked down.

"So you aren't a shift worker like the rest of the crew?" Adri spoke gently.

Jocko looked up and grinned. "No, these guys are definitely great to be around, but I don't work at the plant with them." Then he sobered. "I am groundskeeper for the Wolcott Estate, which means I work at four separate places. My wife and I have lived over the garage at the main estate, but with the baby, we need a larger place, and that means better pay. The Wolcotts have been great to work for, and I was able to swing college and still work, but it's time to really get to work to support my family." He hesitated for a moment before he continued. "This is exactly the opportunity I have been looking for. I sent out résumés just last week but haven't heard back on any of them. The antique world is really what interests me, and I would really appreciate you considering me."

Adri had been sitting back listening to Jocko. Now she leaned forward and rested her elbows on the desk, her hands linked in front of her.

"Jocko, I know you have been taken with this job from the beginning. You've asked intelligent and searching questions, and I wondered about you being a shift worker. So now I know! And yes, I want to see your résumé, and I would like to talk to Gina. Would she be interested in a part-time job?"

Jocko grinned. "Here with you? She might. She loves being a mom, so little Josh needs to be considered, but I'll ask her."

Adri smiled and appeared really relaxed. Something her crew seldom saw. "We are headed in the right direction. Now we need to replace Jocko on the crew. Do any of you have any recommendations?"

Kim straightened up from the door frame. "I would like to tell you about my eldest foster son, Denny. He would be good for the delivery crew, and it would be good for him."

Adri gave her full attention to Kim. "Tell me."

Kim nodded and stepped forward. "He has some disabilities, and at sixteen years of age, he is at the eighth grade level in schooling. We homeschool him, so scheduling would not be a problem. He stopped growing about a year ago but is large for his age, so the lifting and carrying would not be a difficulty, and he likes to work out with weights, so I know he has the strength. He is an eager helper as long as he is given direct and clear instruction. I would be pleased to recommend him for the job, and it would help him see his worth in the outside world."

Adri smiled. "I would like to meet him. Can you bring him tomorrow morning for a job interview? I think that would be a good learning experience for Denny and for me!"

Kim laughed. "Yes, that would be good. I'll try to prep him a little, so he doesn't overwhelm you."

Adri laughed. "Okay."

Dan nodded and added, "He is an enthusiastic young man, but I agree with Kim. He could certainly be a big help around here."

Adri tried to hide her surprise. "So—you all know each other's families, I take it."

Brad spoke up. "Yeah, we belong to the same men's fellowship group and involve all family members in projects and holiday socials. None of us would be strangers to Denny, and he would expect any of us to give him instructions."

"Oh! That explains the camaraderie you guys share!" All four men laughed and voiced agreement. Adri sighed. "I apologize that I haven't made the effort to get to know you all better." She ducked her head, and her cheeks colored. "I have my reasons, but you all have given me nothing but respect, and you care about helping me. I should have made a be-better effort."

Brad grinned. "Maybe your neighbor up the hill is good for you—and yeah, that was cheeky, but you have opened up a little, and we like and respect you even more."

Dan gave Brad a stern look, and even though Adri was blushing like crazy, she saw the look and laughed softly. "Leave it to Brad to say what you all are thinking!"

Complete silence greeted Adri's comment. She ducked and blushed again and spoke softly. "I *have* gotten to know you all a little." She blew out a breath. "Now back to business. Kim, could you bring Denny about nine?" Kim nodded. "Jocko, I would like you and Gina to come about ten if that will work?"

"Yes, ma'am. Ten is great!"

"Good. We may have things figured out before the weekend. Your checks will be ready in the morning, so I'll see you all tomorrow!" Adri sat back in her office chair and smiled as the guys moved to leave and bid her good-bye.

Wow! This is great! I was so nervous, but they were wonderful! And I may have everything I need to keep business running more smoothly! Wow! Adri jumped up from her chair. *I need to tell Max! Wait—where did that come from? Well, he is my friend, and he seems to understand me a little, and I need to tell someone!*

Adri quickly shut down the shop and set the alarm. She hurried up to her house to freshen up. *OH! Max may not be finished reading his book! Well, I'm going to his house anyway! If Max isn't available, I'll tell Betty! She is so motherly and so sweet.*

With her mind made up, she went back into her front room and stopped to look around. Her eyes landed on the chairs around her table in the kitchen. *Those would go perfect with Max's—umm, Betty's kitchen table! I need to tell them I found them chairs!*

Adri checked the time. The sun would be up for a couple of hours yet, so Adri went to her back door. She would take the path up to Max's house, and this would give her a chance to see the path. She wanted to make sure Amanda and her crew had done as good of job as she expected.

She hurried to the hole in the back hedge and didn't have to duck to get through. The trees were thick, and other natural plants were growing along the pathway, which twisted and turned to accommodate the growth, but the path was clear and wide enough for two people to walk side by side. Adri began to understand why Max would have felt the freedom to take the path down the hill. Of course, she had no idea what the overgrowth had been like, but she found the walk enjoyable, even going uphill.

At the top of the path, she stopped and looked around. The path came out about thirty yards from the back side of the garage portion of the house. From this angle, she could see Betty's porch and a portion of the front veranda.

It was toward evening, and Max was so close to the end of the book when he heard the door chimes. His thoughts went immediately to Adri. *Is she here? I'm not expecting anyone.* He quickly read the last page and was very satisfied, so as was his tradition, he typed THE END, saved it, and shut down his computer. He would sleep on it before he sent it off to his publisher.

CHAPTER 7

Adri moved quickly to the front door and rang the bell. After about half a minute, Betty opened the door.

"Adri! What a nice surprise! Come on in."

Adri laughed happily but stuttered her explanation. "I-I know I sho-should have called, but I only have Max's ce-cell number and didn't want to disturb him if-if he was still reading hi-his book."

Betty laughed. "I will give you my cell number, but it's okay that you just came! Come on in."

Adri stepped into the entry and grinned when she told Betty, "I found chairs for the kitchen table! I'll see if one of the guys has time to bring them over tomorrow morning."

"Well, there's no big rush, you know. Come into the kitchen and have some coffee with me." Betty turned toward the kitchen, and Adri followed.

Max rose quickly and opened the library door and heard Betty invite someone to come have coffee. He quickly walked around the bottom of the stair case and saw Adri. She was beautiful in her simple long blue skirt and white ruffled blouse. Her hair was in a French braid hanging down her back. He realized that a shiver of excitement had taken his breath away.

They were almost at the kitchen door, and Adri asked, "Is Max still busy?"

There was a deep voice that responded from behind them. "I was until just this minute."

Adri let out a gasp as she spun around. Max was standing at the bottom of the stairs, and he was grinning. Adri all but ran to him, bubbling with excitement. She stopped short in front of him and told him, "I have something to tell you. I am so excited!"

Max's heart had done double time when he saw Adri with Betty, but now, seeing her excitement, he couldn't catch his breath. She was glowing and looked directly into his eyes. She continued, saving Max from a response that he couldn't seem to form. "I-I did something today, and it has worked out so great, and I wanted to tell you!"

Max couldn't look away from the sweet glowing face, and his eyes crinkled with his gentle smile and told her, "I want to hear!" He glanced up at Betty, who was smiling a soft, satisfied smile. Max's gaze came back to Adri. He held out his arm. "It would be my pleasure to walk with you on the veranda while you tell me your exciting news."

Adri laughed happily and took the offered arm. Then she blushed and asked uncertainly, "Do you have ti-time?"

Max's soft laugh rumbled in his chest. "I have nothing else to do at the moment, and I have all the time you want."

"Okay!" They walked to the front door, Max opening it and closing it as they stepped outside. Adri started recounting her meeting with her crew. Her voice was excited, and her left hand waved often, but she was still shy enough that there were a lot of stutters in her account. By the time she had finished, they had reached the far end of the veranda. Adri spun in front of Max and blushed.

"Now I am embarrassed! Did you even understand anything I said?" Then she ducked her head and fidgeted with her fingers at the waist of her skirt.

Max didn't laugh like she thought he might. He reached out and placed his index finger under her chin and lifted so she could look at his face. When she raised her eyes, she saw his gentle smile and the same gentleness in his eyes.

"Let me tell you what I heard." Max dropped his hand, and Adri nodded slightly. "For the first time, you stepped beyond your comfort level and had an official meeting with your four-man crew." He paused, and Adri nodded, the color creeping into her cheeks.

Max continued, "The end result was that you expect to hire Jocko as your assistant—and maybe his wife, Gina—to help part time in the showroom. And to fill Jocko's place on the delivery crew, Kim's son will interview tomorrow morning."

Adri giggled. "That is exactly the gist of it. How did you make that much sense out of all I said?"

Max shrugged and said seriously, "Words are my business. But you were clearer than you think, even with the excitement."

Adri's cheeks colored again, and there was a trembling in her smile as she said softly, "Thank you."

Max recognized how special the compliment was to Adri. He recognized too how she had really stretched her comfort zone to come to him with her excitement and accomplishment. He was touched deeply by her trust of him. Max cleared his throat, but there was still a slight catch when he told her, "You are welcome."

There was a short silence before Adri reached out and took Max's hand. "I have another surprise for you!" Adri loved the surprised look on Max's face as he gently squeezed her hand.

"Show me!" Max grinned. Adri tugged on his hand and led him across the veranda and down the steps. Max laughed. "Where are we going?"

Adri laughed happily. "Just come along!" She led him around the garage and stopped where they could see the beginning of the path through the trees. Adri released Max's hand and clapped her hands together excitedly and asked, "What do you think?"

Max gave her a startled glance and strode quickly to the path entrance so he could look down the path. Then he turned back to Adri with a big grin. "Now how did this happen?"

Adri ran over to him and took both his hands in hers. She looked at him shyly. "I hired my yard crew to do it. Is that okay?"

Max laughed happily and gently squeezed her hands. "It is very okay with me! What a wonderful surprise!" He paused to search her face before he said softly, "I guess this means I can come to your place the back way?" It was a question because he wanted to make sure he understood her reasoning.

He was so sweet in his gentleness it almost brought tears to Adri's eyes. She shyly pulled her hands away and clasped them together in front of her. "Yes. This is how I came to your house today!"

Max laughed softly. "A two-way path. Wonderful! Thank you, Adri!"

Adri laughed happily. "You really do like surprises! Betty said you did!"

Max grinned. "It's been a really long time since I've had such wonderful surprises, and yes, I love surprises. My parents were really good at it when I was a boy. I guess that's when I picked up that liking." Max's face took on a tender appearance. "You, dear Adri, are very good at surprising me."

Adri felt a tingle of delight skim down her spine. She smiled shyly. "When I was young—uh . . ." She paused and frowned. "I've never told this to anyone." Max waited as she studied his face. Adri still saw the tenderness and sighed. "When I was young, I had so many bad surprises. My Momma encouraged me to imagine surprising others with happy surprises." Her voice dropped almost to a whisper. "You are the first person I have ever wanted to surprise, like I had imagined as a child."

Max's heart twisted in his chest at her admission. He asked softly, "Bad surprises from your father?"

A dark shadow crossed over Adri's face. She clenched her teeth as a shudder visibly went through her, and she answered, "And my brother." The shadow passed, and she almost mumbled, "I won't talk about *them*."

Adri turned toward the path, and even though she tried to infuse brightness into her voice, she failed miserably. "I have accomplished what I came for, so I think I'll go on home."

Max couldn't let her go like this. Her shoulders were slouched and her face pale. He reached out and gently grasped her shoulder to turn her back to face him.

"Adri, don't go, not like this." His voice was soft with a note of appeal. *What can I say to temp her to stay? God, any ideas?* His eyes suddenly sparkled. "Betty always bakes a double fudge chocolate cake to celebrate the finish of another book. If you stay for dinner, the three of us can celebrate with that wonderful cake!"

Adri straightened, and her face relaxed a little. "Double fudge chocolate?"

Max nodded a smile on his face. "With her own recipe for fudge frosting!"

Adri gave a weak smile. "You're pretty good with surprises too." Her voice picked up strength as she finished, "I never say no to chocolate."

Max laughed softly and reached for her hand. "Me either!"

Adri snuggled her hand in Max's and blushed softly. "Thank you, Max." *Thank you for saving me from my own dark and disagreeable thoughts!*

The dinner experience was once again a peaceful and happy affair for Adri. Betty entertained them with incidents and happenings during the delivering of the furniture on Wednesday. Max told the story again about his early morning discovery on Thursday. Adri related some funny and unusual delivery incidents connected to her business.

After the delicious roast beef dinner and the wonderful double fudge chocolate cake, Max offered to walk Adri home. The sun was low on the horizon, and the twilight was not too far away. Max retrieved a flashlight out of a kitchen drawer so they could see the path. As they were about to step out of the kitchen, Betty asked casually, "So, Max, are you intending to grow a full beard and mustache, or was it just laziness on your part?" Her comment being about the two days growth of whiskers Max had on his face.

Max stopped and turned in the doorway to answer Betty. "I haven't decided yet. Why do you ask?" Adri turned also and wondered uncomfortably why Betty would ask such a personal question.

Betty's eyes were twinkling, and she looked mischievous. "What do you think, Adri? Should Max wear a beard?"

Adri felt the bright red in her cheeks, and her whole body felt hot when she noticed both Betty and Max looking at her. She ducked her head and gave it a slight shake.

Betty noticed Adri's reaction, so she laughed gently. "I always thought the right kind of beard made a man distinguished-looking. Max has a great jaw for some whiskers." She laughed again and walked over to Max, trying to ease Adri's embarrassment. "Now you know what I think and Adri, honey, you don't have to answer *me*." Then she reached up and touched Max's cheek. "At least it's soft."

Max had been nervous about Adri's reaction and knew in his heart that this was not a good subject to draw Adri into a discussion. He cleared his throat. "Your opinion is much appreciated, Betty. I am still thinking about it though.

Actually, it's there right now because I knew I'd be shut away and didn't want to take the time to mess with it." Max glanced at Adri, smiled, and then told Betty, "If you are finished embarrassing us, I will walk Adri home."

Betty laughed softly again. "I didn't intend to embarrass anyone, just discussing an unusual occurrence. You two go on now. Good night, Adri."

Adri looked up shyly, her face still displaying some of the blush, but she had a small smile. "Good night, Betty. Thank you again for the dinner and your wonderful cake."

Betty turned to Adri and gave her a quick hug. "You are so welcome, honey, and we would be glad to have you anytime." As she sent them on their way, Betty made a mental note to herself to ask Max later why Adri's reaction was so strong at what she thought was a teasing yet normal comment.

Max turned and offered Adri his arm. Adri shyly smiled and took the offered arm, and they went toward the front door. They were silent until they were headed down the path. There was still enough slanting light from the sun's afterglow, and they didn't need the flashlight. Max apologized. "I'm sorry, Adri. Betty sees our developing friendship and didn't realize we, for the most part, stay away from those kinds of personal things."

Adri ducked her head and was silent for a bit longer and then said nervously, "It's okay." Her voice dropped lower. "I-I agree with B-Betty."

Max smiled to himself and said, "Okay." He would leave it up to Adri if the conversation would continue.

Adri cringed a little and kept looking straight ahead and changed the subject. "Do you want to see the library arrangement tonight or wait until tomorrow?"

"Hmm, you wouldn't mind showing me tonight?" Max slowed and stopped. "I would really like to see it, but if you are too tired or weary, it can wait. You have climbed several mountains today."

Adri looked into Max's eyes and had a puzzled expression on her face. "Mountains?"

"Yes. You were able to generate the courage to meet with your crew. Then you found the fortitude to come to me and share. Those must have felt like very steep mountains to your internal strength. Strength, by the way, that I really admire."

Adri didn't break eye contact, but she felt her face heat up with pleasure at what Max said. Finally, she stepped forward, onto her tip toes and surprised Max with a hug, her arms going around his neck and her cheek resting softly against his. Max felt his heart race with this unexpected move by Adri. His arms closed around her back, and he held her gently, prepared to let go at any time.

Adri whispered so softly he almost missed it. "It is soft!" Then she pulled back slowly, her face a bright red. She searched Max's face and saw a pleased half smile and tenderness in his eyes. She stuttered quietly, "How-how do you do-do that?" She backed up another step as she spoke.

There was a gentle smile now as he asked, "Do what?"

Adri looked down and again spoke, barely above a whisper, "You-you talk like you-you know . . . umm . . . know me-me inside. I-I didn't tell you how-how hard it was."

Max laughed softly. "Oh that! I know you have had a rough history with men because you told me, and you have an all-man crew, and I am a man— your friend and neighbor certainly but still a man." Adri glanced up shyly. Max continued, "So I think you really stretched your inner strength to get through a couple of hours this afternoon. I am pleased with the outcome of your efforts and happy to celebrate with you."

Adri took a deep breath and exhaled slowly. She looked down at the ground and scuffed the dirt with her shoes as she told him, "It *was* a big mountain." She took another deep breath. "I do feel a little weary." Adri looked up and Max nodded.

"Let's get you home then, and I'll come after lunch tomorrow to check out the library display. Okay?" Max didn't move until Adri nodded. Then he stepped beside her and took a hold on her arm with a gentle touch, turned on the flashlight, and directed it at the path in front of them.

They walked in silence until they neared the hedge. Max shined the light across the hedge and he smiled. "I think I can walk right through now."

Adri nodded. "I wanted you to be able to. When I told Amanda what I wanted done with the path, she told me the history. She was the groundskeeper at your house about six years ago when there was a ten-year-old girl living on my place before the original house burned down, and there was a twelve-year-old living in your house with her aunt and uncle. The girls were best friends and used the path. The hole in the hedge didn't need to be very high for children."

Max and Adri stepped through the hedge. "You are good. Getting the story about it and resurrecting the path use!" Adri and Max laughed together. Then Max asked, "That's why you don't live in a graceful southern mansion. Did it burn to the ground?"

"Yes. Faulty wiring when no one was home." Adri led the way up the back steps to her house. The porch light came on when they reached the top step.

"Did you build everything that's here?"

"No, the garage was separate from the house, and the shed behind the garage was already there. I moved the house in and erected the showroom building." Adri punched the code into the door panel and pushed the door open. Then she turned to Max and smiled shyly. "Thank you for walking me home."

Max smiled. "My pleasure. You get a good night's sleep. I think you have a little more mountain climbing to do in the morning."

Adri was serious when she nodded. "I am making some big changes, and I'm nervous about that. I've known for a while that I needed more help but . . ." She let the sentence trail off.

Max took her hand and said gently, "You'll do fine, and I'll be praying for you."

Adri blinked the tears back. *He is so insightful and so gentle.* Adri nodded and whispered, "Good night, Max."

Max squeezed her hand gently, and then released it. "Good night, sweet Adri."

Adri stepped into her house and watched Max until he was back through the hedge.

CHAPTER 8

When Max arrived back at his house, he went to the kitchen to put the flashlight away. Betty was still there, drinking coffee at the table. Max poured himself some coffee and sat down across from Betty.

"We need to talk."

Betty nodded. "I think I put my foot in it earlier."

Max nodded then smiled. "Yes. That kind of interchange is very normal for you and me. I will try to explain Adri's reaction."

Betty sighed. "She was ready to run."

"I know." Max looked down at his coffee cup as he ran his finger around the top of the cup. Then he looked up at Betty's puzzled expression. "Betty, she has had some really bad treatment from men in the past." Betty gasped. "I don't know any details. She won't talk about it. I know that when Adri was ten years old, her mother committed suicide, and in some ways, she seems to have stopped maturing around that age."

Betty nodded. "I've seen her childlike actions and reactions."

"The only reason I know any of her history is because I looked it up on the Internet. She has made one statement about bad treatment by men." He stopped and then asked, "Betty, how do I *not* make mistakes that threaten her? She is so fragile!"

Betty reached across the table and squeezed Max's hand. "You must be doing it right so far. She came looking for you today. And you do reach out to God for answers. I think you'll be fine."

Max frowned. "Yes, but . . . I don't know, Betty. She is so hungry for approval, and so far I think I have said the right things, but does she see me as a man who could love her as a man or as an older man who can just be her friend?" Max stopped, smiled slightly, and continued. "I guess you know I love her already?"

Betty's face lit up, and she smiled. "I knew, wasn't sure you did!"

Max chuckled. "Yeah, I think I knew before Monday was over." He was serious again. "I will need to move slowly though. And I will have to be very careful."

Betty nodded her expression solemn. "I hope I didn't put a halt to her trust of me. I sensed that she is hungry for a mother relationship too. Does she have close friends or family of any kind?"

Max thought for a moment before he answered. "She seems to have a closer relationship with her groundskeeper, Amanda. Since her work crew is all men, I don't think she is close with any of them or their families. She has an aunt nearby but hasn't mentioned her except to say that her aunt taught her to restore antiques. When her past is mentioned, she is tense and shuts off any communication about it." He was quiet for a bit; his hand smoothed through his hair as he said quietly, "I think she needs relationships so much but is really struggling with trust and allowing people close."

Betty nodded in her wise way. "We can help her, and since I know a little more, I hope I make fewer mistakes. Let's pray about it right now and trust Adri to God's care."

Max nodded, and they both bowed their heads to pray.

Adri went to the showroom early to write checks for her crew and made some notes for her interviews later in the morning. Dan came in at eight fifteen, and when she handed him his paycheck she asked, "Are you in your pickup this morning?"

Dan grinned. "Yeah. Did you need me to help with something?"

Adri let out her pent-up breath and realized that Dan would anticipate her. "Yes, I have four chairs at the house that need to go to M-Max's house up the hill." She blushed. "Would you mind . . . ?" The sentence trailed off.

Dan's grin grew. "I don't mind at all. Do you need different chairs moved to your house?"

"Oh! Yes, I do. Umm, there is a matching threesome at the end of the row of chairs. Just three will be fine for now. If-if you could get them, I'll go up and unlock the house."

Dan nodded while he folded the check envelope and pushed it into his back pocket. "No problem. I'll be there shortly."

Adri trotted up the hill and had the door propped open when Dan backed his pickup up to the sidewalk. Dan made quick work of shifting things around, and he and Adri walked out of the house together. When they stopped by the pickup, Adri assured him, "I told Betty yesterday that I would have someone deliver them this morning, so she, at least, will be expecting you."

Dan nodded. He hesitated briefly before he spoke. "Adri." His tone was serious. "I want to tell you how proud I am of you! Our first meeting yesterday—you did very well." Dan looked around the yard before he met her gaze and continued, "I have known you a long time and always thought you had more in you than you let out, and it warmed me all the way to my heart that you stepped up and had that meeting." Adri was blushing, and Dan finished, "We all respect you so much for that effort, and we are all proud of you."

Tears came to Adri's eyes, but she quickly blinked them away. "Thank you," she said quietly. "You guys are the closest thing to family that I have, and that means a lot to me."

Dan grinned. "My pleasure, ma'am. Now I will get these chairs delivered. See you next Wednesday." He gave a brief salute and climbed into his pickup.

Adri stood back and watched Dan leave. She felt so cared for and reviewed Dan's words as she walked slowly back to the showroom. *Why was I stuck with such awful relatives? Other men aren't jerks! Oh, I am sure there are plenty out there, but my crew men are not among them! I guess it took getting to know Max so I could see the good in others.* Adri sighed as she regretted that she had put such a high wall around herself.

Adri stepped back into the showroom and immediately started thinking about the tasks of interviews. She started pacing. *I am so nervous about all these changes. How do I know for sure that I am doing the right thing? Can I work closely with Jocko? He's younger than me by a few years. Surely he's teachable but . . .* She felt a shudder run through her at the next thought. *He is a man, and men want to take over and have their own way! Except Dan just showed me a different side. I can do this—I hope!* The more she thought, the more nervous she got. *I need help with the business, but I don't know if I can do this!*

She looked at the clock. Eight forty-five—she only had fifteen minutes to get it together. Adri jumped when her cell phone rang. Her hands were shaking so much that the cell rang three times before she could grasp hold of it, pull it from her skirt pocket, and open it. It was Max.

Adri's voice trembled slightly when she answered, "H-Hello."

Max's voice was soft as he asked. "You're nervous, aren't you?"

She sagged onto a nearby Queen Elizabeth chair and answered shakily, "Yes. Oh, Max, how do-do I know I'm do-doing the right thing?"

"What is the scariest thing on your mind right now?" Max asked softly.

There was a long silence before Adri worked up the courage to tell him. "Hiring Jocko as my assistant. He-he's a man!"

"Yes, but he has worked for you for a while. How does he seem to be treating you now?"

Adri sighed. "You want me to see him as he is." It was a statement.

"Yes, Adri. Is he respectful now?"

"Yes." She was starting to relax and let a small laugh escape. "He is eager to know more about antiques, and he respects me enough to call me ma'am sometimes, and he seemed humbled that I would consider him for the position of assistant."

"Are you still nervous?" Max asked quietly.

"Oh, Max! Not so much now!" Then she giggled. "You did it again."

There was a smile in his voice. "Hmm, so I did." After a brief silence, he said, "You'll do fine. You know what you need for the business, and you know Jocko. Just put on your business face and tough it out. I have every confidence it will be a good thing."

Adri's face flushed with Max's approving confidence. She sighed softly. "Thank you, Max. How did you know?"

Max laughed softly. "I have this gut instinct that I have learned to respond to. My gut told me to call you, and when you answered, I just knew what the problem was." His voice softened when he continued. "You are on my mind a lot, and I felt like my friend needed a friend."

Max heard a sniff, and Adri's voice was full of emotion. "Oh, Max, now you've made me cry." There was another sniff. "Bu-but happy tears."

"Oh, sweet Adri!" Max cleared his throat and then added, "You will do great. I'll let you go now."

Adri cleared her throat. "Okay. I'll tell you all about it when I see you later!"

Max laughed softly. "I'm looking forward to hearing all about it! Bye."

"Later." Adri closed her phone softly and whipped her cheeks with the edge of her palms. *Max is wonderful—he really is my friend! He believes in me! Me! Oh! Kim and Denny are here.*

The motion buzzer on the gate had buzzed. Adri got up and hurried to her office.

Jocko and Gina left about twelve fifteen, having stayed around to browse the showroom and learn a little about the pricing. They would be back on Monday morning for a full day of training so that Adri would be free to attend the auction on Tuesday, and they would run the showroom.

CHAPTER 9

Adri was so pleased with how everything had come together, and she almost couldn't wait for Max to arrive. She had brought a sandwich and tea with her for lunch, which she ate at her desk. After she had tidied everything, she went to the entry door and stepped out into the sunshine. It was another beautiful spring day, and she was sure Max would use the path to come over.

Adri leaned back against the corner of the building, relaxing in the sunshine and keeping an eye on the spot where Max would appear around the corner of the fence. When she spotted him, she called out and waved before pushing away from the building and ran to meet him.

Max was grinning and lengthened his stride, and they met in the middle of the drive. Adri stopped short. "Oh, you brought something with you!" She had spotted a small plastic container in his hand.

Max nodded. "Actually two things. Betty said you should have a piece of cake to finish off your lunch. She taped her cell phone number to the lid so you would have that too." Max held out the container to Adri.

She laughed happily as she took it. "She is going to spoil me!"

Max laughed. "She's trying! The other thing—" Max reached into the back pocket of his jeans and brought out a folded piece of paper. "Payment for the bedroom set."

Pink color crept up Adri's face, and she said quietly, "There was no hurry."

Max chuckled, "Maybe not, but I already have a running tab so thought I should at least get started."

Adri blushed again and agreed, "Okay." She tucked the check into her pocket and then reached for Max's hand. "Come on, I want my cake!"

Max snuggled Adri's hand into his and let her pull him toward the showroom. *This morning must have gone well! Adri is very upbeat. Of course, I could think she is glad to see me, her friend, but I think it is more than that. I think she feels highly successful because of what she accomplished this morning.* Max opened the showroom door, and Adri pulled him along to her office door.

Adri released Max's hand and motioned for him to have a seat. She went to the coffee counter and picked up a plastic spoon before she went and sat behind her desk.

"Betty is so sweet! Did you tell her I never say no to chocolate?"

"No, didn't say a word." Max sat back in the chair and stretched his legs out in front and asked, "So how did it go this morning?"

Adri gave him a cheeky smile around the piece of cake she was chewing. After she swallowed, she said, "You'll have to wait. Cake first."

Max threw his head back and laughed heartily, and Adri joined in the laughter. When Max caught his breath, he said, "You really are serious about your chocolate. Go ahead and enjoy!" Max sat and watched her with amusement, and Adri went back to the cake.

The room was silent until Adri was fishing for the last crumb. After she captured it, she held the spoon out and asked, "Do you want the last of it?" Adri shivered when Max laughed again. She loved the sound of his chest-deep rumbling laughter.

He shook his head. "No, you go ahead." Then he chuckled again as she carefully licked it off the spoon. "Now are you ready to share about your morning? You have an amazingly light spirit, so my guess is that it went well."

Adri jumped up from her chair and whirled around to the front of the desk. She laughed happily. "It went great—great—great!" She clapped her hands enthusiastically and continued. "Oh, Max, I was falling apart before you called, and I just barely got myself pulled back together when Kim arrived with Denny."

Max straightened up in the chair. Adri sat down in the other chair and reached for Max's hand and continued, "Denny saw me and came right over to me and told me I was so pretty, and he hugged me! At least Kim had mentioned Denny's disability, so I didn't make a scene like I could have, but I wasn't real comfortable with the hug. Denny is at least as tall as you and bulkier, so I just kind of held my breath and invited them into the office." Adri laughed softly. "A week ago, I wouldn't have been able to handle an approach like that, let alone accept a friendly hug from the male of the species."

Max grinned and asked, "What brought about the change?"

Adri blushed and squeezed Max's hand. "You."

Max chuckled softly. "Me? What did I do?"

Adri blushed even more as she ducked her head before she looked up, right into his eyes. Her voice was soft when she said, "You gave me a friendly hug after I asked, and I wasn't threatened or taken advantage of."

Max looked into Adri's sparkling blue eyes and smiled tenderly. "You discovered a different kind of man in me?"

"Yes." Adri broke the eye contact and pulled her hand back to her lap. "You are a very different kind of man, and you are teaching me so much!"

Adri moved off the chair and went to the coffee counter. "Would you like a cup of coffee? It's fresh."

Max recognized that Adri needed a distraction. He had felt the pull, the spark from their eye contact and was sure that Adri had too but didn't know probably what that was all about. He smiled and agreed, "Yes, a cup of coffee would be nice."

Adri took her time pouring two cups of coffee. Then instead of handing it to Max, she set his cup on the desk in front of him and went around the desk to sit in her office chair again. She sipped her coffee as the thoughts zipped through her mind. *Max had to know what I was going to say, and I'm not sure what happened when I looked in his eyes. He had a tender expression, but there was something else. I felt it clear to my toes! Okay, Adri, get it together. Tell him about your morning. I know he wants to know how it went!*

Adri looked at Max but not in his eyes. She smiled.

"Anyway, I asked Denny some questions about handling special furniture and about how to be around people, and he gave real clear and good answers. I had just pulled out the paperwork that needed to be filled out when a customer came in. Denny jumped up and wanted to go get it. Kim and I both convinced him that he needed to fill out the paperwork while I would go to wait on the customer." Adri giggled. "As it turned out, I needed some help after all. The table that my customer wanted to see was behind a couple of heavier ones, so I asked Denny to help. He was very courteous and gentle with the furniture and stood with the table until the customer paid for it, and then he carried it out and carefully put it in her car." Adri sat back and clapped her hands and laughed happily. "The customer was so pleased. She tipped him, and he was overwhelmed, and I told him he had the job. He couldn't wait to tell Kim."

Max laughed too. "Did he hug you again?"

Adri blushed. "Yes, and I returned his hug this time."

Max smiled. "That's my girl! What kind of disability does he have?"

Adri couldn't answer right away. A shiver had gone through her when Max said "my girl", and she concentrated on the sensation. Finally, she answered, "Umm, Kim says he is slow. He is sixteen years old and struggles at the eighth grade level. They homeschool him. Kim didn't tell me, but I think he is maybe ten or twelve in emotional years."

"A new experience for you, and you came through with flying colors! How about Jocko? How did that go?" Max questioned gently.

Adri jumped up again and danced a little jig. "I was on a roll. Kim and Denny were still here when Jocko, Gina, and Josh got here. Denny knew them and had to play with the baby before he was ready to go. Then Brad came to get his check. So we were actually seated in my office before Jocko introduced me to Gina and Josh." Adri moved around in front of the desk and stood in front of Max. "What a sweet baby! I even got to hold him when Gina excused herself for a few minutes!"

Adri laughed happily and fluttered her hands gently before she swung back around and sat in the chair next to Max.

"Here I go again—getting off subject. Anyway, I asked leading questions of both of them and just let them talk. Then—" Adri looked down at her hands, smoothed her skirt, moved a lock of hair to the back of her shoulder, and sighed. She finally looked at Max as she continued. "I asked Jocko some very pointed questions about what he thought his job would be. He never once got uncomfortable or aggravated, and I was pretty blunt. The thing that really got him the job though was when-when he said, 'You are the boss, and I respect you, and I am willing to do any task you assign me to do, and I intend to do it to the best of my ability, and I won't be afraid to ask questions.'" Adri paused and stood up. She paced to the coffee counter and back before she met Max's eyes and smiled a sweet, happy smile. "He couldn't have been more sincere, and I really believe that he will work with me and not try to take over. So I have an assistant and a part-time showroom helper!"

Max grinned and stood up and laid his hands on her shoulders. "Good for you! Business woman, extraordinary!"

Adri laughed and then reached out and hugged Max, resting her cheek on his shoulder. Max gave a firm hug in return and leaned back so he could see her face. "When you talked about being blunt, you seemed to regret something."

Adri nodded and stepped away from Max. "I may not have been out of line as a business owner, but I felt like I was being mean with my questions. I've never done this kind of interview before, and it was real uncomfortable."

Max tilted his head to the side and asked, "What was your meanest question?"

Adri looked at Max with a startled expression and then ducked her head and thought a minute. When she looked up, her face was pale instead of flushed. "I-I asked him if-if he thought he-he had the right to change the bookkeeping methods or the showroom layout without my con-consent."

Max had to hold back a smile. "That sounds acceptable to me. Is that when he told you that you are the boss and he respected you?"

"Yes." A little color came back into her cheeks. "Yes. But my experience in the past—well, that kind of question would have been answered with a belligerent tone or a disrespectful shrug or an 'I don't care' attitude." Her checks were very pink now. "I had a couple of delivery men that displayed those kinds of attitudes in spite of Dan's intervention."

Max did smile now. "Well, there you go. It sounds like Jocko is a man after my own heart!"

Adri gave him a little smile. "The question didn't sound offensive?"

Max shook his head. "If I wanted to be hired for a job and was asked that question, I would take it in the spirit it was meant and try to answer as smoothly as Jocko did."

Adri thought for a little before she sighed. "Okay. I wasn't mean then?"

Max answered tenderly, "No. Adri, you did good!"

Adri laughed happily. "Now I need to show you the library setup! Oh wait, I need to put Betty's number in my phone!" She rounded the desk and sat down to accomplish that and then bounced up again. She reached out and grasped Max's hand. "Come on!"

As they were weaving their way to the back of the showroom, Adri asked, "Did you and Betty like the chairs Dan brought over this morning?"

Max pulled Adri to a stop, and she faced him. He was grinning. "Yes! We were both excited at how well they went with the table!" Then he looked puzzled. "But I thought you said you couldn't find any?"

Adri laughed. "That's right. Didn't have any out here in the showroom, but they were in my house at my kitchen table, so we switched things out, and now you have chairs."

Max protested. "But those are yours!"

Now Adri giggled. "They were like all the other furniture in my house or out here in the showroom. I will sell any of it if someone wants it." Then she was serious. "The only thing I won't sell is the small writing desk that was my mother's." A sad expression crossed her face. "It's the-the only thing I have left of her."

Max was stunned at this revelation. Even the antiques that he was sure surrounded her at home weren't family heirlooms. Max took a deep breath and said softly, "That's okay then."

Adri lit up again. "Come on, we are almost there!" They walked around two smaller rows of antiques. Then Adri stopped and exclaimed, "Ta-da! What do you think?"

Max turned a full circle. "This is wonderful! Even in this large room it gives the impression of cozy. I can see that you mixed a few styles, but they go nicely together." He turned back to Adri with a smile.

She was glowing. She pointed to some pictures lined up nearby. "I picked those out for the library and the master's bedroom. You need to decide if you like them well enough to look at every day."

Max walked over and squatted in front of them. He considered each one carefully. He stood and backed away and looked for a bit longer. "Yes to all but the last one. It's too busy for my peace of mind. I could see it in the dining room or on the stair wall maybe, but not in my quiet places."

"Okay. We won't take it right now. I have another picture that you might like better, but we'll have to dig for it."

Max stood in the center of the setup and turned a full circle again. Adri asked, "Do you like the rugs?"

Max looked down at the one he was standing on and then at the fireplace setting. "Yes. They contrast beautifully and will bring out the individual colors in the drapes."

Adri laughed happily. "You learn fast!"

Max grinned. "I'm trying. It must be the company I'm keeping!"

Adri laughed again and spun around. "Let's go find a replacement picture!"

Max followed Adri back through the maze of furniture. Of course, his thoughts went to Adri, his eyes observing her as she walked gracefully ahead of him. *She dresses to fit in. I wonder if the long skirts and ruffle blouses are really her style or if it is a deliberate choice. Probably her style. She was wearing something similar at the courthouse. She carries it off with grace and style with her tall slenderness and seems really comfortable.*

Max was startled out of his thoughts when Adri announced, "Here we are! I can't hang all the paintings and prints, so I'll need to sort through, uh, this cart I think." There we two large roller carts under a large display of smaller framed paintings and prints.

Max offered, "Can I help?"

"Yes, when I find the one I'm looking for." She bent slightly and began to carefully flip through the paintings in the cart. "Some of the frames are fragile, and even though there are hinged and cushioned spacers, they need gentle treatment."

Max was standing so that each picture was briefly visible as Adri moved them. A white-framed painting caught his eye, and he put a hand gently on her arm to stop the movement. "That white-framed one would go with the Italian bedroom set."

Adri straightened up, her eyes soft and a sweet smile on her face. "That's exactly right! Are you interested in the Italian set with this picture, for your rose-colored spare room?"

Max chuckled. "Yes. Ever since you suggested it, I liked it more as I thought about it."

"Well, let's just pull it out and put it with the bedroom set!" Max stepped closer to Adri and reached for the painting of an Italian street market, only a few people in a waiting pose, in the early morning light. His movement brought his arm in direct contact with Adri's arm, and Adri felt the shiver that raced through her, clear to her toes. Max didn't miss her reaction. Adri jumped to the side and was blushing furiously.

CHAPTER 10

Max carefully lifted the painting to a secure place on the floor. He had his own reaction to the touch but felt it was more important to help Adri deal with her reaction and overreaction. Max's face was serious and his eyes tender when he turned back to Adri.

"It's okay, Adri. Do you understand what happened?" he spoke softly.

Adri was still blushing, her eyes continued to focus on the cart of pictures. She shook her head slightly and whispered, "It wasn't the first time I-I felt it."

Max nodded seriously. "It wasn't the first time for me either. Don't be afraid of it."

Adri rushed the words out before she could change her mind. "But I've hugged you and held your hand and didn't . . ." She shook her head. "What—why . . . ?"

Max gave a soft, tender laugh. "Didn't you ever have a boyfriend that you felt attraction for?"

Max realized that was definitely the wrong question. Adri went pale. She bit her bottom lip. Her hands trembled when she clutched them together at her waist. Max knew that right now he could not approach her, so he used words.

"When we hugged and when we held hands, we did that as friends. The touches that tingle, those tell us that we are attracted as man and woman. It is very natural when we like the appearance of someone. And we were both traveling the same thought path, which is very appealing. It can be subconscious or at the front of our minds." His voice dropped to a tender, quiet timber. "It's okay, Adri."

Adri stared at him for an endless moment. *I can tell Max. I've never told anyone everything! I can tell Max! I can! He'll understand.* She blinked and whispered, "M-Max, I-I had a couple of dates in-in college but-but never . . . not that. And he only-only tried to kiss-kiss me once. I pulled a-away. He-he wasn't nice." Adri's hands went up, and she covered her flushed face. Max saw her shoulders shudder. Adri was remembering the college experience.

Max asked quietly, "He ended up being a real jerk, didn't he?"

Adri's hands dropped. She was pale again. *Keep talking. Get it all off your chest!* Unshed tears sparkled in her eyes. "He and-and two of his friends kept asking for dates, and I re-refused, but they-they started following me-me everywhere. My sorority sisters took turns being with-with me the rest of the spring sem-semester so I wouldn't have to face any of th-them alone." Her voice dropped to a whisper. "The-the dean wouldn't le-let me get a re-restraining or-order."

Max shuddered at what Adri said. His voice was angry but soft. "The dean was a real jerk too!"

Adri blinked to try to dispel the tears. The more she tried, the more the tears came, and they were running down her cheeks. *I hate what they were trying to do to me, and it hurts so badly.*

Max pulled a handkerchief from his pocket and held it out to Adri. Instead of taking the cloth from Max, she hesitantly stepped toward him. *Will he still accept me? Will he help the hurt go away?* Max was watching her face and saw the fear and uncertainty.

"I am still your friend, Adri," he told her softly.

Then Adri was in his arms. He held her tenderly as the tears turned to sobs. *He is my friend—a friend I really need right now. Please, God—thank you, God.* They lasted a few minutes, and when the sobs stopped, she spoke huskily. "You understand. Th-thank y-you."

Now, Max gently rubbed one hand up and down her back and told her. "I think I do understand. I am so sorry you went through that."

Adri sniffed and pushed back slightly. "The worst th-thing—I found o-out that those three had made a pack th-that one of-of them would ge-get me into bed. With-without the protection of my sorority sisters, I-I . . . Oh, Max!" There were new tears, but they were quiet tears now, and Max gently dabbed at them with his handkerchief.

A shudder ran through Adri, and she set her face with a determined expression. She shuffled back a half step and took the handkerchief from Max. Her voice was still a little husky, but it was firmer.

"That was seven years ago. Now that-that I-I have told the whole stor-story, it is time to let it go." She balled the used cloth in her hand and looked at Max. She spoke with quiet reserve. "I felt you would understand and wanted you to know."

Max's hands were resting on her shoulders, and he squeezed gently. "Thank you for trusting me. I am willing to share this burden with you and help any way I can."

Adri couldn't pull her gaze from Max's. She saw such wonderful tenderness. "You-you have already he-helped. It doesn't hur-hurt so much now."

Max's chocolate brown eyes went almost black with the thrill he felt at Adri's words, and he smiled. "I'm glad!" Max's voice had a slight gruffness when he add, "Once again, you have shown me how much courage you have."

Adri blushed at Max's words. Then she smiled shyly. "I need to freshen my face. I think the picture I was looking for is three back from where we stopped."

Max chuckled. "I'll look, if that's okay."

Adri nodded as she turned to go toward her office and the restroom.

Max watched her go and allowed his thoughts free rein. *She must have been terrified—horrified in that experience! And the scars went deep. God, make me worthy of her trust! I know you brought us together, and I know it is your work that has given Adri the courage to share deeper things with me. It's scary that she trusts me so much! Please be with me in all this. Be with Adri.*

Max heard the restroom door open, and he turned back to the cart of pictures and found the one Adri had indicated. It was a perfect replacement, and he was still looking at it when Adri came up beside him.

"What do you think? Do you want that one?"

Max turned his head and smiled, noting that Adri looked fresh and more contented.

"Yes. It is a perfect choice. Are you this good with all your customers?"

Adri laughed happily, one eyebrow going up and her eyes sparkling with joy. The laugh and the sweet beauty was taking Max breathe from his lungs.

"Usually. Once in a while, I haven't asked the right questions to get a feeling for a customer's wants. That's when I have to work a little harder for a sale."

Max finally had his breath back and chuckled. "I have a feeling that you have a lot of repeat customers because of that gift. That and your love for what you do, selling antiques that you love."

Adri's face flushed beautifully. "Yes. I have an amazing number of repeat customers. In the first year that I opened, I helped with a whole house, like I am doing for you." The blush deepened and she added shyly, "At least I guess I will help you . . ." Her voice faded with a tad of doubt.

Max grinned. "Yes, sweet Adri. I would very much like you to help me furnish my entire home. I have no desire to seek help elsewhere."

Adri nodded with a sweet smile. "Let's get these two paintings to the other side of the building."

Max picked up a painting in each hand. He gave Adri a smile. "I've got them. You lead the way."

As they approached the front door, the gate buzzer went off. Max stopped when Adri did. "I'll stay here and wait."

Max nodded and asked, "Since I've decided on the library setup, what can I do while you wait on your customer?"

"We need to gather it up and put it at the loading dock. You could just push it toward the back until I get there."

Max nodded and moved past Adri as the customer came in the front entrance. He nodded and smiled as he continued on his way and noticed the long look she gave him.

The customer turned to Adri, and Adri greeted her. "Hello, Mrs. Sykes. Did you decide you wanted the pendant after all?"

Mrs. Sykes was a small slender woman in her fifties and had been coming to look at antique jewelry since Adri had opened the business. She was a bubbly and blunt lady and didn't hesitate to speak her mind now.

"Yes, yes. But, Adri, what a dish that young man is! Did you hire some help? Are you going to give *him* some serious attention? He looks very dashing with those whiskers on his jaw. You couldn't do better, you know. You should be giving thought to settling down and having babies!"

Adri was blushing because she was sure Max had heard everything. She laughed and answered, "He's a customer, and yes, he is getting a lot of my attention right now."

Mrs. Sykes laughed too. "Good. Good. Do you still have that pendant I was looking at a few weeks ago?"

Adri assured her, "Yes, it is still here. I have some new pieces that you might like to see too. I bought them on the Internet with you in mind." They moved toward the jewelry display, and the conversation turned to business.

Thirty minutes later, Mrs. Sykes left bubbling about her purchases, three pieces instead of one.

When Adri joined Max at the back of the building, he had accomplished quite a bit, even the rugs were rolled up and ready to move. When Max looked up at Adri's approach, his eyes were twinkling, and there was a broad smile on his face.

"Are all your repeat customers that outspoken?"

Adri blushed furiously and laughed. "No. Mrs. Sykes is a special treasure on that score!"

Max laughed.

Adri continued to look at Max and said shyly, "I agree about your, uh, whiskers and-and a few other things." Adri's blush deepened.

Max grinned and bowed at the waist. "Why, thank you, kind lady!"

Adri straightened her shoulders and moved toward the back wall and the walk-through door.

"You got a lot done. Now we'll move it to the loading dock."

She stepped through the door and pushed a button and then stepped back through and closed the door. There was a motor sound, and the wall began to separate at the center. Eight-foot panels moved behind and continued to slide as another panel moved back. Soon the wall was just two eight-foot stacks of panels at the outside walls of the building.

Max watched the wall in amazement. When the wall stopped moving, he grinned. "Great setup! I'm impressed!"

Adri laughed. "I had a terrible time finding someone who would install this. I had the idea and got someone to design it, but the people to install—well, I had to pay in advance and write in the contract that the responsibility was mine if it didn't work." Adri laughed again. "The designer has had three calls from the installer for more similar designs since then."

Max grinned. "Have either one of them paid you a finder's fee?"

"No, but the designer is in high demand these days. She calls me from time to time to thank me for trusting her."

Max's face registered surprise, and then he laughed. "A woman designer. Makes sense. Some women rise up with wonderful new challenges."

Adri nodded emphatically. "Now we move the rugs first, then paintings and smaller furniture to the back wall of the dock. The larger items follow, and then we will move the Italian bedroom set. The guys load the large items first and then fill in with smaller items."

Max was curious. "Is your truck large enough to hold all two rooms?"

Adri smiled as she went to one end of the large area rug. "Oh yes. The guys are good packers, and there will probably be room left over with these two rooms." She pointed at the rug. "You get that end, and we'll move this first."

Max bent and grasped the end; Adri picked up the other end. Max asked, "It's not too heavy for you?"

Adri smiled. "Not a bit. I'm used to this kind of thing." They set down the rug in the dock area. "Oh, Max! I almost forgot. Jocko made a suggestion for the library, and I need to tell you about it!"

"I'm listening!"

"Follow me." Adri moved away from the dock area and wove gracefully into the maze of furniture. She stopped at a large bookcase. It was free standing and had amazing cutout work on the sides with elegant shelves, edged with the same design. When Max caught up and was standing beside Adri, she continued. "Jocko hadn't seen your library room, but he was aware that some of these houses didn't have built-in library shelves. He suggested you might want something like this in there since I confirmed that there were none built in."

Max's eyes widened as he took in the beautifully worked cherrywood shelf. It stood eight feet tall, and he was sure it was nearly eight feet wide.

"This is magnificent!" He looked around. "Is there just one?"

Adri laughed happily, again stealing Max's breath. "This is the only one out here. There are five more in storage, all in wonderful shape, just as this one is!"

Max chuckled. "Six shelves altogether. Great! Let me see if I can guess where you would put them!" Max thought a minute. "Fill the two corners at the far end of the library with four of them, and the other two could go in my office area to replace the condo shelves there."

Adri laughed and clapped her hands. "Good job! Excellent placement, but to keep the cozy look, we need to put a chair, a table, and a lamp in each corner for reading nooks!"

Max laughed too. "Of course! Now we have to find those pieces!"

Adri grabbed his hand and pulled. "I have sets you can look at! Max, this is so much fun!"

Adri led him to a place where chairs and tables were set up in cozy arrangements. These were all sets, and each table that matched had matching lamps on them.

Max exclaimed, "Wow! There is a good number to choose from! But it will be easy. The nook set-up needs to be lighter in color to contrast rather than match, don't you think?"

"Exactly! There are two medium oak sets and the lighter varnished Spanish style that may be too ornate. What do you think?"

Max laughed. "Does furniture talk to you?"

Adri went serious instead of laughing. "Yes. I don't admit it very often, but there is one set that is talking to you, isn't there?"

Max nodded slowly. "The oak set with the beige and green-striped cushions."

"Great choice! Do you like the lamps?"

Max considered the lamps and looked around. "I think the green and gold lamps instead."

Adri moved into the arrangement and switched out the lamps. "Now, is this right?"

Max grinned. "Yes, very right!"

"Well, let's just get these things to the back as well!" Adri picked up the lamps, and Max grabbed a chair. They arrived at the loading dock and were setting things down when the gate buzzer went off again.

Max laughed. "That buzzer made me jump! I didn't realize you had a buzzer back here."

Adri shrugged. "I need it to get my attention. I don't spend a lot of time sitting in my office."

CHAPTER 11

Adri headed toward the front, and Max went back to get the other chair. Adri arrived at the front when Jocko opened the door and Gina stepped in holding a sleeping Josh.

Adri smiled happily. "Well, hey there. What are you doing back here?"

Jocko grinned. "We've been out looking for a place to live." He sobered. "Nothing within five miles seems to be available right now. We wanted to come back and see if you, by chance, know of any place big enough for us."

At that moment, Max set something down with a thud, and Jocko looked around Adri. "You have someone here?"

Adri nodded. "Max and I are moving his purchases back to the loading dock."

Jocko's face brightened. "Hey, can I give a hand? House hunting is depressing. I need to cheer up!"

Gina put a hand on Jocko's arm. "Maybe they want to do it!" There was a mischievous smile on her face.

Adri blushed, catching Gina's meaning. "Yes, Jocko, you can help. We have just barely started." She looked at Gina with the sleeping baby in a chest pouch. "Gina, would you like to get comfortable in the office?"

Gina laughed. "No, thank you. I don't want to miss out on the action!"

Adri laughed too. "Okay, you three come on. All the action is at the back."

Jocko and Gina followed Adri to the back. Max had just set down the side tables for the reading nooks on the loading dock and turned around as they approached.

One of Max's eyebrows went up, and he grinned. "Jocko! I know you! You work at the Wolcott estates."

Jocko stepped forward and held out his hand to Max. "Hey, Max. Good to see you again. And yeah, I worked for the Wolcotts until today. I have a new job now, here with Adri."

"It's good to see you too. Adri told me she hired an assistant." Max released Jocko's hand and turned. "You must be Gina and Josh. I don't think we've met."

Gina smiled. "No. It's been a while since you've been around I think. Mrs. Wolcott complained to me just the other day that she hadn't seen you in a while!"

"That's true. I think the last time was Connor and Abby's anniversary celebration. And that was almost a year ago." Max chuckled. "I didn't realize it had been that long!"

Jocko asked, "Have you seen John and Carol lately? They're expecting again."

Max laughed. "Yes, I had a meal at their house a couple of weeks ago. Number 5 is due at the end of summer."

Adri had just been standing, listening. The pieces started to fall into place, and she wondered why Max hadn't told her he knew Jocko. *For that matter, why didn't Jocko mention that he knew Max? Their connection is the Wolcotts. I've never heard of them.* Adri felt an uncertainty creep into her thoughts.

Max glanced at Adri and saw the uncertainty on Adri's face and wondered about it.

Jocko asked, "So what can I help with?" He was glancing between Adri and Max.

Adri nodded toward the rest of what remained of the library setup. "This all needs to go to the loading dock, and Max decided to take the bookcases you suggested, so those need to be moved out of storage."

"No problem! I would much rather be here doing this than out talking to landlords that have no vacancies. I don't guess either one of you have information about a possible rental?" Jocko had moved toward a larger piece of library furniture as he asked the question.

Adri shook her head. "Not something I hear about."

Max grinned. "No, haven't got a clue."

Jocko shrugged. "Mrs. Wolcott told us that we would find the right place at the right time, and until then, we can stay where we are. I owe them a lot for all their encouragement and don't want to take advantage."

"You know they will never see it that way," Gina spoke softly. She turned to Adri and explained. "They treat us like family."

Adri nodded. *Family. Something I don't know about—at least the feeling of belonging. I need to distance myself for a bit. I am really sad right now.*

Before Adri could move away, Jocko spoke again. "Hey, Adri. It would be your call but wondered about Denny and I delivering all this for the library tomorrow. The library is on the ground floor, so it would work with just two of us."

Adri felt her face pale, and her insides clinch up with dread. *What have I done? Jocko is already trying to take over!* There was strain in her voice when she told him, "I'll th-think about it." Then she swung away and said quickly, "I need something from my house." And she nearly ran toward the front and pushed out the door of the building.

Max had seen the sadness and the flight reaction when Gina mentioned family and then the total rigidness and how pale she became at Jocko's suggestion. *She's overreacting. Too much of the past hit her in the face right now. I need to go see if I can help her.* He glanced at Jocko and then Gina and saw their worried expressions.

"Jocko, carry on. I'll be back in a few minutes."

Jocko nodded. Max strode purposefully to the front and out the door. He didn't have to look for Adri. He heard her. She was standing at the corner of the building, and she was gasping for air. He knew immediately that she was hyperventilating and needed to be calmed. Max went quickly to her. He grasped the nape of her neck and pulled her face against his shoulder and murmured softly.

"Everything is okay, Adri. Draw breath in slowly through your mouth." She wasn't calm enough to obey. "Slowly, slowly. That's right. Slowly. Now slowly out through your nose. Slowly."

While giving instructions, Max was gently massaging the nape of her neck with one hand, his other hand between her shoulder blades, holding her firmly in place. He knew she needed to breathe back in the air she had expelled.

"Time to take in another breath through your mouth slowly. No, don't move, just pull in breath. That's right. Now slowly out through your nose."

Adri felt Max's gentleness. She heard the quiet confidence in his voice and the soothing motion on her neck. By the time he was encouraging the third breath in, she began to relax, and the breath was more easily taken in and then let out. She relaxed even more when Max encouraged, "Don't stop yet. Once more." Max waited and felt the tension leaving Adri's shoulders. "One more time." When she had followed the instruction, he gently moved his hands to her arms and moved her back from him so he could see her face. He noticed the color was back, and he asked gently, "Better now?"

Adri was trembling slightly, but she nodded jerkily. When Adri reached out, Max brought her back to his chest and held her tenderly. When the trembling stopped, he spoke softly, "This day has been a little of an overload for you, hasn't it?"

Adri nodded against his shoulder.

Max prodded gently. "Tell me."

Adri stiffened and pushed back. Her face was pale again. "Jocko is already trying to take over!" Her voice strengthened. "You heard him about the delivery!"

Max nodded. "I heard him say it was your call, meaning it is your decision."

Adri's eyes widened, showing her confusion. "Did he say that?"

"Yes. Everything else he said was a suggestion, and the decision is all yours."

Adri looked away from Max and then back. "I-I overreacted, didn't I-I?"

"Let me ask you something." Adri nodded. "If this situation had taken place Thursday instead of today, while he was just one of your delivery crew, how would you have reacted to this same suggestion?"

Adri dropped her head and shook it. She took a deep breath, straightened her shoulders, and finally looked up into Max's eyes. "I would have been glad for the suggestion and actually asked him to work it out. It would be fine because I trust him with deliveries."

Max just tilted his head and asked, "What really changed? Jocko or your attitude?"

Adri covered her face with her hands and sighed. Then she dropped her hands in disgust. "Oh, Max. My attitude or rather the fearfulness of-of men taking over."

"Okay. Now what are you going to do?" There was a slight smile on his face, and his eyes crinkled at the edges.

Adri took another deep breath. "I think you will get your library furniture tomorrow, and I need to go ask Jocko to arrange it."

Max's smile filled his face now. "That's my girl!"

Adri gave Max a shaky smile. Then she reached for his hand and squeezed it. "I am so glad you were here! Thank you!"

Adri moved away from Max and turned toward the door. She asked, "Are you getting tired of rescuing me? You are doing it a lot!"

Max chuckled softly. "I'm glad you trust me so that I *can* help."

"Yes, me too." Adri meant it, and the question flashed through her mind. *How can I trust him so completely?*

Max opened the door, and they went in. Adri had her confidence back and went straight to the back where Jocko was pushing the last bookcase onto the dock.

"Jocko, call Denny and ask if he can help tomorrow. Time shouldn't be an issue, right, Max?"

"No. Any time is fine."

Adri nodded and continued. "I have a ten o'clock appointment here, and then at one o'clock, I have a tour bus coming, just so you know my schedule."

Jocko pulled out his cell phone. "I'll call him now. I think the earlier, the better."

Adri smiled. "Good, let me know when. I need to go to my office and make an invoice."

As Adri moved away, her face flushed a little. *I feel like I should apologize, but I don't know what to say, how to explain. It's really amazing that I even let Max in that close. I might need to be alone this evening and give it some thought.*

Jocko arranged to pick up Denny, and they would be there at eight the next morning. After Jocko and Family left, Max asked Adri to join him and Betty for dinner, but Adri knew she needed alone time and maybe an early night, so she promised Max she would be available Saturday evening.

Adri worked her way through her evening ritual and thought about the day and the successes and what felt like the failure when she overreacted to Jocko's suggestions. Her face colored every time she thought of it and how disappointed Max probably was with her. Yes, she remembered how reassuring he was and his straight-forward attitude, but she wondered if deep down inside, he was getting disgusted. *Oh, Max! When will you give up on me? I am such a mess!*

When she crawled into bed, she knew that sleep might be a problem, so she decided to read a little in the book, *Trail to Life,* to redirect her thoughts. After reading the first chapter, she was feeling sleepy, so she put the book down and refused to think about anything, except what she had read, and she finally slept soundly.

Chapter 12

When Adri awoke for the start of her Saturday, she felt rested and strangely at peace in her spirit despite her wonderings about Max. She had hoped that he was being completely honest with her, so she hurried down to the business just before Jocko and Denny arrived.

As the guys were loading the truck, she just stayed out of the way and observed Jocko's directions and Denny's willingness to do everything right. Adri decided that she was really pleased with the job they were doing. After they pulled out, she was busy with rearranging the showroom to fill in the gaps.

Her morning appointment was with Mr. Carl Canton and Ms. Jessica Walker. They were soon to be married and wanted advice on antique furniture and other things that they could use in the wedding and then place in their home. This was a challenge but also a lot of fun. These young people were in their midtwenties and were fun and enthusiastic with common sense thrown in.

Jocko popped in briefly about eleven thirty to give Adri the check for the delivery and promised to arrive on time Monday morning. Since she was busy, they didn't discuss how the delivery had gone.

By twelve thirty, Adri's customers were happy with their selections and paid for their purchases. Adri assured them that yes, she could store their things until they were ready to use them at the church.

She barely had time to eat a bite of lunch before the tour bus arrived, but she was ready for them and greeted the spry octogenarians as they poured in through the front door. These kinds of tours were usually wild and crazy because of the questions and whims of the people that came with the tours.

Adri was always in her element with these situations, except today, there were two older men who could not be classified as gentlemen; and before the group had even been there an hour, Adri was beginning to feel harassed, and the time started to drag. Her smile was starting to fade. The men kept trying to corner her and were making innuendos about physical play and not the nice kind.

Adri finally latched on to the tour organizer, Lisa Dunnally, and insisted she needed to stick close. After taking this defensive mode, the older men positioned themselves where they could watch her every move, and they stared at her continuously, still making her feel violated.

Adri was very relieved when Lisa announced that they all needed to be back on the bus in thirty minutes. Because of her past experiences, Adri was impatient to see the last of this tour group. She usually accompanied the group to the bus to bid farewells, but today, as the last person exited, she closed and locked the doors, went to her office, and collapsed in her chair. She was fighting hyperventilation, and she was shaking all over. She used a paper bag from her bottom desk drawer to regain normal breathing, but before the shakes stopped, she was crying hard, sobbing tears. When the tears finally stopped, she was exhausted, and all she could do was sit there and feel the hatred once again building toward her father and her brother, and she latched on the hatred of the two dirty old men that she had suffered that afternoon.

Adri finally went to her house and decided that she needed to shower and hoped to wash away the awfulness of the afternoon. It didn't really help, but she was able to at least work toward a better frame of mind.

Adri walked up to Max's house alone on Saturday evening. It was about an hour before dinner time, and she took her time. Her thoughts jumped to the questions from the night before. *It still bothers me why Max never mentioned that he knew Jocko. It feels like something is going on behind my back. And Max didn't even seem to be dismayed about my problem. I haven't hyperventilated in a really long time! Too many changes in my life at one time, I guess. I really like Max, but now I am wondering if I trust him too much.* Adri sighed and muttered to herself. "Get a better attitude, Adri. You are going to Max's house to enjoy the company and the food. Lighten up!"

During dinner, Max and Betty told Adri how the delivery had gone, and Max showed Adri the library after dinner. Max told Adri, "Jocko said he thought there were some small area rugs that would make the reading nooks a little more tempting. What do you think?"

Adri nodded. "Yes, there should be a matching pair that would fit in there."

Max noticed Adri's reserve and wondered about it, so he asked, "Did we set this up right?"

Adri smiled. "Oh yes. The setup is good, almost like I had it in my showroom. It looks good."

Max turned to her. "You seem tired tonight. You've had a busy day. Do you need to go home?"

Adri nodded and turned to the library door. Adri said good-bye to Betty and thanked her again for the wonderful dinner while Max went for the flashlight.

They were both quiet as Max walked Adri down the path toward her house. Max was puzzled by Adri's reserve. *Have I done something to upset her? She wasn't enthused about the library like I thought she would be. God, give me the insight and the right words when the time is right.*

It had been a busy day, and Adri was starting to feel it. She felt the body weariness and was sad that she was struggling with so much baggage from the past that seemed to be transplanting into the present.

Max made sure the flashlight was shining on the path as it was quite dark with a light cloud cover. The weather man was predicting rain the following day. As they stepped through the hedge, Adri commented, "Betty really is trying to spoil me. I mean cream puffs for desert and chocolate filling too!"

Max chuckled. "Yeah! You know why, don't you?" They had reached the back porch, and the security light came on.

Adri faced him. "No, I don't know why, but it is nice!"

Max grinned. "She told me that it's not right that you eat alone when you enjoy being at my house for a meal. She says she wants to temp you to more meals."

Adri smiled a little. "Bless her heart. I am used to eating alone, but"—her face blushed—"I do really like eating with you and Betty. It's always so relaxed and calm. And of course, the food is always wonderful!"

Max chuckled softly. "Betty is a jewel." Max hesitated and then gently touched Adri's cheek with his bent knuckle. "You have a good night and sweet dreams."

Adri blushed again as she reached up and touched Max's cheek. Then she turned quickly and punched in the code to open the door. "Good night, Max." She stepped into the house. Max smiled gently and turned to leave. Adri watched until he was through the hedge before closing the door.

She had just turned on the kitchen light and reached for a glass, had it in hand when the gate buzzer sounded. The glass slipped from her fingers and went crashing into the sink when she heard a car motor rev and then turn off. It felt like all the blood drained out of her body. *Have they come back? Oh god, I can't face them! I've got to call the police.* Her phone was in her hand when it rang. It was Max.

"M-max." Her voice was trembling.

"Adri? Were you expecting someone?"

"N-no. I-I was just going to call 911."

"I'm almost back to the hedge. I'll knock twice at your back door. Now call the police."

"Ye-yes." She disconnected and then punched 911. When the dispatcher answered, Adri had to stiffen her spine and force herself to say who she was, where she was, and what the problem was.

The dispatcher asked if she was alone. Adri heard the two knocks. Adri opened the back door and stuttered into her phone. "My-my neighbor is-is here wit-with me."

The dispatcher warned them to stay in the house and told Adri that two patrol cars were on their way.

Adri closed her phone with trembling hands and almost collapsed into Max's arms. Then she started hyperventilating.

Max immediately took charge of Adri, talking to her and soothing her as he had the day before. His thoughts were racing. *What is she so afraid of? I'm here, and the police are on their way, but this reaction must be something more. God, help her to calm and give her courage to talk to me. This is scary. Twice in two days.*

Adri was in Max's arms, and he was speaking softly, reassuringly, but Adri couldn't seem to listen, to hear him for all the terror in her brain. *It's them! They've come back to ruin the rest of my life! I know it's them! Oh god, take them away!*

Max wasn't getting anywhere. Adri was still gasping helplessly. Max gripped Adri's arms in a tight hold, tried to get her eyes to focus on him, and raised his voice. "Adri! Adri, listen to me!" Adri's panicked eyes finally focused on Max's face. "You have to breathe slowly in through your mouth. Do you hear me?"

Adri fell against Max's shoulder and tried to listen. Max softened his voice and coached her steadily, over and over. It took more breathes this time, but he finally felt her trembling, with almost normal breathing. He bent and lifted her into his arms and carried her to the Victorian sofa in the front room. He sat down beside her and cuddled her close, continuing to reassure her with comforting phrases.

She had almost stopped trembling when the gate buzzer went off, making her jump and stiffen. Flashing red and blue lights danced across the front window curtains. Max said softly, "It's okay. The police are here."

Adri shuddered and took a deep breath. Her voice was husky and low when she spoke. "I guess the-they'll want to ta-talk to m-me."

"I'm sure they will, but right now, they are checking out the car," Max reassured her.

Adri clung to Max. "I-I am so afraid it's the-them," she whispered.

"Who? Adri who are you afraid of?"

Adri could barely say it. "Ch-es-ester a-an-and Ch-Char-Charles."

"Chester and Charles?"

Adri nodded against his shoulder. Max asked another question. He wanted to make sure he had it right. "Your father and brother?"

Adri shuddered and nodded again.

Max glanced out the window and told Adri, "I think an officer is coming to the house. Are you going to be able to talk to him?"

Adri pulled away, squared her shoulders, took a deep breath, and answered, "Yes."

She remained seated until the officer rang the doorbell. She got up and walked to the door.

"Ms. Winfield, it's Officer Dennis," the officer called from the other side.

Max followed her to the door and stood behind her as she opened the door. Adri was pale but had an amazing calm in her voice. "Officer, whose car is it? Was someone in it?"

Officer Dennis tilted his head slightly and answered, "The man in the car is passed out drunk, and the car belongs to his neighbor. This man has done this before, and it is amazing that he made it two miles this time."

There was a slight tremble in her voice when she asked, "Was he alone?"

"We believe so, but there are two officers searching your property as we speak. We want to make sure he *was* alone."

Adri nodded and asked, "Do you have questions for me?"

Before the officer could answer, his radio squawked, and a question was clear from the other end. *"Request instruction about a hole in the back hedge."*

Max stepped forward and explained the connection to his property and that he had come back to Adri's place that way shortly after hearing the car in her yard. The officer gave instructions to check the back side of the hedge, and the voice answered in the affirmative.

Then Officer Dennis asked for a clearer description of events and timing. Adri, with Max's help from time to time, filled him in on the details, and he made notes. His radio squawked again, and the only thing that was understandable was two different voices reporting "all clear." Officer Dennis informed them, "You heard. The search has cleared your property. The tow truck should be here within the next half hour, and then we will be out of here as well. Be sure and call if anything like this happens again."

Adri blew out a long breath. "Th-thank you, Officer Dennis."

The officer gave a brief salute and turned to leave.

CHAPTER 13

Adri closed the door and locked it with a trembling hand. Max took her hand in both of his and asked softly, "How are you?"

Adri shook her head slightly and turned her face away from Max. Her thoughts churned in her head. *I overreacted again. Max is going to get really tired of being around me. I am a mess, and men can't stand a mess. They want to be the center of everyone's attention. Oh, I know Max is different—but how long can that last with me?* Adri shuddered at her bitter thoughts and tried to pull her hand away from Max's hold.

Max held on and suggested, "Let's sit. I'm not leaving until everything is quiet again." He tugged gently and led Adri to the sofa. He handed her glass of water and watched her drink and then took it back and set it down before he sat a small distance from her.

Max studied her pale face. *She still doesn't trust me completely. Is she afraid that I will shun her or make fun of her? I would really like to know what else happened to her in the past. God, help me to ask the right questions. Help her to share her burden with me.*

"Adri, I am still your friend. Will you tell me, first of all, why you were so afraid it was Chester and Charles, and second of all, why that terrified you so much?" Max's voice was gentle, and his eyes didn't miss the panic that spread across her face when he asked her to tell him.

She's not going to tell me about her father and brother. What else can I get her to talk about? Something has shifted for her in her mind. I could see it on her face. God, give me an opening here. Help me! Wait; there is something she has mastered. I'll ask about that.

"Okay, sweet Adri. I have a completely different question to ask. Maybe you will tell me something else." Max got up and walked to the window and noticed the tow truck, and he told Adri quietly. "The tow truck will be coming through the gate." Seconds later, the gate buzzer sounded.

Adri got up and came to stand by Max. They both watched the activity outside. *Max seems different all of a sudden. I was trusting him, but the threat, the notion that I would have to face my worst nightmare, I think I put walls up again. Is he responding to that? Can he really sense my withdrawal?*

Adri sighed and went back to sit down. "What . . ." She had to stop and clear her throat, and she suddenly felt shy, and it came through her voice. "Max, what did you want to ask me?"

When Max turned from the window, he saw her shy glance down at her hands and then saw her look at him, but she was still pale.

"I have seen you do something, three different times, and I wonder how you can do it."

Now Adri's eyes jumped up to meet Max's gaze. "What have I done that puzzles you?"

Max relaxed, not realizing how tense he had become when Adri wouldn't communicate. "When you were sharing about your crisis in college and when you missed something and thought Jocko had taken over and again tonight. You were falling completely apart. Then you were calm."

Adri looked puzzled. Max held up his hand and continued. "In fact, you flip a switch when a conversation is going a direction you don't want it to. You seem to be recalling bad memories, and then suddenly, you are calm or even chipper, and the conversation goes in a direction that you want it to."

Adri blushed. She twisted her fingers together in her lap. "You want to know how I can do that?"

Max was relieved to see color back in her face, and he was relieved that she seemed to be open to this conversation. "Yes, I haven't encountered anyone who does it the way you do it."

Adri gave him a half smile. "I learned it from my Aunt Dixie. She had it down to an art. Come sit down, and I'll tell you about my aunt."

Max moved to the sofa, nodded, and said softly. "I'm listening."

"I was terrified the first time I saw her do it. She was ranting and raving at a piece of furniture that she was working on. Something wasn't going right. Mind you, she never used any 'blue' words, but she sure could verbally rip into that furniture. What stopped her ranting was the phone ringing, and I wasn't sure she should answer it. She did, and I couldn't believe how calm and responsive she was to the caller. It's like—well, you used the phrase, 'she flipped a switch.' She finished the phone call and fixed the problem with no more yelling." Adri smiled, and Max chuckled.

"I could picture it when you were describing it. What a deal!"

"The next time I witnessed a tantrum was when we were going to town and her pickup quit. First, she made the phone call to her mechanic, and then she got out and voiced a few dire deeds she intended to do to the pickup and kicked and hit the exterior. When the mechanic arrived, she was calm and clear about what happened just before it quit, and the mechanic found the problem, and we were on our way. Tantrum gone like it never happened." Adri laughed softly this time. "I am not as high-strung as Aunt Dixie, so it is a little different.

I learned it really well with some of my professors in college and then used it more with difficult customers. I internalize the part that upsets me and show only congeniality."

Max nodded and said softly, "The first time I came to your showroom, you didn't hide it quite so well. I knew you were taking deep breaths to calm down after I 'came in the back way.'"

Adri blushed bright red and explained, "That's because . . ." She went shy. "Because you surprised me. I didn't expect you to do that."

"Why didn't you expect that of me?" Max's question was sincere.

"Because I saw you as a thoughtful and deliberate kind of person at the courthouse."

Max grinned. "I wasn't quite myself that day. I just wanted to see you again."

Adri smiled. The gate buzzer went off, and Max got up to look out the window. "They look like they are all leaving." The gate buzzer sounded two more times. The yard out front was clear now.

Adri nodded, even though Max was still standing with his back to her. Adri began chewing on her bottom lip and clench her fingers together. This is what Max saw when he did turn around.

He asked quietly, "Is there another time you want to ask me about? Something else that surprised you?"

Adri nodded, and there was a stilted, almost accusing sound to her voice. "Why didn't you tell me you knew Jocko?"

Max groaned silently. He remembered the uncertain expression he had seen on her face when he and Jocko greeted each other. Now he knew what it was about and also recognized that her trust in him had been shaken by that one small thing. He also realized that to Adri, it was not a small thing. Maybe taking her back to the unpleasant surprises she had suffered by her own father's doing.

Max came and sat down on the sofa and turned to Adri. "Adri, do you remember the first time you told me about Jocko?"

"Yes. When I told you I had met with my crew."

"The only thing that identified Jocko to me was that he wasn't a shift worker like the others."

Adri nodded.

Max continued. "The second time we talked about Jocko, you were very nervous, and my concern was to build your confidence."

Adri nodded again.

"The third time was again in excitement yesterday afternoon. You did talk about Jocko and Gina and Josh. I had not met Gina and honestly did not remember her name, even though the Jocko I knew, I did know he was married. It did not occur to me that I would know someone that worked for you." Max leaned forward, directly in front of Adri's line of sight. "Granted, there are probably not very many men named Jocko, but I had no reason to think I would know him, and I was surprised to see him yesterday evening."

Adri sighed. "I've embarrassed myself—again." Adri got up and walked to the window to stare out at the darkness.

Max came and stood behind her. He didn't touch her, just spoke softly. "You don't have to feel embarrassed with me. I understand from what you have said that your past puts some things into shades of gray that really bother you. I don't mind helping by talking you through things."

"But, Max, it must seem to you that you have to keep repeating things like a broken record. How long will it be before you are tired of having to do that?"

Max put his hand on her arm and turned her toward him. "Adri." His voice was so gentle she immediately looked into his gaze. "I want to see you healed and whole and free from the past. If you need me to help you, I will never tire of talking you through things."

"I see." Adri looked down, her eyes settling on the V left from the two buttons that weren't fastened at his shirt collar. She continued, "Max, my life has changed a lot in the last week, and I really feel like I need to deal with fewer things." Adri stopped. She wasn't sure she could finish.

Max lifted her chin with one finger so that she was looking at him again. "It's okay, Adri. I need to back off and let you deal with business right now. I will do that. You have my phone number and Betty's, so if you need anything, anything at all, you call. We are your neighbors, your friends, and we are right up the hill. Is that what you need right now?"

Tears came to her eyes, and there was a husky sound in her voice. "I'm sorry, Max, but yes, that is what I need."

Max nodded, leaned forward, and brushed his lips gently across her forehead. "Betty and I will be praying for you. I'm going home now."

Max turned and moved toward the back door. Adri hesitated for a moment and then followed. Max picked up the flashlight off the cabinet and stepped out of the door and said softly, "Lock up. Talk to you later."

Adri didn't stand and watch this time. She gently closed the door and locked it and then turned and went to her bedroom.

CHAPTER 14

Max was amazed that even with the drama at Adri's place, it was only nine forty-five when he walked in the house and discovered that Betty had retired for the night. He had hoped she would still be up so he could talk to her. He knew he was too unsettled to sleep, so he went to the library and sat in his office chair. He sat tapping his fingers on his desk while his mind paged through the week. Finally, he prayed. *God, I am not sure what's really happening right now. You know where my heart is. You know what is really going on with Adri. I trust her to you. I feel like I have deserted her, but she agreed that I needed to step back. Help me to be sensitive to your wisdom and leading. In Jesus's name. Amen.*

Max turned to his computer and decided to look up his family tree. He was curious to find out if somewhere down the line he was related to Adri's family. He was pretty sure Chester was some kind of relation, and he was curious. It didn't take long. His great-great-grandfather, Maxwell Winfield, had a brother, Charles. Charles Winfield had a family but was charged with treason and put to death. His son, John, had a criminal history and died in prison; and John's son, James, married rich and squandered the family fortune. He died at the age of fifty from a heart attack. Chester was James's son. Chester's son, Charles, would be Max's cousin five generations removed.

Max was amazed that the whole line, five generations, seemed to have been the "black sheep" of the family. He sat back and pondered this insight. Then something strange brought him up short. *It shows Chester's first wife and that Charles is the son of Chester and Denise. So what happened to Denise? Adri's mother is Margaret. But it doesn't show her or Adri in the family line.*

Max punched keys and did another search and then another. He found no indication, not even a marriage license to show Chester and Margaret had ever married or a birth certificate to show Adri's birth. Marriage licenses and birth certificates were public record. Who was Adri's father?

Max was completely mystified. He looked at the clock. It was almost midnight. He shut down his computer and went slowly upstairs. He wasn't sure he would sleep with the mysteries he had discovered, but he needed to try.

Sunday morning was as dreary and overcast as the weather man predicted. The clouds were heavy with occasional heavy rain that would turn to drizzle. Then another cell would move over and bring another heavy downpour. The weather really suited Adri's mood. As tired as she had been the night before, she hadn't been able to find sleep until the wee hours of the morning. Then she had only slept fitfully as she kept dreaming she couldn't breathe, and even though she looked for Max in her dreams, she couldn't find him and would wake up gasping for air.

A downpour with thunder had brought her out of the bed at seven, and she didn't even want to try to sleep anymore. After fixing coffee and toast, she decided that she would try to read the book she had picked. She wasn't sure that was a good idea because she was trying hard not to think about Max, and it was one of the books he had given her.

She settled herself and began to read at the second chapter. She discovered that the plot was so intriguing that she got into the book and lost all track of the weather and the time.

Adri finished the book by midafternoon and discovered she was hungry. The last time she had sat and read a book with this much enthusiasm, she had still been in high school. Max was an excellent author, and because of the history, Adri was doubly thrilled.

Adri went and fixed a sandwich and some soup, and as she sat down to eat, her thoughts went to the heroine of the book. Adri actually identified with her in a lot of ways. *Men didn't become the plague of her existence until she was a grown woman, but she sure had to deal with a lot of garbage then. But she didn't let the fear rule her actions. I know there is a lesson here for me.*

I have shown Max a lot of different parts of me. The carefree person that finds joy in old houses and antiques and celebrates. The person that plans surprises and acts like a joyful kid when he is pleased. The emotionally handicapped person who fears too much. Agh! He has been amazing through it all, but how long will it last? I want him to see the best of me, but he has seen the worst of me too. I have lived with my biggest fear for seventeen years. It's been worse through college and after I set up the business. Aunt Dixie wasn't my protection anymore. I really did trust her for that, even if there weren't a lot of hugs or a lot of celebrations. I'm beginning to wonder if I'll ever grow up and behave normal.

Then there is the big question. Why do I want Max to—what do I want? Max is wonderful! I wouldn't even know if I could love him. I have no examples to follow. Okay, so he is a great friend. I and he—well, we are attracted to each other—at least according to his explanation. Now is when I need a girlfriend or a mom to talk to, and will it even be possible for me to handle it if Max disappoints me?

Adri stood suddenly, picked up her lunch dishes, and carried them to the sink. She went still at the sink, and a prayer came to mind. *God, if you care about me at all, I need some help. I feel lost in a forest of uncertainty, and I want Max to stay in my life, but I sent him away last night. Help me figure this out. And please let my decision to hire Jocko and Gina for the business be a really good decision.*

Adri went to her desk and pulled out her laptop and opened an auction web page. She needed to quit thinking because she really didn't think she had the answers, and she needed to review what was selling this week and decide what she would buy.

Adri wasn't really sure why she felt so upbeat Monday morning. She was up early, fixed a good breakfast, snagged her laptop, and headed for the showroom. Jocko and Gina would be coming in at nine, but she wanted to print out pictures of auction items. She had found several room sets that she wanted to show Max before the auction on Tuesday.

Adri kept telling herself this was business, but she got a little breathless every time she thought about seeing Max, whatever the excuse was. After printing the pictures, she placed them in folders, the things to show Max in one folder, Tuesday's auction in another, and the rest in another folder.

Jocko and Gina came in right on time, minus Josh. Adri greeted them and asked, "Who's taking care of Josh today? It would have been okay to bring him."

Jocko nodded. "We know, but Mrs. Wolcott and my mom thought it would be easier for us if we left him with them. They said we could fully concentrate on our training without him needing our care."

Adri smiled. "That is so sweet! Your mom knows the Wolcotts too?"

Jocko grinned. "My mom has been Mrs. Wolcott's housekeeper and cook since before I was born. My dad was the groundskeeper until he passed away ten years ago. My brother and I grew up there!"

Adri felt the sadness trying to push in again, but she wasn't letting it. Instead she smiled again and said softly, "That's why they treat you like family!"

Jocko and Gina both laughed and nodded. Adri asked, "Are you ready to get the inside scoop on the antique world?"

Their enthusiasm was contagious, and Adri happily began their training. She led them to the checkout desk and introduced them to her system. The morning went quickly. They didn't hesitate to ask questions or affirm something that wasn't quite clear. There were two customers in who just wanted to look, and at eleven, Adri asked them, "Do you think you can handle things for a couple of hours? I have some errands to run."

Jocko grinned. "I guess you have your cell phone in case we get stumped?"

Adri reached in her pocket and pulled out her cell phone. "It's on and always with me. I'll try to be back for sure by one so you can go to lunch."

Gina laughed. "No hurry. Mom packed us lunch, and we brought it with us. We are good on that score."

Adri laughed too. "Okay. I'll just grab some things from my office and get going then. This afternoon I'll want to spend some one-on-one time with Jocko. I'll eventually want Jocko to help with the auctions, so we need to talk about that."

Jocko was surprised but grinned. "Sounds great!"

Adri collected her bag, the bank bag, and the folder to show Max, and she was on her way. She went to town and took care of two errands before heading for Max's house.

She felt shy when she rang the bell and even more shy when Max opened the door. Her cheeks colored as she met his gaze.

"Hi, Max."

Max grinned, and then one eyebrow went up, and he asked, "Hi yourself. Is it business?" He pointed to the folder in her hands.

Adri blushed even more and smiled. "Yes." She was excited now. "I have some pictures to show you! I have an auction tomorrow and another on Friday, and I think we can get some more of your rooms set up!"

Max chuckled. "Come on in. Let's see what you have." *Oh my! It is so good to see her, and she is happy! Thank you, Lord!*

Adri moved past Max and led the way to the formal sitting room. She opened the folder and held out two pictures.

"This set up would go really well in here with the white walls and eggshell drapes. The dark color a perfect fit. You can see by the pictures that as far as furniture, it is a full set. The sofa and two chairs are dark charcoal and two more chairs are light charcoal. The extra pieces are the cherrywood and it is French from about 1820."

Max studied the pictures and then the room. "I can picture this, and I like it!"

"Okay! Now the breakfast room!" Adri swung around, but Max stopped her with his hand on her arm. Adri and Max both felt the tingle, and there was a brief pause.

Max cleared his throat as their eyes met. He cleared his throat again and asked, "The breakfast room?"

Adri laughed happily and covered his hand with her free hand. "Some call it the informal dining room or the breakfast room. It is usually located on the east side of the house to let the morning sun in." Adri released Max's hand, and Max drew it back.

"Oh. You are talking about that smaller room, off the kitchen behind the library." Max had a comical expression on his face.

Adri laughed again. "That's the one."

Max admitted sheepishly, "I wondered about that room. If the realtor told me, I forgot. It's pretty bad when a man doesn't even know his own house."

Adri smiled. "When you were growing up, you didn't have a big house, did you?"

Max grinned. "Not this big. We had one dining room, a play room, a front room, and a kitchen on the ground floor and bedrooms upstairs. It was pretty much the same as all our neighbors' houses."

Now Adri turned and grabbed Max's hand. "I want you to look at the room before I show you the pictures."

Max chuckled and walked beside her. As they approached the kitchen door, Betty stepped into the hall. "Adri, honey, I've set a place for you for lunch. You can stay, I hope."

Adri stepped forward and hugged Betty. "Yes, but it will need to be a working lunch if that is okay with you and Max."

Betty smiled. "Not a problem, just so you don't talk the whole time. You need to eat too!"

Adri nodded and stepped back. "I will eat."

"Okay. It will be ready in ten minutes." Betty turned and went back into the kitchen.

Adri and Max moved together toward the breakfast room. Max said softly, "I'm glad you are staying."

Adri blushed, smiled, and nodded. She stopped in the doorway arch.

"Look at the room. Then I'll show you the pictures."

Max did notice the extra sunshine, even though it was noon. To prevent glare in the room itself, the walls were a soothing shade of medium blue-green. The drapes for the wall of windows were a patterned green.

"Breakfast room. I like that. Even lunch would be great in here."

Adri's voice was excited. "Yes! Now look at these pictures! This is Italian, and the color is described as greenish white."

Max took the pictures and considered them. He asked, "It appears delicate, small."

Adri nodded. "It is called petite. The table has leaves, so it will seat four, six, or eight, and the table comes with eight chairs. There are two petite sideboards and a petite buffet. It's a good size for fit for the room size but sturdy and very serviceable. What do you think?"

"So you think it is sturdier than it looks?" Max sounded doubtful.

"Yes. I will admit that these pictures don't do justice to the petite. I have seen other sets and can assure you it is sturdier than it looks."

Max nodded and handed the pictures back to Adri. "I'll think about it over lunch. Let's go see what Betty has for us today."

Adri smiled shyly. "Okay!"

CHAPTER 15

After Max said the blessing for the food and they had helped themselves to the salad and tuna casserole, Adri flipped her folder over and pulled a scrap of paper from the back. She handed it to Max.

"Your house was featured in a magazine almost twenty years ago. There are room photos, and you can see how the house was for Robert and Louise Conrad."

"That is the previous owner. Are you copying any of the rooms?" Max asked.

Adri gave him a cheeky smile. Max blinked. *I love that smile! It lights up her whole face.* Max almost missed Adri's answer. "No. At least not yet."

Max chuckled. "I don't know if we should look at this then. I might have you move out the furniture I already have so it can be replaced like the old days."

Betty objected. "Don't you dare! Adri has done a wonderful job, and I know you like it!"

Max chuckled again. "Yes, Adri is doing a wonderful job. I am curious though about how the previous owners had things."

Adri blushed and informed them. "This house has historical significance too. It was part of the underground railroad."

Betty sat back, astonished. "Well, Max, you aren't the only researcher around here! That is amazing!"

Max had an amazed look on his face as well. "I guess you know where to look for this kind of thing. The realtor mentioned historical value, but he didn't say what."

Adri laughed. "I know that you have a wine cellar too. Something I didn't find when I was touring the house. But the last owners didn't use it for a wine cellar."

Max grinned. "Well, I was kind of holding on to the information as a surprise for you. Now you've spoiled the surprise!"

Adri smiled. "I'm a pro about history. No secrets from me. I know about the extra room upstairs and the attic."

"Okay, so what was that extra room used for?" Max had a puzzled look on his face.

Adri laughed. "You'll just have to look it up on the Internet." She smiled. "We haven't talked about the rooms"—she blushed softly—"the rooms that could be a while before they're occupied."

Max knew she was referring to the nursery and kid's rooms. "Hmm, do you think you have found something for one of them?"

Adri nodded shyly. "For the girl's room."

"Show me what you have."

Adri thumbed through the folder and pulled three pictures out. The pictures showed the canopy bed and the rounded curves on the armoire, vanity, and chests.

"This is high-end colonial with the rounded edges. The smaller size is perfect for a girl three to sixteen. It comes with a step bench so little ones can climb into the bed."

Max was looking at the pictures as Adri was describing them. Betty had gotten up and was looking over Max's shoulder.

Betty exclaimed, "I have three granddaughters that would love that room set up with this!"

Max chuckled. "Yes. Annie, Candi, and Alice. They would spend all their time there!"

Adri smiled. "Are you interested then?"

Max looked up quickly, remembering Adri's sadness when family was mentioned. He was relieved to see that she was truly smiling. Max grinned.

"Yes, but this may be hard to top for the boy's room."

Adri laughed. "Oh, ye of little faith! Something really nice will show up. When is the next family reunion?"

Betty laughed. "If you are talking about my family gathering, it won't be until the end of June. Same week every year."

Max nodded. "Easy to plan for that way—for everybody!"

"Well, I may have something by the end of April. We'll just have to wait and see." Adri pulled out her phone. "Oh. I'm already late getting back. Sorry to eat and run, but I am training today."

Betty hurried to the refrigerator. "Wait just a half a minute. I'll send your pudding with you."

Adri laughed. "It wouldn't be chocolate by any chance?"

Betty already had a small container filled and pushed the lid on. "It is." Betty hurried over and handed it to Adri. "Enjoy!"

Max asked, "Can I keep these pictures?"

"Yes, that's your copies. Now I really need to go." Adri swung toward the door, and Max followed.

"I'll walk you to the door." They walked down the hall, and Max opened the door. Adri stretched a little and kissed Max quickly on the cheek before she stepped through the door.

Adri said over her shoulder. "I read your *Trail to Life* yesterday, a really good book, and I really prayed like I thought God would hear me. Talk to you later."

She was about to open her car door when Max called out to her. "I am so proud of you, sweet Adri!"

Adri blushed, gave a small wave, and got in her car.

After Max shut the door, he turned around, and Betty was coming toward him with a smile on her face.

"What?" Max asked.

Betty chuckled. "I heard what you said to Adri and wondered what that was about."

Max walked toward her. "Let's go eat our pudding, and I'll tell you."

"Good idea!" They moved to the kitchen, and both sat down. "So?"

Max grinned. "I think good things are happening with Adri. How did she seem to you today?"

Betty thought for a moment. "Confident. Relaxed. Happy."

"My thoughts exactly. On her way out the door, she kissed my cheek and told me she had read *Trail to Life*, and she prayed 'like God would hear me.' Her words." Max stopped and really felt the impact of her words, his heart beat increasing and a lump forming in his throat.

Betty smiled. "Well, bless her heart!"

There was a silence as they both enjoyed their own thoughts and their pudding.

Max suddenly spoke. "I don't know what she prayed, but I sure know that God has answered a prayer for me. I prayed she would find satisfaction in her work decisions and that she would find peace in her personal life. Today, I think, she is finding both!"

Betty nodded. "When she mentioned she was training, she did seem upbeat. That is positive."

"Yes. And she was not backing away from me in any way. I hope my book gave her some positive insights. She thought it was a really good book."

"Well, it is a good book, and the main character had some really hard times with men. Maybe she recognized herself in parts of it." Betty laughed softly. "You are good at what you do, and you always pray that your writing will touch lives. Double prayers answered."

"So right. Let's pray together now for Adri and with praise."

"Yes, let's do that."

When Adri got back to the showroom, Gina greeted her happily.

"I'm sorry I didn't get back as soon as I thought," Adri apologized.

Gina laughed. "That's okay. We have done fine, I think. I want you to check out my invoices, but I think, and Jocko said I did fine."

"Where is Jocko?" Just as she asked, he called out.

"I'm back here. A customer asked about an armoire, and I was checking in the storeroom."

Jocko approached quickly and all but slide to a stop in front of Adri. "I didn't think to check there before he left, so I'll need to call him."

Adri laughed. "Do we have what he wanted?"

"I think so. He'll want to see it, I'm sure."

"Who is it?"

"It's a guy from Kentucky. He'll be around another couple of days. Name is Wallace Dorsey." Jocko had pulled out a scrap of paper from his pocket to double-check the name. "Have his phone number right here."

Adri smiled. "I take it you have been busy while I was gone."

Gina and Jocko answered at the same time. "Sure have."

Adri shifted her bag to her shoulder and held out a box to each of them. "These are yours."

Gina questioned, "What is it?"

"Well, open them and see." They followed instructions.

Jocko grinned. "Business cards? With our own names on them?"

Adri laughed. "You will find out in the antique world that people like to know who they are dealing with. These will give you credibility and will keep the customers happy."

Gina smiled. "I feel like I've moved up in the world! My name is on a business card with a reputable business!"

Jocko echoed, "Yeah, I'm impressed!"

Adri laughed. "You are both too easy to please! You wanted me to look at something?"

Gina went over to the business desk and picked up some invoices. "First ones we've done, so thought it would be good to let you check and make sure we did it right."

Adri took the invoices and glanced over them and then she looked up startled. "You sold a whole British bedroom set? And delivery on Thursday morning with a question mark?"

Adri saw Jocko and Gina look at each other worriedly, and Jocko asked, "Were we wrong?"

Adri smiled and invited, "Come into my office. The only thing you did wrong was something I didn't tell you about." Jocko and Gina relaxed and moved into Adri's office with her. "Have a seat. You've only had two hours of training, and I was going to cover the rest of this yet today, so let's just say our customers jumped ahead of us." Adri sat in her office chair.

"All the invoices are fine. Two repeat customers with name and address, one new customer with name and address and phone number. When an order totals more than five thousand, the cheapest item is free, or in this case, the cheapest two items. The bedside tables—since we sell these as pairs, they are one price. When I make out an invoice, I start with the most expensive and so on. That way, when I get to the bottom, I'll know what the total will be and can type free on the cheapest."

Gina nodded. "That makes sense. Mrs. London didn't even ask about a lower price, and I'm glad because I'm uncertain about dickering." Gina jumped up. "After the invoice was printing, she decided she wanted a picture too." Gina went to the coffee counter and picked up a framed painting that was leaning there. "I put it in here so we could save it for her. She said she'd pick it up next time."

Adri laughed happily. "We'll just rewrite this invoice when we do the delivery one. She can be pleasantly surprised that she is getting it free!"

"So we can fix it and get more business! Oh, but it's a painting and more than the side tables!" Gina looked dismayed.

Adri reassured her. "That's okay. A few hundred dollars is not a problem. Especially if she comes back for more furniture."

Adri turned to Jocko and asked, "I guess you helped decide about the delivery date?" Jocko nodded. "Tell me what you were thinking when you set it."

Jocko nodded again. "When you go to auctions, we usually spend the next day picking up auction items. It made sense to me that delivery couldn't happen until Thursday."

Adri nodded. "Is the nine o'clock hour okay with her?"

"She said any time Thursday was fine, just not before nine."

"Jocko, that is exactly the kind of independent thinking I want from my assistant. You know enough about how the deliveries work to come up with a plan that we don't have to juggle. Getting as close to the customers' wishes is what we aim for. I am pleased with both of you taking care of things. It increases my confidence that the business will be handled when I am not here." Adri sat back with a smile. Jocko grinned, and Gina laughed.

"Now, this is something I decided over the weekend. You have already proved yourselves. Every single order that totals over five thousand, you will get a commission above your salary and wages. So, Gina, you have earned a commission today." Adri wrote the amount on a scrap of paper and handed it to Gina.

Gina's mouth dropped open at the amount. "That's a lot!" She exclaimed as she showed it to Jocko.

Jocko blinked and then turned to Adri. "That is a lot. Adri, isn't that too high a percentage? Commissions are a common practice, but I would not have expected that much! You have overhead and item cost—well, I could go on and on."

Adri laughed. "I juggled numbers before I came up with the percentage, so I wouldn't offer if I couldn't afford it!" Then she said seriously, "You may not have worked too hard on today's sale, but believe me, there will be times when you will earn every penny while working to keep the customer happy and returning." Adri continued, "Now, Jocko, you need to make a phone call. Then you and I need to spend some time going over auction details. Gina, we will be available, but handle what you can." Gina nodded, pulled some business cards out of her box, and left the office.

The gate buzzer went off as Gina stepped out. She laughed. "Time to go to work!"

Chapter 16

By the time Adri had shut down and locked up the showroom on Monday evening, she was tired, but it was a happy tired. She thought about the prayer she had prayed the day before. As she walked to her house, she prayed again now. *Okay, God. You have my attention. Was this whole day answers to what can happen if I put you in charge? But, God—well, I'm sure you know how hard it is for me to trust. Is it okay to act naturally with Max? Am I important to you? Am I important to Max? Who can I talk to about all these feelings that are stirring in me? Am I falling in love? No, am I learning to love Max? I am confused about that. Is he just using his advanced knowledge he's gained from writing, or does he feel something for me that could be special? Okay. Enough. I will try to let you lead me and heal me. I guess that will have to do for now.*

Adri went in and fixed a simple meal and had just finished washing her few dishes when her phone rang. She opened her phone. It was Max.

"Hi, Max. Have you had a good day?" The question was shy.

Max chuckled. "Yes. The best part was you being here for lunch."

Adri was still shy. "Thank you."

"Was your afternoon as good as your morning?" Max asked lightly.

Adri laughed. "I didn't tell you I had a good morning! But yes, the whole day has been terrific!"

"I am so glad to hear that. So Jocko and Gina are going to do a good job for you?"

"Not just good! They did great today!"

Max let out a breath that carried over the phone. Then he spoke softly, "I hope I don't put a damper on your day."

Adri's voice trembled only a little when she asked, "How would you do that?"

"Well, I'm still not sure about that dining room setup for the breakfast room."

Adri laughed happily. "No problem. I am going to get it anyway. If you don't want it, somebody will!"

Max sighed. "Good. I do know it would look a whole lot better than what was in there before. After looking at those pictures, I am so relieved that your recommendations run in a very different direction."

Adri had to smother her giggle. "Max! I'm surprised! There is actually some very interesting history behind the previous owner's furniture, and you are into history."

Max had heard the smothered giggle, and now Max laughed his deep rumbling laugh. "Adri! Stop teasing! You didn't like it either!"

Adri laughed now. "Are you sure?"

Max's voice softened almost to a caress. "Yes, I'm sure."

Adri blushed and said shyly, "Well, you are right."

There was a small silence as Max dealt with the breathless feeling he had at Adri's tone of voice and soft statement. "You are going to auction tomorrow. Is it local?"

"Anything within a two-hour drive is considered local, but this one is only a forty-minute drive. I'm glad it's that close. I am not a fan of road trips. In a couple of weeks, I will have Jocko bring the truck to an auction that is four hours away."

"Hmm—you may not like road trips, but that doesn't seem to stop you."

"No. When they have something I really want, I go for it!" Adri laughed and added, "After all, I do know my furniture!"

"What will Wednesday be like for you?" Max asked gently.

"I actually get to stay in the showroom and wait on customers. Jocko will be directing traffic or relieving me in the showroom when I need to come set up your sitting room."

"When do you plan to come to do that? I have a lunch appointment from about eleven to one thirty."

"We can work around that. I expect it will be afternoon before they bring that back. I'll give you a call Wednesday morning when I have a better idea." Adri felt her excitement rise again as she anticipated seeing Max.

"That is a good idea. I don't want to cancel the lunch appointment. I am meeting John Wolcott, my longtime friend. I'm looking forward to that." Max gave her the information in a casual tone. He wanted her to start to become familiar with people in his life.

There was a smile in Adri's voice when she said, "I wondered what you were doing with all your free time. That must feel a little strange to you."

Max chuckled. "It is a little strange. When I am working, I will go ahead and do these kinds of things, but then I plan on working later into the evening or get up early to make up the time."

There was a brief silence. Then Adri said seriously, "Max, I want to apologize for Saturday evening." Adri hesitated, and Max waited as he felt she had more she wanted to say. "First of all, some people in the tour group I hosted upset me. Then I was a little out of sorts that the library could turn out so good without my input. And I really was terrified when you came back to my house. I was sure the car—well, I told you. Sometime soon, when there is time, I do want to tell you about *them* and why I am still afraid." Her voice was a little shaky as she finished.

Max replied gently, "I accept your apology, even though I don't think I have anything to forgive you for. As for the rest, I will be glad for you to share that burden when you are ready."

There was emotion in her voice when Adri told him, "Thank you, Max. I hate being so messed up, and I really am trying to rise above it."

Max assured her gently, "You are a remarkable person, and, Adri, I know God can help you clean up the mess you feel." When Max paused, he cleared his throat, but there was still some emotion. "And I believe that you are really on your way to healing. Sharing the load is a step forward, and I am glad you choose me to share with."

"Oh, Max." Adri sighed. "You really are special."

"Thank you, sweet Adri. You have had a busy day, and I am guessing it will be an early morning tomorrow, so I need to let you go." Max was pushing to the positive.

Adri had a smile in her voice. "Yes, early tomorrow, and yes, I do need to go now. Thank you for calling. It's a special ending to a good day."

Max's voice indicated a smile too. "Special for me too. Good night, Adri."

"Good night, Max."

Max was up early the next morning. He awoke about four and couldn't go back to sleep. He kept rerunning the phone conversation of the night before and felt like he needed to do some more research. He got up and got ready for his day and went to the library. He tried several locator sights, trying to find out where Chester and Charles Winfield were currently living. He wasn't getting anywhere.

Over breakfast, Max talked about his frustrations with Betty.

Betty asked, "Max, why is it so important to get that information?"

Max rubbed his chin whiskers and told her, "Adri is still terrified that her father and brother will come back. I don't know why. She says she wants to tell me. I thought that maybe I could locate them and find out by keeping track of them if I could protect her somehow."

Betty shook her head. "Max, God is the ultimate protector. Put it in his hands."

Max nodded and ate in silence for a moment. Then he asked Betty, "Did I tell you that I wasn't able to find a marriage certificate for her parents or a birth certificate for Adri?"

Betty gasped, "No! That is strange, isn't it?"

"Very strange since those are public record. Chester's first wife, Denise, is apparently still living, and there are no divorce papers for them either. And Denise is Charles's mother."

Betty shook her head in dismay. "Wonder if Adri is aware of any of that. Surely she would be working to figure it out if she was."

Max shook his head. "As terrified as she is at just the thought that she might have to see her father again, I don't think she would want to stir the waters, especially if he were to find out."

"So you are working on the assumption that she does not have a clue about any of it?"

"I am. She was only ten when her mother died, and unless her Aunt Dixie told her anything, assuming she knew anything, Adri wouldn't know where to start finding any answers. I am sure of that." Max was starting to wish he wasn't aware of any of Adri's past except what she has told him.

Betty sat up straight and asked, "Have you thought of contacting Dixie Winfield? Isn't she distant family to you?"

"I've thought about it, but other than telling her I am distant family and wanting to get in touch with Chester, what could I ask her without trespassing on her life or Adri's for that matter?" Max shrugged, having no answers.

Betty told him softly. "Pray about it and look for God's direction. If he wants you to ask more, he'll give you the words."

After they finished eating, Max helped Betty clear the breakfast table. He told Betty he would be in the library.

Betty responded, "I'll be prayin' you get your answers or some peace."

"Thank you, Betty."

Max went into the library and walked around, soaking in the peaceful, cozy feeling of the room. And he prayed. *God, there are so many thoughts and mysteries swirling in my head. I want answers, but again I will wait on your timing. You know all the answers, and I trust your wisdom. Bless Adri in her travel and her business. Amen.*

When Max's prayer ended, he found himself back at the library door. He just stood there for a moment and then decided to go upstairs and decided to clean out the "girl's" room. He would move his condo furniture and all the miscellaneous it now contained into "the extra room" on the second floor of the house. That room was across the hall from the guest rooms and didn't have a traditional door but a wall panel that separated and turned sideways. This had been one of the hiding places for the Underground Railroad.

The girl's room would have its permanent furniture by the end of the week, he thought. He took the steps two at a time and went to work.

Max had the couch halfway out of the room when a thought hit him. He stood up straight. *Adri loves this house! She is filling it with her favorite styles with an eye toward harmony in each room! Okay, I understand now why she wasn't enthused about the library. She wanted to make it right herself. She did before the furniture was delivered but didn't get to actually place it. So to be sensitive to her, I will make sure she supervises every other room in the house!*

He finished emptying the room and then hurried downstairs to let Betty know what he had done. She assured him she would have time to clean the room that afternoon.

Chapter 17

Max went into the library and pulled up the yellow pages on his computer. He easily found Dixie Winfield under antiques. Her business name: *Dixie's Restorations.* Max dialed the number.

"Dixie's Restorations, Dixie speaking."

"Hello. Max Winfield here."

Dixie was a straightforward person and responded. "Don't you mean A. Maxwell Winfield?"

Max chuckled. "Yes, ma'am!"

"You are a distant relative of mine and you write historical novels," Dixie told him.

"Yes. Are you familiar with my work?"

"I am. Became a fan about three years ago. You tell a good story."

Max chuckled again. "Thank you. I enjoy doing it."

"What can I do for you, Max? I'm sure you have a reason for calling," Dixie asked.

Max didn't even hesitate. "I've been checking out my family tree, and I'm confused about some names that seem to be missing."

Dixie's tone was firm. "The black sheep of the family don't list all their sins." The next words were bitter. "My *brother* Chester Edgar Winfield is still married to Denise Louise Canton Winfield, and their son is Charles Samuel Winfield, their only child. If either one of them have fathered any other children, no one knows about it."

Max was a little taken aback. "Okay, but—"

"My sister Connie made a good marriage with a man who loves her," Dixie interrupted. "Connie and I made a pact years ago that we would not procreate a line of genes that contained poison. We are both childless."

Max swallowed before he asked, "Who is Adrianne Margaret Winfield then?"

Dixie's voice softened. "Awe, now we get to the real reason for the phone call. I wondered how long it would take you after moving in next door to her business. I love that girl, but she does not have a single drop of Winfield blood in her."

Max sighed. "I already suspected that because I found no marriage certificate for her mother and Chester, and I could not find a birth certificate for Adri."

Dixie's voice hardens again. "Of course not! Chester coned Margaret into a sham marriage because he knew she was an heiress. She was already carrying the baby when the sham took place." There was bitterness again. "After all, Chester was still married. He had already spent everything that Denise brought into the marriage, and he had just got through all the paperwork to make Denise a ward of the state and needed another source of income."

Max asked, "Where is Denise that she would be a ward of the state?"

There was a deep sigh on the other end of the phone. "Chester had driven her crazy. She tried suicide too, which damaged her brain. She is a permanent resident of a mental hospital." Dixie's tone changed again, coming across gentle. "Margaret was so fragile, and I befriended her immediately. I wanted to help her, try to protect her from Chester. After her parents died and she came into her inheritance, I helped her set up an irrevocable trust for Adri so that Chester couldn't spend it all. Adri received the lawyer's name and the paperwork on her twenty-first birthday."

Max was a little confused and asked, "Why does Adri still believe she is a Winfield? Do you know who she really is?"

Dixie sighed. "Margaret wouldn't tell me. She believed that Chester would find a way to kill Adri if she shared that information. Nothing I said assured her that I could keep the secret." There was a lot of sadness as she continued. "As much as I tried to help Margaret, it wasn't enough. We had papers drawn up to make me Adri's guardian in the event something happened to Margaret. That was just two weeks before she took her life. I should have tried harder to get her and Adri away . . ." Her words drifted off.

Max was silent for a moment before he asked. "There has to be a true birth certificate on record somewhere. When is Adri's birthday?"

"That is something else I am not sure about. Margaret told me, and on the fake birth certificate, it is June 1, 1982. I have researched to find the real birth certificate. I know the year is correct, but Margaret left for about a month around that time, so the real month and day could be different." Dixie paused. "I don't have any idea how she ever got away from Chester at that time, and I am completely in the dark about why she came back."

Max changed the subject. "Why are you so willing to talk to me?"

Dixie's response was immediate. "Honey, I can hear in your voice you are deeply concerned about Adri. She needs to know that she has a better heritage than the black sheep of the Winfields and the blackest one of all, Chester. Please help her truly find herself. She carries some really deep scars, and she needs to heal."

Max affirmed that statement. "Yes, she needs to heal. She has admitted to me that she is a mess, and I have seen direct results of some of the scars that she has not verbalized yet. Did she hyperventilate a lot as a child?"

"Oh mercy! That is happening again? Yes. When Chester and Charles were around, it happened as many as ten times a day. Margaret was really concerned for her. Once Adri was living with me, it happened once in town when she thought she saw Chester down the street. Then there was a stressful time during college when it happened frequently in a two-month period. She had sorority sisters looking after her then. As far as I know, it didn't happen after that."

"She had a lot of stresses last week, and it happened twice in two days' time. I was able to help her past it both times. The last time was when someone drove onto her yard after dark, and she wasn't expecting anyone. In her mind, it had to be Chester and Charles. That one really scared me, and I don't scare easily," Max told Dixie.

"Well, I was right. You love her, don't you?" Dixie said softly.

Max answered immediately, "Yes, ma'am!"

"Good. She needs happiness in her life. What else do you want or need to know?"

Max hesitated before he said, "I need Chester's—" A buzzer in the background interrupted him.

Dixie said hurriedly, "I just had a customer walk in. I thought of something else I want to tell you. Can I call you back? This customer could take at least thirty minutes."

"Yes. Call me back when you have time. Do you have my number?"

"Got it. We'll talk in a bit." The line went dead.

Max wasn't sure what to think about the new information. One thing he did know: if he ever encountered Chester, he wasn't sure he would be able to hold back his anger toward the man. *God, forgive me, but if his sister hates him, he must be unspeakable. What did Adri suffer at his hands? No wonder her dealings with men are so guarded. God, keep her in your care today.*

Max turned to his computer. He would do some research while he waited for Dixie to call back. He had a really good search engine, and he knew how to use it. *I want to see if I can find Adri's real birth certificate. Now I at least have a close date, and I might find it this time. Surely her mother would have given her at least a permanent first name and probably middle name. There is too much government interference for that to change very much.*

Max typed in the dates first, a month on either side of June 1, 1982, then typed Adrianne, and searched. Nothing came up in the state of West Virginia, so he was in the process of searching neighboring states when his phone rang.

"Hello. Max here," Max answered.

Dixie was a little breathless. "The customer just wanted some information, so it didn't take as long as I thought." Dixie stopped and took a deep breath. "I wanted you to know that Adri might have all the information she needs for her real identity. Margaret made me promise that when Adri left Chester, I *had* to take her writing desk too. She was very insistent about that. I have wondered many times if she left something in that desk for Adri."

"Did you ever encourage Adri to look through the desk?" Max asked.

"No. And I never looked either. That is special to Adri, and she treasures it. It has gone everywhere with her." Dixie's voice softened. "Maybe I should have at least suggested Adri should look carefully through it."

Max asked another question. "Is it the kind of desk that might hold a hidden panel or a false bottom in the drawer?"

"I don't think so, but like I said, I never checked it out. Because of its small size, we have never had to empty it to move it." There was almost a gasp when Dixie asked, "She still has the desk, doesn't she?"

Max answered solemnly, "Oh yes. She told me it was the only thing she had left of her mother and that it was the only piece of furniture she owned that she would never sell."

Dixie's voice relaxed. "Good. I am a believer and strongly believe that God will lead Adri to the information when the timing is right in her life. Because I was hesitant to deal with all the questions, well, that may be one reason, but something will point her to the answers when God says it's time for her to know."

Max affirmed that. "I believe the way you do. God's timing is important!" Max hesitated before he asked, "I have another question for you. Did Margaret know that she was in a sham marriage?"

Max heard Dixie catch her breath and then sigh. "Yes, but not for the first nine years. None of us except Chester knew. When her inheritance came to her, Chester was demanding she turn it all over to him. Because there was no marriage license on file at the courthouse, she couldn't turn it over to him with a simple signature like he wanted. Turns out, Chester couldn't lay his hands on any of it, which was a blessing." Dixie's voice got soft. "Finding out about the sham marriage just about sent Margaret over the edge. She already knew that Chester was devious, selfish, and wanted what he wanted when he wanted it, but finding out that they weren't really married . . ." Dixie took a deep breath. "I was there when Margaret confronted Chester about their marriage. She had already sent Adri and Charles away to boarding school but didn't want to face Chester alone. Max, it is the only time I ever saw her challenge Chester, and when he admitted the truth, she verbally laid into him and told him exactly what she thought of him. He was so angry I had to step between them to stop him from harming her. Fortunately, I am a large, strong woman, *and* I threatened to call the police."

"Do you know why she stayed? Why didn't she leave and separate herself from his evil?" Max asked.

Dixie answered in a whisper, "Adri." She took another deep breath. "I went with Margaret to help her pack, and Chester started drinking. When we came back downstairs with her suitcases, he threatened Adri. When Chester drank, he was more laid back, but the tone of voice he used, Margaret and I both knew he meant it. His words, 'You walk out that door, Adrianne is dead.' Margaret passed out at his words, and when she came too, he added, 'You are writing me a check for fifty thousand dollars every month for the rest of your life, or you will never see your daughter again.'"

Max couldn't stop the words. "Oh god, *no!*"

"Adri was Margaret's world. Chester knew that," Dixie continued.

Max sighed and asked, "Margaret must have had some kind of income to satisfy Chester. Was she getting something from her parents while they were alive?"

"No. Margaret had two of her own high-producing oil wells, and that income came directly to her every month. She had signed those over to Adri, the transfer to be done on her death. She was determined that Chester receives nothing after he cashed the last check she left for him the day she died." Dixie chuckled. "Adri didn't know about that income until she received the trust. I made sure it channeled back into the trust. There was enough just off those two wells for her to finance the start-up of her business." Then her voice was somber. "Adri asked a lot of questions then."

"I guess I am missing something. Adri didn't know she was inheriting from her mother?"

"No. When she came to live with me, I supported her and taught her a work ethic. She got good enough at restoring furniture that she had saved enough to pay for her first two years of college all on her own. Without her help, except in the summer, I did dip into the trust so she could finish college. No one knew she was rich, not even her." There was a note of uncertainty in Dixie's voice.

Max approved. "Having a work ethic is good. I put myself through college, even though I could have dipped into my own inheritance."

Dixie chuckled softly. "Yes, I know, and you have done very well for a very long time."

"How do you know so much about me?" Max asked.

Dixie laughed a hardy laugh now. "I have friends in high places, and I know how to look up about high-profile people on the Internet."

"I'm not that high profile. And friends? Like who?"

Dixie laughed again. "That's for me to know. But seriously, Max, I am very glad you are in Adri's life now."

Max needed to ask. "A big reason I called, Adri is terrified that Chester and Charles will show up on her doorstep. Do you have any idea where they are?"

Dixie was bitter. "I make it my business not to know where they are. My sister, Connie, reported to me about seven years ago that they had moved to San Diego, California. That is the last information I have."

"Another question, are you and Adri close now?"

Dixie's voice softened. "There was a serious breach between us when she found out about the trust. I'm not sure she has really forgiven me yet. We communicate by e-mail and phone from time to time, and she still sends furniture my way, but we are not as close as we used to be." Dixie's voice was sad, and she added, "I thought I was doing the right thing by her."

Max felt gentleness toward this woman he had never met. "Dixie, I like you. In your own way, you are remarkable, and I am pleased to call you cousin."

There was a brief silence before Dixie told him, "I have work to do and, Max, call anytime. It's been good to talk to you, and I'll help anyway I can when it comes to my sweet girl. Take care of her, okay?"

"You've got it! And, Dixie, thanks for taking such good care of her early on."

Dixie chuckled. "Yeah, yeah. Take care, Max."

CHAPTER 18

The trip to the auction was uneventful for Adri, and she had plenty of time to examine the merchandise before the bidding started. She was the successful high bidder on all the things she had come for, except it was now midafternoon, and the sitting room set for Max was still further down the docket, and she was growing impatient.

All her earlier purchases had cost less than she had budgeted, which was nice for her. But waiting around for the last purchase was wearing on her. One of her least favorite things to do was drive after dark, and it was starting to look like that was going to happen. She had encountered several other dealers she saw on a regular basis and visited with them earlier.

With her impatience growing, Adri left her chair and went to the back of the building.

She pulled out her cell phone and decided to step outside and call Jocko to see how things were going at the showroom.

When Jocko answered, she asked quickly, "Do you have time to talk for a few minutes?"

"Yes, ma'am. What's up?" His voice was cheerful.

"Is everything going okay? I have a wait and thought I could check in." Adri was trying to keep her voice conversational.

Jocko sensed a slight tension though. He responded, "Things are good here. Gina just sold some jewelry, and Josh wants her attention, so I'm alert and on duty."

"Good. Have you had any big sales today?"

"Yes, a dining room set this morning and a bedroom set this afternoon. Busy with deliveries on Thursday. Everything okay there?" Jocko asked Adri.

Adri's voice was hesitant. "Yes, I think so." Then she added, "I'm feeling unsettled about something, but I'm not sure what it is."

"Have you been able to get what you went for?"

"Right now I am waiting for the sitting room furniture to come up. The auctioneer is slow. It's a different one than they usually use, and things seem to be dragging out." Adri sighed. "Oh, and yes, I have gotten everything else I came for."

Jocko could hear the stress in Adri's voice, but he wasn't sure what to do about it. He finally said, "I guess it will be dark then before you are headed home."

"Yes, and maybe that is why I am tense. I don't like driving after dark."

Jocko had an idea. "Gina can handle things here. I could bring the truck and load it up and come back with you."

Adri's response was surprised. "Oh!" She thought for a moment. "No, Jocko, I'll be okay. I guess it's just been a long day, and you need to get Gina and Josh home on time."

"Okay. If you change your mind, let me know. I'd be happy to do it, and Mom could come get Gina and the baby."

Adri tried for cheerful. "I need to get back to the auction. I'm glad you are handling things there. Thank you."

Jocko was cheerful. "We are pleased to do it. Call if you need me! Talk to you later."

Adri answered, "Later." Then she disconnected.

Adri pushed her phone into her pocket, paced a little while chewing on her bottom lip. Then she shook her head and went back into the building with purpose. The chair she had vacated earlier was occupied now, so she looked around and found another in an almost empty row. There was a couple that looked vaguely familiar, sitting mid row and a man she had never seen before at the other end of the row.

The auctioneer was trying to get more money for a set of armoires, finally sold them, and the next item up was a nice English bedroom set. Adri decided to bid; after all, she was running short on quality bedroom sets. After raising the bid a few times, she realized that she and only one other person were bidding. It was the man at the other end of the row she was sitting on, and out of the corner of her eye, she saw he was getting agitated that she kept bidding. Upon realizing that, she put in one more bid. The auctioneer kept looking at the man for another bid, but he didn't make one. He just sat back in his chair with an angry red face and glared at Adri. Adri got the bedroom set. She, all of a sudden, felt real uncomfortable about that, but she wasn't about to approach the man and offer the set back to him.

When the sitting room sofa and chairs came up, there were several bidders, and the price kept going up. That didn't bother Adri until she realized that the only other bidder left was the man at the end of the row. As the bidding continued, she also realized that he was bidding to drive up the price. Adri finally got the set but had spent a thousand more than she had intended. Next for auction were the rosewood accessory pieces. Again, the bidding was brisk at the beginning. As her bids became higher, she realized the man was again driving up the price. Adri was determined to have those pieces and finally got them, again over her limit.

Adri had never experienced anything like the intimidation she felt from the man at the end of her row, so when the auctioneer pounded the gavel and said, "Sold to number 21," Adri hurriedly rose from her chair and went quickly to the cashier to finish the auction paperwork and pay for her purchases.

As she finished writing her check, she felt the hair rise on the back of her neck. She was sure the man was nearby, but she wasn't about to look. She hurriedly gathered her paperwork and headed for the exit. She was grateful to see a guard in uniform standing near the exit, and she stopped.

She asked the guard if he would escort her to her car.

The guard was agreeable and held the door open for her to exit ahead of him. He walked with her and saw her safely into her car. As Adri turned the key and started the car, she could feel the onset of breathlessness, so she sat still and concentrated on slow, deep breaths, hearing Max's voice in her head. When she felt back in control, she put the car in gear and pulled into the street. She was hoping the trip home would be as uneventful as the trip over had been, except the sun had just set, and she would be making the trip in the dark.

Adri was alert to her surroundings, and the first ten minutes were quiet. As she stopped at a red light in a small town she had to pass through, headlights shone behind, she then pulled into the other lane, and a black truck pulled up beside her. As she glanced sideways at it, she recognized the angry man from the auction. She observed that it was a Ford F-250. When the light changed, she pulled through the intersection, and the truck pulled in behind her, almost tailgating.

Adri felt a shiver of fear as she tilted the review mirror to minimize the glare of the truck's headlights. The truck continued to follow the next few miles, and Adri decided she couldn't lead him to her business and house, but she didn't know where to go. Her hands were shaking as she pulled her phone out of her pocket.

She hit speed dial, and Max picked up immediately. "Adri?"

She squeaked out of her tight vocal cords, "Max, I need help. I have an angry bidder from the auction following me, and I can't go home. I don't know what to do."

Max's voice was tense. "Where are you?"

Adri was gasping a little, and Max immediately told her in a soothing voice, "Calm down and take a slow deep breath." He realized he should not have let his anxiety into his voice. He had a sense that something was wrong and let it show. Max heard her follow his instructions and then asked calmly, "Where are you now, Adri?"

Adri was able to respond. "I'm on Jefferson Road near Fourth."

"Okay. You can go to the Wolcott Estate where Jocko lives. You are less than ten minutes from there. Go to Eighth, turn right, and go eight blocks to Truman Road and turn left, two blocks. Call Jocko and tell him to open the gate and wait for you at the drive. I am in my car and on my way there now."

Adri's voice trembled. "At Eighth turn right, Truman Road left and two blocks." She pulled in a deep breath. "I'm calling Jocko now." She disconnected and almost dropped her phone before she hit speed dial for Jocko.

He answered quickly, "Hey, boss."

Adri had to take a slow breath before she could talk. "Jo-Jocko. I-I need your help!" Adri had to take in another slow breath. "Max sent me to the Wol-Wolcott Estate. Some-someone is following me in a bl-black Ford tr-truck. I-I . . ." Adri gasped as the black truck swung in front of her, almost clipping her front bumper as she was approaching Eighth.

Jocko was alarmed now but calmly asked, "Adri, what do I need to do?"

"Open the front gate and wait for me-me." Adri stayed in the right driving lane until the last minute and jerked the wheel to the right turning lane, running the red light as she turned onto Eighth, barely making it before the traffic crossed the intersection.

Jocko answered firmly, "I'll be there. Do you want me to stay on the line?"

Adri gasped, "N-no. I need to watch my driving." She disconnected. As she checked the rearview mirror, she saw the black truck charge out into the intersection and cut several cars off as he continued his pursuit.

Adri pushed her speed a little. She was almost two blocks ahead of the truck and wanted to keep it that way until she could get to the Wolcott Estate. At the same time she was trying very hard not to hyperventilate. Fortunately, the only stoplight on this street was at Truman road, and she hoped she could hit a green or yellow light.

She looked in her rearview mirror again and moaned. The truck was catching up. One more block to Truman. Traffic was thinning, and Adri decided that whatever the light was, if it was safe, she was going through it. She stayed in the right lane, and the truck was less than one hundred feet behind her when the light turned yellow. She sped up and without using her blinker, swung into the intersection, hitting the brake just as she swung the wheel and turned onto Truman. She hit the accelerator again to get out of sight of the truck. The black truck squealed his tires as he hit the brakes and stopped, almost into the intersection.

Adri guessed she had come about a block and a half when she rounded a curve and saw Jocko standing almost in the street. As she hit the brake so she could make the turn into the driveway, she spotted a police car parked at the curb just past the drive. She quickly took the car out of gear, turned it off, and unbuckled as she pushed the car door open. Adri found the courage with the extra adrenaline coursing through her to get out of the car and run to the police car.

Just then, the truck came around the curve, and she had a clear view. Adri shouted as she approached the cruiser. "I am Adrianne Winfield, and that black F-250 has been chasing me, and I'm pressing charges."

The officer in the car nodded, and as the black truck sped by, the cruiser's flashing lights and siren came on. Jocko grabbed Adri around the waist and pulled her back quickly as the officer took off in pursuit.

The fight left Adri, and she would have crumpled to the ground if Jocko hadn't still been holding her waist with his strong arm. Well, not all the fight. As the police car rounded the curve down the street, Adri yelled, "Men are jerks." And she shook her fist in the air and then completely collapsed against Jocko.

Jocko could feel Adri trembling and then start to gasp for air. He scooped her up and carried her through the estate gate. He was about to set her down into the open door of her car when Max's car swung into the drive and pulled up beside them. Adri had caught her breath, but she was still trembling. Max jumped out and ran around the front of his car and lifted Adri into his arms.

"I think she passed out," Jocko told him.

Adri's arms lifted and circled Max's neck. "No, I didn't," she said it slowly. "I was just too weak to stand."

Max spoke softly, "Did you hyperventilate?"

"No. I was close, but I kept hearing your voice in my head and kept breathing deeply when I needed too."

"I'm glad. Will you be able to stand if I set you down?" Max asked.

Adri sighed. "Yes, just don't let go."

Max set her on her feet, keeping one arm around her waist. "Okay?" he asked her.

Adri drew in a deep, cleansing breath. "Yes. Umm, Jocko, that man is a jerk, n-not you."

Max's eyebrow went up at Adri's comment, and then he looked at Jocko, who was beet red in the face. Max had to work at not smiling when he asked Jocko, "What is that about?"

"After the police car left, Adri shook her fist in the air and yelled. And believe me, I have never ever heard her yell." Jocko stopped and went red again.

Adri giggled a tension release for her, and she told Max, "I yelled men are jerks."

Now Max let the chuckle go and hugged Adri. "Good for you! That's my girl!"

CHAPTER 19

Adri was still giggling, a helpless but tension-releasing giggle. When she looked up, she saw a statuesque white-haired lady coming down the drive at a spry pace toward them. Adri covered her mouth as she gasped, "Oh!"

Both Max and Jocko looked to where Adri was looking. "Jocko, is everything all right?" she called out.

Jocko went quickly to her and gently took her arm. "Yes, ma'am. Watch your step. It's shadowy out here."

They continued to Max and Adri. Jocko introduced them. "Mrs. Wolcott, this is Adri Winfield, my boss. Adri this is Adrianne Wolcott."

Mrs. Wolcott smiled. "I am pleased to meet you, Adri." She held out her hand to Adri. Adri took it, and before Mrs. Wolcott released, she gave an extra squeeze, and the smile was so gentle.

Then Mrs. Wolcott turned to Max. "It's about time you came to see me, Max."

Max chuckled as he took half a step to receive her hug. "Hello, Grandmother. It is an unconventional visit, but I am here."

"Is there a reason to stand out here in the drive, or will you come up to the house?" The invitation was extended to everyone, but Mrs. Wolcott's eyes were on Adri.

Adri ducked her head and looked up with a blush in her cheeks. "I-I'm so sorry to barge in on you. I kind of had trouble on the road coming back from an auction and-and . . ."

Max picked up the explanation. "She couldn't get to her place, so I directed her here when she called about her trouble."

"Adri called me to meet her here at the gate. I called the police, and I am expecting them to report back here," Jocko finished.

Mrs. Wolcott had a puzzled look on her face as she followed the conversation. Then she laughed softly and told them, "You have given me a clear explanation of why you are here, but I still don't know what is going on, so maybe Jocko could stay here until the police return, and meanwhile Max and Adri can come up to the house for some hot tea."

Adri protested, "Oh, we shouldn't intrude."

"Nonsense. No intrusion and . . ." Her voice softened with sympathy. "If you have had a scare on the road, you need to come in at least for the tea to calm your nerves."

Adri looked at Max. He smiled softly and gently squeezed Adri's hand, a hand that she suddenly realized he was holding. "It's a good idea." He told her gently.

Max handed his car keys to Jocko and drove the ladies up to the house in Adri's car.

They settled in a small sitting room halfway down the hall. Mrs. Wolcott handed the tea around. As she settled in her chair, she asked Adri gently, "Are you all right, Adri? You look a little pale."

Adri's hands started to tremble. Max noticed and reached over to steady her tea cup and saucer. Adri answered slowly, "I-I think it is reaction. Can I-I not talk a-about it ri-right now?"

Max told her quietly, "It's okay if you're not ready."

Adri looked into Max's eyes and felt calmer. She nodded and sipped the tea slowly.

Max turned to Mrs. Wolcott. "Grandmother, you are looking well. You're staying busy, I'm sure."

Mrs. Wolcott nodded and told Max, "Oh yes. Two new great-grandbabies have been born since I saw you last." She laughed softly. "You have a new look, and it looks really nice. How long have you had that beard and mustache?"

Max grinned. "About a week. It was something I thought I would try. Not sure I need to look older and more distinguished, as I've been told, but I like it."

Mrs. Wolcott laughed again. "Actually, I think you look younger and more dashing!"

Max chuckled. "Grandmother, you always did know the right thing to say."

Adri was still sipping her tea, and thoughts floated in. *First, Betty teased him about his whiskers, and now Mrs. Wolcott comments on them. Is this normal for people who like each other—well, maybe love each other? Sure wish I knew more about that. I guess I have a lot to learn.*

Adri jumped slightly and almost spilt the little bit of tea left in her cup when the door chimes rang.

Mrs. Wolcott stood up. "That is probably Jocko and the police. Catrina will let them in."

A diminutive lady with Jocko's facial features stepped into the doorway. "Mrs. Wolcott, the police are here." She stepped aside, and Jocko and the police officer stepped into the room.

Mrs. Wolcott gestured and invited, "Please come in and have a seat."

Jocko moved into the room and just stood near the doorway. The police officer came in and stood in front of Adri.

"Ma'am, I am Officer Woods. You spoke to me briefly at the street."

Adri nodded. Max was relieved to see color in Adri's cheeks now. "I am Adrianne Winfield. I'm sure you have questions for me."

The officer glanced at the chair nearby and answered as he moved to the chair. "Yes. I will tell you up front that there were several angry driver's that called in and complained about the driver of the truck and turned in his plate numbers, so we will have several traffic citations against him. I do need you to tell me as best you can what you experienced."

Adri nodded again. She reached for Max's hand and began recounting the auction incident that seemed to start it all. She stuttered from time to time while relating her fear and the scary parts of the drive. Occasionally she shuddered with remembered angst, but she was clear, and her voice remained steady throughout the account.

When she finished relating that she had phoned Max and Jocko for help, the officer turned to Max first. "What was your reasoning in sending Ms. Winfield here?" he asked Max.

Max identified himself first and then replied to the question, "I practically grew up around here, and I knew the house was back enough from the street to limit access, and the estate has a gate to use if needed with security notification if there was a breech. And Jocko lives on the estate and would be available, or at least hoped he was available to help. And it was a closer location than any other place I could think of."

Officer Woods asked Adri, "Have you ever been here before?"

Adri shook her head. "I trusted Max to tell me right."

The officer nodded. Adri continued before the officer finished writing in his note pad. "Jocko is my employee, and I know him, so it was a good idea."

The officer smiled. "Yes, ma'am."

Then he turned to Jocko and asked a few questions to clarify things.

Officer Woods checked a message on his phone and then stood and turned to Adri again. "Ms. Winfield, a patrol car is here now with our suspect, and I would like you to come outside and identify the man. You said you didn't know him but said you would recognize his face. Is that right?"

Adri shuddered. Max squeezed her hand gently. Adri told the officer. "Yes, I will know his face."

"Would you come with me then? They are waiting to take him to booking." Officer Woods turned toward the door.

"Can Max come with me?" Adri asked.

The officer said that would be okay but asked that everyone else remain in the house. As they approached the extra cruiser in the drive, Adri trembled slightly. An officer was standing near the back door and opened it as Officer Wood indicated Adri should stop ten feet away. Max put his arm across Adri's shoulders. The officer by the car said something to the man inside. As he turned his head to look out of the car, Max stiffened beside Adri and exclaimed, "Nate Caffrey?"

Adri looked at Max and asked, "Do you know him?"

Officer Woods touched Adri's arm and asked, "Do *you* recognize him?"

Adri looked back at the man in the car just as his face took on the angry sneer she had seen earlier in the day. Adri stuttered, "Ye-yes that is him."

Officer Woods waved his hand to the officer by the car. The car door closed as Officer Woods blocked Adri and Max's view of the car. He told them, "Let's go back to the veranda. Mr. Winfield, I have a few more questions for you."

Max nodded and ushered a trembling Adri to the veranda. Officer Woods had a few words with the other officer, and the cruiser left. Officer Woods joined them on the veranda.

"Mr. Winfield, how do you know that man?"

"I did an interview with him about three years ago. I am a writer and wanted some input on judicial history, and he was recommended as an expert in that field. He is Professor Nathanial Caffrey," Max explained.

Officer Woods nodded and asked, "Did you interview him one time?"

Max answered, "The first interview brought more questions to mind, so I interviewed a second time. He seemed quite knowledgeable about what I was interested in."

Officer Woods thanked them and handed first Adri and then Max his card. "That includes my cell phone number. Don't hesitate to call if you think of anything else."

Adri reached into her skirt pocket and handed the officer her business card.

The officer's car had just disappeared down the drive when Max said slowly, "It bothers me that a tenured professor at a university would do something like this. He wanted that bedroom set, so why didn't he keep bidding?"

Adri said thoughtfully, "I think there may be extra value in that bedroom set to him, but he probably ran out of source, money to pay for it. If he wanted it for sentimental value, I would think there would be disappointment, and it isn't unheard of for furniture to change hands at these auctions before it's paid for. He could have approached me to deal. So I don't think it was sentimental. If there is something illegal—"

"The police need to examine it before it's moved," Max finished. "Adri, can you call the auction place and get them to have security move it behind lock and key?"

"Yes! I'll call . . . Oh, I need my handbag!"

"Where is it?"

"By the sofa, where I was sitting."

"I'll go get it." Max turned toward the door. Adri put out a hand to stop him. "Will Mrs. Wolcott . . ."

Max smiled. "I'll give her a brief explanation. She'll understand."

Adri nodded. "Bring Jocko back with you. He needs to know what is going on."

Max nodded and went in the house.

When Max and Jocko returned, Adri and Max filled Jocko in on what they were thinking. Adri called the auction house asking to talk to the head of security and explained reasons for putting the furniture behind lock and key. The head of security, James Holland, was happy to comply. Then she called Officer West. After Officer West spoke to his captain, he called back to arrange to meet Adri at the auction house at eight fifteen the following morning. He said he would bring a detective with him.

Adri sighed. "Another day turned upside down. I need to call Gina—Jocko, will it disturb her and little Josh to call now?"

Jocko looked at the time on his phone. "No, she probably just finished his bath, so they are just cuddling." He grinned as he said the last.

Adri smiled softly. "I'll be as quick as I can."

Adri talked with Gina about working again the following morning. She was agreeable and said she would leave Josh with Jocko's Mom so she wouldn't have interruptions.

When she finished the phone call, she turned to Jocko. "I still need you to go with the crew to organize the hauling. There will be some specific instructions. I'll have that organized in the morning."

Jocko nodded and then turned to Max. "Do I need to bring your car over in the morning? I am assuming you are taking Adri home now."

Max agreed, "Yes, I was just going to ask if you would do that for me. You can just park it there at Adri's as I have a lunch with John and am guessing I won't have much time."

Adri looked at Max with a puzzled look on her face and asked, "Why would your time be tight?"

Max's expression was gentle. "After what you have been through today, I am not letting you go back over there by yourself. I am taking you."

"Oh!" Adri's face flushed a little. "Thank you! I was wondering if I could do it alone."

Max assured her. "You don't have to." Then Max asked, "Are we set for now? Are you ready to go home?"

Adri nodded and turned with Max to go to her car. A soft voice spoke behind them. "Is everything all right? I wondered if you were still here." It was Mrs. Wolcott.

Max and Adri turned as one back toward her. Max smiled. "We aren't using our good manners right now. We should have come to say good night."

Mrs. Wolcott laughed softly. "That's okay. You are leaving now?"

Adri moved away from Max and stood in front of her. "Thank you so much for the tea. It really did help me."

Mrs. Wolcott smiled and reached out and hugged Adri. "You are so welcome, my dear."

The hug had been so unexpected that Adri's cheeks were flushed when she moved back. Adri stuttered a little. "It was nice to-to meet you. I-I am starting to-to feel the lo-long day and need to-to go home."

Mrs. Wolcott smiled gently. "Yes, you need to go. Is Max taking you home?"

Max stepped up and assured her. "Yes, Grandmother. Jocko will bring my car in the morning." Max reached and gave her a hug. "We will say good night now."

Mrs. Wolcott laughed softly as she responded. "I am so glad you still consider us family, even if you have been absent. Good night to you both."

Chapter 20

When Adri and Max arrived at the auction house, one of the partners greeted them and ushered them to where there was a group of people. Adri recognized the security guard that had walked her to her car the evening before. As they approached, Officer Woods came toward them. Another man came with him. Officer Woods introduced them to Detective Alan Morris.

Detective Morris filled them in. "We wanted to talk to all the security that was working yesterday afternoon. One reported that a man fitting the description of our perp was caught going through drawers, after the set was sold. The guard who escorted you out reported that same individual asked who you were as he was leaving. The guard didn't know your name so couldn't tell him what he wanted to know." Detective Morris checked his notes and continued. "You spoke with the head of security last night, James Holland. Is that right?"

Adri confirmed that. "Yes. Mr. Holland assured me that he and another guard would personally lock up the furniture set."

Detective Morris nodded. "We are ready to go check out the furniture then. I understand that you have worked with antiques for a long time and would be aware of where to look for secret compartments. We may need your help with the search."

Adri took a deep breath and answered, "Yes. You just need to tell me what to do."

The detective called out to Mr. Holland. He jangled the keys and led them to a locked room at the back of the building. After he unlocked and opened the door, he stepped back to allow the four of them into the room, and then he stepped in and stood in the doorway. He told Detective Morris, "We wore gloves when we moved it so as not add to any fingerprints."

Detective Morris nodded and turned to Adri. "Officer Woods and I will do a traditional search and dust for fingerprints. This could take a while."

Adri just nodded. Officer Woods and the detective began their search. After the drawers and obvious surfaces had been examined with no results, they began the fingerprinting process. To everyone's amazement, there were only a few prints to be lifted.

Detective Morris handed Adri a pair of gloves. "It's up to you. Find any hidden places you can think of."

Adri nodded and approached the bed headboard first. She felt at the edges of first one leg and then the other. She found the small indentation she was looking for. She pulled a small screwdriver out of her pocket, reached down, and turned the screwdriver a half a turn, and everyone heard the click. Adri placed both hands at the side of the back panel and gently eased it open. She looked up.

"Detective, you will want to see this." Adri stood and backed away, leaving only one hand on the delicate panel to hold it steady.

The detective moved to get a full view. He saw the twelve-by-twelve-square-inch cut in the center of the solid wood headboard. Taped inside the cutout was a small package wrapped in brown paper. The detective snapped a couple of pictures, dusted for prints, and removed the package. He asked Adri to close the panel. After that was accomplished, the detective asked, "Will there be other compartments?"

Adri smiled. "Oh yes! I tried the head board first. If there is a compartment in there, that means there will be others. This maker is especially fond of hidden places."

Adri went to the pieces with drawers and pulled a small tape measure from her skirt pocket. She pulled out drawers, measured outside depth and inside depth. Out of twelve drawers total, two she removed from the furniture and turned upside down on the floor. She again used the screwdriver and exposed compartments with contents.

While the detective was busy with the drawers, Adri asked Officer Woods to help her turn the vanity mirror. When that was done, she told them. "This mirror has been replaced, and the compartment has been removed." She showed the officer how she could tell, and he made notes.

Then he asked, "You are sure about this?"

The detective joined them, and Adri explained again how she was certain. The detective was thoughtful. "I see what you mean. The hole has been filled in too. Does that devalue the piece?"

Adri shook her head. "Only to someone who wanted a mirror with a compartment."

Detective Morris asked, "Are there more compartments?"

Adri moved to the foot board of the bed. "This piece and the back of each of the stand-up pieces may or may not have compartments."

Adri checked the foot board and found no indentation. Then she moved behind the other pieces. Officer Woods stayed close now and watched her search. Adri had a sense that the officer all of a sudden didn't trust her, and she had no idea why. She found an empty compartment at the back of the vanity and found a large compartment at the back of the armoire. This was the real payday. Larger packages filled the entire space.

While the detective processed the armoire and its contents, Officer Woods questioned Adri. "Do all antique dealers know about this kind of thing? The hidden compartments?"

Adri thought about it. "If they have been in the business a while, they probably would, if for no other reason than a customer has shown it to them. Furniture restorers would definitely know this."

"So some dealers might not be aware of this feature?"

"Yes, that is possible."

"Did you buy this set by this maker just because you thought it would have the compartments?"

Adri stared at the officer. What was he really asking? "I told you yesterday evening that I bid on it as an impulse since I had talked to my assistant, and he told me they had sold another set out of my showroom."

"You are more knowledgeable than most. You would know about the hiding places and would expect to find something in them." Officer Woods said it in an accusing tone.

Adri's back stiffened. "Because it was an impulse buy, I did not research it or even look at it before auction. I did not know who the maker was until this morning when I inspected the back side of the headboard. The maker's name is there at the top."

Officer Woods walked over to take a look at the headboard and then wrote the name on his pad. He came back to Adri. "You would be familiar with maker's styles. You must have at least suspected the maker."

Adri didn't have an answer for him. He continued, again accusing, "You didn't find compartments on three pieces that could easily have them. What are you hiding?"

Detective Morris was packing the last of the packages into a plastic crate and spoke. "That's enough, Woods. Ms. Winfield has been extremely helpful in spite of the inconvenience."

Officer Woods wasn't done. "You could have intentionally missed some compartments so you could keep what is hidden. Are you sure there are no more compartments?"

Adri turned red in the face and told the officer with hard sternness in her voice, "The only way to be absolutely sure there are no more compartments would be to completely disassemble every piece, and I do not believe whoever put things into this furniture would go to that much trouble."

There was sarcasm in the officer's voice, "Oh, but Ms. Winfield, you would know how to do it and put it back together, wouldn't you?"

Max and the detective both began to move toward them.

Adri held up her hand, and that stopped them both. Her voice was like steel when she spoke. "You, sir, are out of line. I am an experienced antique restorer, and yes, I know how to dismantle and rebuild antique furniture." Adri went pale, and her voice shook slightly as she continued, "However, I am sure the Auction House will provide you with the origin of this set, and you will perhaps find the packer. Now you *will* excuse me, I am done with you."

Adri drew in a breath and held it as she moved past the guard into the hall. When she let the breath out, she began to hyperventilate. Max was right there and pulled her to him. He soothed her with his voice and his hand on the nape of her neck. She recovered quickly, and they both stood and listened to a raised voice in the room.

It was Detective Morris speaking. They had missed what Officer Woods might have said. "Woods, you are not to speak to Ms. Winfield unless it is to apologize. And it better be a pretty fancy and sincere apology. Ms. Winfield is a real lady, and believe me, she tolerated more from you than she should have. Your captain will hear about this, and I'd like you off the case."

Officer Woods protested, but the detective cut him off. "It will be up to your captain, but he'll know what I want."

There was silence and then a shuffling, and Detective Morris appeared in the doorway holding the crate of evidence. He nodded at them and said, "You are free to go. We need to keep your furniture set locked up here for the time being, but I will be in touch."

Adri smiled slightly. "I understand. Thank you, Detective."

He nodded again and watched as they moved to walk away.

Max and Adri were quiet as they left the building and made their way to the car. They were each busy with their own thoughts. Adri was still shook at the officer's attack, and Max was thinking how proud he was of Adri.

Max opened the car door for Adri and handed her into the car. He noticed how pale she was. "Adri, he was being a real jerk right now. Let it go."

Adri looked up and asked, "But why? I was just doing what they asked me to do!"

Max squatted by the car, reached out to touch her cheek so she could look at him. "You were amazing! First of all, you knew exactly what you were doing, and then you stood up to Woods, all on your own! Let it go."

Adri sighed. "The only reason I was able to talk back was because I knew you and Detective Morris were ready to back me up." Then she gave Max a small smile. "I was pretty amazing, wasn't I?"

Max smiled, and his eyes sent a tender message. "Yes! I am so proud of you!"

Adri smiled happily then and nodded.

During the trip back, they had relaxed conversation and just enjoyed each other's company. Max walked Adri to the showroom, and then he left for his lunch with John.

Gina was waiting on a customer when Adri walked in, and a few minutes later, another customer arrived. Adri was finally able to send Gina home at noon, and she stayed busy with a steady stream of customers. It was a quarter to three when Jocko arrived. He told Adri that the truck was on its way.

Adri laughed and said, "I have been really busy, and you might be too. I'll take the path up to Max's house."

Jocko grinned. "We put the dinette set, the small colonial bed set, and the Italian bedroom set in the truck as you instructed, so Max will get his surprises. Have fun!"

Adri laughed again and waved as she went out the door. She was a little breathless as she arrived at the top of the path. It was going to be fun surprising Max again.

CHAPTER 21

The crew had moved in all but the two medium gray chairs and placed things where Adri directed. Max was pleased. "I really like this room. With this furniture, it appears large but cozy. It is so amazing what the right furniture does for a room!"

Adri laughed. She looked around toward the front door. "Wonder what is taking so long with those last two chairs." She reached out and took Max's hand. "Let's go check on them."

They moved out the front door. Brad and Denny were up in the truck, and Dan and Kim were on the ground, waiting for the other two to hand them some furniture.

Brad looked up. "Sorry about the wait. Denny set these other two chairs behind some big stuff."

Denny grinned. "Yeah, 'cause you told me too." He clapped his hands and added, "Sorry, Ms. Adri."

Adri smiled. "No problem. Maybe you should just lift that table down. Then you could get to the chairs."

Kim grinned. "Good idea. Denny, grab that end. Dan and I will get it down here." The table was moved carefully over the lip of the truck and set on the veranda.

Max eyed it and turned to Adri. She was smiling broadly. Max's eyebrow went up, and he asked, "Your choice for the breakfast room, I take it."

Adri laughed. "Look it over. If you still don't like it, they will load it back up."

Max went over to it and examined it, giving it a gentle shake. The crew was shifting and unloading. Kim set two dinette chairs by the table, and Max examined them as well. He turned to Adri and grinned. "Okay. You were right. They can unload the rest of this set. It's sold!"

Adri laughed and hugged Max. Then she turned to her crew. "You heard the man." They all agreed and were busy again.

Max pulled Adri back into a side hug and teased her, "You planned this! Another surprise! And I've learned a lesson. I shouldn't question your choices in furniture."

Adri laughed happily and told him, "The other surprise is they have the Italian bedroom set loaded at the front and the girl's room colonial. We are filling four rooms today!"

Max threw his head back and laughed the rumble in his chest, giving Adri tingles down her spine, clear to her toes, and she laughed with him.

After the crew had the breakfast room set up and was working on carrying the two bedroom sets upstairs, Adri was excited to show Max all the neat features of the breakfast room set. The buffets had storage at the bottom for the table leaves, and this set had hidden compartments that she gleefully opened for Max. He smiled a lot and just plain enjoyed Adri's enthusiasm and joy.

After all the bedroom furniture was upstairs, Adri supervised the setup of each room with Max and Betty's input from time to time. Finally, things were set to Adri's satisfaction.

It was first thing Thursday morning, just after Adri arrived at the showroom that Detective Morris called. He told Adri, "It was very wise of you to call us about the possible use of the furniture. We have a line on a drug smuggling ring that could be international. Our suspect will not be released on bail. I thought you might want to know that."

Adri took a deep breath and let it out slowly before she spoke. "Yes, Detective, that is a big relief to know that I will not have to encounter him by accident. If I can be of further assistance, you know how to reach me."

Detective Morris told her, "You have helped us so much and turns out we have someone here in the department who is somewhat of an antique fan, and he went back and double-checked your furniture and confirmed that you had found all the hidden panels. Just wanted to let you know that the officer on the case had absolutely no call to attack you the way he did." Detective Morris chuckled and continued, "I really appreciated that you gave him what-for. He deserved it!"

Adri sighed and told him, "That was a big thing for me. Thank you."

"The other thing you need to know is that the department has no further need to hold your furniture, so it is yours to pick up any time. The auction house is aware and will assist any way they can."

Now Adri laughed. "No, thank you. I will call the auction house and tell them to sell it at their next auction. I don't want it!"

Detective Morris chuckled again. "I don't blame you. Ms. Winfield, you have a nice day!"

"Good-bye, Detective Morris."

After she hung up, she wasted no time in calling the auction house to make arrangements for the bedroom set to be resold. Then she called Max.

"Good morning, Adri!"

"Yes, Mr. Winfield, it is a good morning!" Adri laughed.

Max chuckled. "Mr. Winfield?"

Adri laughed again. "Yes, sir! I have good news!"

"Well, ma'am, you best tell me what it is!"

"This is fun!" Adri laughed and paused before she told Max, "The news is that Detective Morris called this morning! The suspect is staying in jail. They have leads to find a drug ring, maybe international! They have released the furniture, but the auction house will resell it at the next auction, and the detective was glad I gave Officer Woods 'what-for,' his words. Because he deserved it!" Adri had run out of breath.

Max laughed. *What a treat to hear her so confident!* "Wonderful! I told you that you did good! This really is good news!"

"Yes!"

There was a pause. Max asked, "What does your day look like?"

"Well, it will finally be a normal day. First one this week. Since we have been so busy, the showroom needs some serious rearrangement, and Jocko will be here. The first day we will actually work together here. Was there a reason you asked?" Adri asked.

Max chuckled softly. "Yes. I would like to invite you to lunch today. Betty has a new recipe, and I would rather not be her only—"

"Don't say it!" Adri interrupted. "It will be delicious, and yes, I would love to come and be a taste tester!" They both laughed. "But the time needs to be flexible."

"Yes, we both know that. So we will eat when you get here."

"Oh, and I have some more pictures to show you! The auction tomorrow has some real jewels!" Adri was excited.

Max's smile carried across the phone waves. "What rooms are we filling this time?"

"Well, maybe not filling. Not sure what you intend to use the wine cellar for . . . Anyway, I'll have a picture of a magnificent antique pool table and a huge armoire that with a few interior modifications would work as an entertainment center. And there is a sweet Spanish bedroom set that would work in the nanny's room and another Italian set, much different than the other, for the other spare bedroom!" Adri was so excited in giving the information that Max was almost speechless.

He responded, "Wow!"

Adri's excitement continued. "There is so much room in my showroom now, and storage is almost empty, so I have my eye on a lot of other things! The truck may need to make two trips if I buy it all!"

"I think I just heard the buzzer," Max commented.

"Yes, it is probably Jocko. He has a tendency to be early."

Max laughed. "I probably should let you go then."

Adri laughed. "But I called you!" They both laughed. "I will see you around lunchtime because I really do need to go." She was suddenly shy and said quietly. "Later, Max."

Max responded gently, "Later."

Later that day, it was almost closing time at the end of a busy day. Jocko had already left thirty minutes earlier. He needed to go check out an apartment they had heard about.

When the delivery truck returned, it backed up to the loading dock. Adri wasn't expecting that. She knew that Kim and Denny had gone home from their last delivery, so it would be just Dan and Brad with the truck. Adri quickly flipped off the "open" sign and hurried to the back. She arrived in the loading dock area as Dan was opening the back sliding door on the truck.

"What do we have here?" Adri asked him.

Dan grinned. "Mrs. Williams was tired of the Spanish style and wanted you to have it."

"What do you mean have it?"

Brad chimed in, "She has bought so much from you, and she said you deserved a nice tip and wants you to have this."

"Oh my!" Adri stepped into the truck and walked through, looking at the Spanish dining room antiques. As she came back through, Brad had already unfastened a large urn to take off the truck.

Adri hooked the toe of her right shoe on a buffet table leg and pitched toward Brad. He had the urn in his hands, and as Adri bumped him, the brass urn plunged down and hit Adri on her left foot, the one she had moved forward to try to catch her balance. She let out a loud moan and collapsed to the floor of the truck. Brad set the urn back where he had moved it from. He quickly squatted in front of Adri.

"I am so sorry. Oh, Adri, I was too careless. I am sorry!"

Even though she had sturdy shoes on, she was sure her toes were broken and maybe the in-step of her foot as well. She clenched her teeth to try to stop the moans as she rocked back and forth in pain.

She managed to speak through the pain. "Brad, there's an ice pack in the refrigerator in my office. Dan, help me out of here and get my shoe off. I can feel it swelling."

Dan, first of all, helped her stand, and then he lifted her in his arms and carried her to a small settee nearby in the docking area. He tried to gently remove her shoe. She gasped in pain, and the tears filled her eyes as the shoe came off with difficulty. She told him to leave the sock on. Brad returned with the ice pack, and both men stood there looking helpless as she gingerly placed the ice pack around her foot. She took her shawl off her shoulders and wrapped it all up, tying the shawl's ends together to secure it.

When she looked up, she saw the same helplessness in their faces that she felt. She took a couple of deep breaths. "I will need to go to the emergency room. Which one of you has the most time this evening?" Brad said he did. "Brad, go get my car. The garage code is 1020. The keys are in the car. Dan, go to the house and get my bag off the table near the door and bring the pair of crutches that are in the closet behind the front door. The key code to the house is 2324. Reverse the code to lock it again." They both went to do her bidding.

Adri laid her head back against the settee back and closed her eyes. Max's face flashed into her head. *This hurts so badly. Max would know how to take care of me.* That thought shook her a little. *I want to be cared for by Max.* That thought shook her even more, but it stayed there and kept replaying. She moaned again as a pain shot up her leg. Then her head jerked up when she heard her name in Max's voice.

"Adri!" She wondered if she was seeing and hearing things. Max was coming up the steps by the dock, taking them two at a time. He hurried to her. "Oh, Adri, my sweetheart! Brad told me what happened." Max knelt at her foot and was reassured the ice pack would stay in place and then stood quickly. "I am going to carry you to the car and get you to the ER."

Adri just nodded, her face registering the pain.

Brad had the car nearby as Max carried her down the steps. Brad opened the passenger door, and Max set her down gently on the seat and buckled her in. Brad was distressed and said, "I am so sorry. I should have waited until you were back out before I tried to move anything. This is awful!"

Adri tried to reassure him, "I just need a doctor's attention and a little time. I'm sure I'll be okay."

Dan returned with her bag and the crutches. She told him, "I'll take my bag. The crutches can go back to the house." She had to pause and grit her teeth to stop another moan. "Make sure everything is closed up and locked up and go home. You can come back tomorrow and unload the truck." The last of her instructions were breathless as the pain almost overwhelmed her, and tears came to her eyes.

Max was in the driver's side of the car and started the engine. Dan assured her, "We'll take care of things. Go!" He gently closed the car door and stepped back.

Max put the car in drive and reached for Adri's hand. "You can cry, sweetheart. It must hurt terribly!"

Adri leaned her head back and let the tears quietly run down her cheeks. She turned her thoughts away from the pain to the wonder of Max appearing as she thought of her need of him. *How did he get there right then? Was it his instinct again? Was it God telling him I needed him? God, is this your work?* A moan escaped her lips as the pain took over again.

Max squeezed her hand gently. "We're almost there."

Chapter 22

The X-ray had shown that the three middle toes were broken, and all five toes were bruised, and the in-step was not broken but had deep tissue bruising. She received a shot for the pain and then left the ER with a bottle of prescription pain meds and a bottle of over-the-counter anti-inflammatory meds.

The doctor's instructions to her were to stay off her foot and keep it elevated as much as possible for a week. After the swelling went down, she should wrap her toes together, and they had shown her how to do that, the nurse using her fingers as the doctor taped them. While she had her foot up, they had told her the schedule for icing it. Max was able to stay with her the whole time, except for when she went for the X-ray.

The shot for the pain had really eased things for her, and as soon as Max had turned the car onto the street, Adri asked him, "How did you know to come at just the right time?"

Max asked softly, "Why was it just the right time?"

There was emotion in her voice when she answered, "I nee-needed you to-to come take care of me." Adri took a deep breath and continued, "Dan and Brad seemed to feel as helpless as I did. We have never had an accident since I opened."

Max turned his head briefly and smiled at Adri. "I was actually coming to look at area rugs just before closing. The rugs we talked about needing for the reading nooks in the library. About halfway down the path, I heard the truck pull in and had a sudden urge to hurry and arrived just as Brad was opening the garage. He did seem relieved to see me and immediately filled me in."

Adri rested her head back against the seat and told Max, "When you came to me, I thought for a moment I was imagining you. I had just thought about needing you." Adri raised her head and glanced at Max's profile and then ducked her head and blushed. "I think I am saying too much."

Max said gently, "It's okay. Sometimes we say things more freely under the influence of medicine."

They were approaching the turn to Adri's place, but Max didn't slow down to turn. Adri asked, "Where are we going?"

The car crested the low hill and turned into his drive. "I hope from what you just said that you will allow me to continue to take care of you." Max stopped the car near the front step, and Betty opened the house door wide, hurrying toward the car. Max's voice was gentle and persuading. "You can't get around on your own, and Betty and I are here for you right now."

Adri gasped and was shaking her head. She didn't have time to voice a protest as Betty pulled the car door open and leaned in. "Oh, sweet girl! You can be assured that Max and I will take really good care of you!"

Max had turned the car off but was still sitting in the driver's seat and angled toward Adri. There was such a tender look in Max's eyes. Adri sighed. "I guess I really am pretty helpless right now. I ne-need you-you and Betty."

Max reached out and gently touched her cheek. "I'm glad you will allow us to be your good friends and neighbors. I'll come around and carry you in." His smile was tender.

Betty took Adri's handbag, and Max lifted Adri out of the car. When they were in the entry, Max asked, "Can we settle you in the library for now? There are some things we need to make arrangements for."

Adri just nodded against Max's shoulder where her head rested. Betty hurried ahead and placed pillows on a settee. Max and Betty fused over her until she insisted she was comfortable.

Betty told her, "You need to eat. First I'll bring an ice pack and a glass of water. Then I will get you a tray of food. It'll be light and hopefully appealing." When it looked like Adri was going to protest, Betty assured her, "Max hasn't eaten either." Betty hurried out of the room.

Max sat down on the occasional table in front of the settee. He asked softly, "Do you need to call Jocko about the auction tomorrow?"

Tears came to Adri's eyes, and she blinked them quickly away. "Yes. I am so tired right now. I really messed up. I hardly ever walk into the truck. Oh, Max, I am so stupid!"

Max reached over and placed his index finger gently on Adri's lips. His voice was a little stern when he told her, "None of that. You and Brad both need to understand that accidents happen. He was pretty upset that he was responsible for your injury. You weren't at fault, and he didn't do anything to cause what happened. Okay?"

Tears came to Adri's eyes again. "Yes, you are right. I was just so excited about the dining room set they brought back, I didn't think!"

Max handed Adri the tissue box. Betty came back with the ice pack and glass of water. Max told her, "The doctor told you to keep the pain under control, so I think you need to take the pills now."

Adri nodded. "Please give me my handbag."

Max handed it to her off the occasional table and asked, "Do you want to put the ice pack on, or shall I?"

Adri sighed. "You can. I'm too tired."

Max applied the ice pack. Adri jerked only a little when the ice pack touched her foot. Adri had the pills in hand, and Max handed her the glass of water. Max asked softly, "Is it okay if I take your other shoe off? I think you would be more comfortable."

Adri gave him a half smile. "Yes, please."

Betty came in with a tray of food and asked, "How do you want to do this? One tray for both of you."

Max looked around and then suggested, "Let me pull this table a little closer, and I can just hold the tray on my knees."

Betty nodded approval and handed the tray to Max to arrange on his knees. Betty told them softly, "I'll be in the kitchen if you need anything."

Adri saw the full tray, and tears came to her eyes again.

"Oh, sweetheart, don't cry right now. This is a good thing." Adri blinked back the tears, and Max continued, "That's my girl. You are weak and tired right now and need nourishment." He pointed at the tray. "What do you want to start with?"

Adri blinked again and studied the tray of food. There was cheese and crackers, three different fruits, two bowls of chocolate pudding, and two mugs of hot cocoa.

"The hot cocoa."

Max grinned. "Good choice." He picked up a mug and carefully handed it to her. She took it, blew on it a little, and took a sip. Then another sip.

"I can reach the tray if you move just a little closer."

"Does that mean the food appeals to you and you are ready to eat?"

"Yes, please." She put her mug of cocoa in her left hand, and Max scooted a little closer as she reached for a piece of cheese and a piece of apple.

They were silent as they both helped themselves to the food. When Adri's mug was empty, Max asked her if she wanted more.

"No, thank you. I don't need anything to drink right now." Max took her mug from her and set it out of the way, and he was happy to see that she kept eating.

After eating a good portion, she finished a strawberry, sighed, and said, "I think I am ready for the pudding. How did Betty know to bring two chocolates?"

Max laughed. "That is Betty's cure for a cloudy day or anything that bothers a person. Her motto is that you can never have too much nutritious chocolate around."

As Adri let the first spoonful of chocolate pudding slide down her throat, she smiled. "I like her motto!"

Max smiled. "So do I." He looked at her, assessing her countenance. "I think you are doing a little better now."

She smiled. "I'm doing a lot better. I was hungrier than I thought!" When she finished her pudding, she asked shyly. "May I have a glass of ice water now?"

Max smiled. "I'll get it." He stood with the tray and went to the kitchen to get a fresh glass of ice water.

When he returned, he told her, "It's time to take the ice pack off."

Adri nodded. "Could you please do that?"

Max nodded and bent over her foot and gently removed the ice pack. When he straightened, Adri's eyes were closed, and she said, "I am so tired. Can I just rest for a bit before we fix anything else?"

Max spoke softly. "Yes, you can rest."

"If I go to sleep, be sure and wake me in thirty minutes. It is getting on to eight o'clock, and I still need to make some phone calls." Her voice grew softer, and Max noticed that she had barely finished speaking and had already relaxed into slumber.

Max moved to a chair a short distance from the settee and began a mental list of what still needed to be accomplished yet this evening. *I think we need to send Betty to pick up some things from Adri's house. Hopefully Adri can contact one of her guys to meet Betty there so she isn't alone. Adri needs to talk to Jocko this evening and maybe again in the morning. Wonder if Jocko is aware of what has happened. Maybe I should call him to give him a heads-up. I don't have his number. Oh, I know . . .*

Max pulled out his phone and placed a call to Mrs. Wolcott.

After she answered, Max spoke. "Grandmother, it's Max."

"Hello, Max." There was a slight tremble in Grandmother's voice.

Max was curious about the tremble and expected her to say more. When the silence lengthened, Max asked, "Am I calling at a bad time? I'll only keep you a minute. I need Jocko's phone number."

Mrs. Wolcott's voice was soft, and there was still a tremble when she answered, "Not a bad time. I'll get Jocko's number for you." There was a silence, and then she came back with Jocko's phone number.

When she finished, Max asked softly, "Grandmother, are you okay?"

Max heard her take a deep breath. When she answered, her voice was stronger. "Jocko was here at the house when one of the crew called him—Dan, I think—and told him about Adri's accident, so I am aware of it." Her voice faded at the end.

"Okay. With your tender heart, you are worried about her. The update is that the three center toes are broken, and she has deep tissue bruising. She needs to stay off that foot for a week, for sure, and the healing will be slow. You can pray for her."

Grandmother had emotion in her voice when she told Max, "I am praying. We all are."

Max reassured her. "I brought Adri to my house so Betty and I could look after her. I am with Adri now. She is sleeping. She won't be alone until she is mobile again. And since Jocko already knows about the accident, I will let Adri call him when she can handle it."

Grandmother's voice was trembling again. "I will tell Jocko. Thank you, Max." She hesitated. "I need to go."

"Okay, Grandmother. Talk to you soon."

When Max disconnected, he was puzzled about Grandmother's emotion and seeming distress. If Adri was family, it would make sense, but Grandmother had only met Adri two evenings ago. Of course, he understood that Grandmother would have been drawn to Adri's sweet personality, just as he had been, but it still seemed an overreaction on Grandmother's part.

He bowed his head and prayed—prayed for Grandmother and for Jocko and for Adri's crew, especially Brad, and then spent considerable time praying for Adri.

CHAPTER 23

At eight thirty, Max went and bent over Adri. He placed one hand softly on her shoulder and with the fingers of the other gently touched her cheek as he spoke her name. "Adri."

She opened her eyes slowly and looked a little confused. "Max?"

"Yes, sweet Adri. You need to wake up and make some phone calls." Max removed his hands and straightened.

Adri started to move to sit up, but the pain in her foot as she moved it caught her unaware, and she cried out. Max placed both hands on her shoulders and told her, "No, stay where you are."

Adri caught her lower lip between her teeth, and tears shimmered in her eyes. "I wasn't aware. I forgot."

Max asked gently, "Okay now?"

Adri nodded, and Max straightened again.

"I need a drink of water." Max picked up the glass from the end table and handed it to Adri. "Thank you." She sipped slowly and then handed the glass back to Max.

Adri sighed. "You said I need to make phone calls."

Max nodded and sat down on the occasional table. "Let me tell you what I was thinking." Adri nodded. "First of all, make a list for Betty of a few things you might need from your house tonight and in the morning. Then you maybe could call one of your crew to meet her there so she won't be alone." Adri nodded. Max continued, "You do need to call Jocko about tomorrow."

Adri thought for a moment. "I'll start the list. Where is my handbag?"

Max gave her a gentle smile. "There on the floor beside you."

Adri blushed. "Maybe I am not as aware as I thought." She picked up her handbag and dug in it for a little and came up with a small spiral notebook and a pen.

"While you are working on that, I'll go get Betty."

Adri continued writing and nodded her head in agreement.

As Max left the library, he was thinking. *She was a little druggy when she first woke, but that nap seems to have helped her a lot. She seemed to be thinking clearly when she started her list.* Max went into the kitchen and told Betty what the plan was.

Max checked the time and realized the ice pack needed to go back on, so he got it out of the freezer and asked Betty, "Do we have another one of these?"

Betty shook her head. "No, that is the only one. I checked."

"Maybe Adri has one you could bring over. I'll ask."

While Max was gone, Adri paused in making the list and decided to see if Brad would be able to help yet tonight. He was the closest, and she was sure he needed to be reassured.

Adri shifted so she could get her phone out of her pocket. She hit speed dial for Brad, and he answered immediately.

"Adri, how are you?"

"Hi, Brad. As long as I keep my foot still, I do okay. I am calling to ask a favor."

Brad responded immediately, "Name it."

"I am at Max's house, will be here at least until I am mobile again. Betty needs to go get some things for me from my house, and I would like for you to come pick her up and help with that."

Brad was eager to help. "I can be there in fifteen minutes and will be so glad to help. What did the doctor say about your foot?"

Adri sighed. "The three center toes are broken, and the whole front of my foot has deep tissue bruising. It will take a while to heal."

Brad started to apologize again, and Adri stopped him. "Brad, accidents happen. Max told me earlier—now listen closely—I wasn't intentionally at fault, and you didn't do anything intentionally to cause what happened. Now take it to heart. I had too."

There was a long silence before Brad responded. "I told you the man on the hill was good for you, and now he is good for me. Thank you, Adri."

Max and Betty had come into the room as Adri was telling Brad about her injury and heard the rest of what she said. Betty whispered to Max, "Another rescue times two." Max just nodded.

Adri asked, "Fifteen minutes then. See you soon." Brad affirmed, and Adri disconnected.

Adri turned her head and spoke to Max and Betty. "Brad is coming here to pick you up, Betty, and he will assist you as you need."

Betty came over and was a little flustered. "He didn't need to come get me!"

"Well, no, I know that, but I think he will sleep better if he sees I am doing okay."

Max chuckled softly. "Now you sound like me—you're taking care of Brad."

Adri blushed and reminded him, "You set a good example."

Max grinned and asked, "Is the list finished?"

Adri nodded. "Almost. Then I'll have Betty read it to make sure she understands." There was a silence as Adri wrote quickly and then handed the note pad to Betty. "After you read it, I'll have a few instructions."

Betty looked down at the list and then looked up at Max and smiled. "She read our minds. Ice pack is the first thing on the list!"

Max chuckled softly. "Hmm."

Betty finished reading. "It's all clear. What are the instructions?"

"There is a wicker clothes hamper and a wicker trash basket in the bathroom. Everything out of the bathroom can go in those. There are a couple of wicker chests in the bedroom and a couple of pairs of shoes, and everything I need out of the dresser can go in one of those. I won't need any of the jeans, just skirts and blouses, and bring those on hangers please."

Betty nodded and smiled. "You are very organized with all this. Is there anything else you can think of?"

"Yes—uh—in my office in the showroom are my laptop computer and the two file folders lying on the desk. One folder says Auction, and the other isn't labeled, but they are stacked together." Adri rubbed her forehead.

Max asked softly. "What is it?"

"I can't remember if I put a blank check in the Auction folder. Betty, you will need to look in that folder, and if the check isn't there, you'll need to call me."

Betty smiled. "No problem. I guess Brad knows how to get in?"

"He knows how to get into the showroom and my office. To get into the house, I wrote the numbers at the top of the list." Betty looked and saw the numbers and nodded. "To lock the house again, reverse the numbers. Brad may not remember that."

Betty nodded just as the door chimes rang.

Max handed the ice pack to Betty and asked, "Will you put this on for Adri while I get the door?"

"Sure thing."

"Just lay it on top of the coverlet. It's too cold to go directly on my skin. When you get back with my things, I'll put on a thick sock," Adri instructed Betty.

"That's a good idea." Betty completed her task gently, and Adri only jerked once during the process.

Max and Brad came in the library, and Brad came quickly over to Adri. "Can I see it?"

Adri actually laughed and then told him, "No." She was still smiling. "I just got comfortable with the ice pack. I'll let you look when you come back."

Brad grinned. "My kids want me to describe it to them in the morning. That's really the reason I asked. Kids get some weird ideas sometimes, so I will probably make it sound worse than it really is. But I am curious as well."

Adri laughed again and saw some of the tension leave his neck and shoulder muscles. *He was glad to hear me laugh.* "Okay. One condition though. You can't take your guilt back when you see it. That is already in the trash. Right?"

Brad was serious now. "Yeah. Max already talked to me to make sure too. So I can't lug the guilt around, or you will all know it." Then he grinned. "Besides, it will give me one up on the rest of the crew. I can describe it to them as good or as bad as I want to."

Everyone laughed, and Adri warned, "You best be truthful."

"Yes, ma'am." He turned to Betty. "Mrs. Betty, are you ready to get this errand done?"

Betty smiled. "Yes, let's get it done."

Brad took her arm, and they left the room.

Adri sighed. "The meeting with the crew has opened so much more for me. They are all my friends. I just wouldn't let myself be their friend." She looked up at Max. "I owe you so much."

Max took a seat in a nearby chair and assured her, "You don't owe me anything because your knowledge and experience in the antique world and your choices for my home more than make up for anything you think you owe me. And there is so much more." The last was said almost as a caress.

Adri blushed a little and was silent for a moment and then told him, "You are my best friend. I have told you things that I would never have dreamed of telling anyone. You are so solid to my emotional hang-ups. You so completely accept me, mess and all."

Max smiled softly. "Thank you. And you are not such a mess right now. You have come a long way."

"Yes, because I trusted you to understand, and you always have."

There was a brief silence. Adri mused. "I need to call Jocko. He will need to go to the auction tomorrow. There is no way I can go." She looked down and then up with pink in her cheeks. "After I talk to Jocko, I-I need to ask you something I need an answer too!"

Max smiled. "You can ask me anything you want."

Adri nodded and picked up her phone off her lap and hit speed dial for Jocko's number.

Jocko answered softly, "Hello, Adri, how are you?"

"Did Dan or Brad call and tell you what happened?"

"Yes. Dan called. How are you?"

"I'll be laid up for a while. The pain pills are working, and as long as I don't move it, the foot doesn't bother me much." Adri paused then continued. "I need you to go to the auction tomorrow."

Jocko took a deep breath. "Are you sure you are ready to send me to an auction? Are you sure I am ready for that?"

Adri laughed softly. "I am about as sure of that as you are! But listen, Jocko, you know how auctions run. I have all the information you need for what I want, and I have been very pleased with everything you have done for me, so yes, I will send you and believe you will do just fine."

Jocko cleared his throat before he answered. "Thank you, Adri. I am still a little nervous, but I really appreciate your confidence in me."

"Now, I am at Max's home, and I will have the auction folder and a signed check here. You need to be here by eight fifteen in the morning. Since the auction is only a thirty-minute drive, that will give you time to view the furniture to make sure it is in good shape." Adri stopped and then added, "But you know that. Sorry for being so bossy."

Jocko laughed. "Ma'am, it is so comforting to hear you say all that! It reassures me that you may be laid up, but you are not out of commission!"

Adri blushed and laughed too. "Anyway, if you have any questions, you can ask them when we meet in the morning."

Jocko assured her, "I will be there on time, and I know you will still answer your phone, even if you can't be at the auction."

"That's right! No guarantees what shape I'll be in though."

"Adri, we are all praying for you, and I believe you will get very good care. We can all just put up with grouchy if we need to."

There was emotion in Adri's voice when she answered that. "Thank you." Adri cleared her throat. "Gina will need to work all day tomorrow. I hope that isn't a problem?"

"Not a problem. She has already made all her arrangements and will be there to open in the morning. She's a little nervous but knows you and I are as close as the phone."

"I know she'll be fine. You are both great help, and I really appreciate your eagerness. I am not nervous about tomorrow at all!" Adri sighed. "Now I need to go. See you in the morning."

"Good night, Adri. We will continue to pray."

"Good night."

Adri sighed as she disconnected and laid her phone back in her lap.

Max said softly, "Are you okay? You are taking care of Jocko too."

Adri smiled. "Yes. When I told him his first day on the job that eventually he would be going to auctions, he was truly surprised and humbled. I know he will do just fine."

CHAPTER 24

"I wish Betty was here, but I can't put it off any longer." Adri sighed again. "I need the ladies' room."

Max stood and smiled. "I'll get you into the bathroom, and since it's small, maybe you can manage."

Adri just nodded. Max removed the ice pack and the coverlet and gently picked Adri up.

Max had just got her situated on the settee again when they heard voices in the entry.

Adri sighed again. "Guess I better get on my happy face. That's hard though after all the moving around."

Max soothed. "You did better than I thought you would. Just think positive. You'll do fine."

Adri nodded. "Oh, I didn't ask if you had a mattress set for that bed that I guess I'll be using."

Max nodded. "My spare room at the condo had a queen-size bed. The bed is even made up already. And it sounds like you'll have a little time for the happy face. I think they are carrying things upstairs."

Max and Adri were quiet while listening to the activity at the stairs.

Eventually, Betty and Brad came into the library. Betty hurried over to Adri. "Here are the folders. I thought you might want everything else upstairs. You get the room with that beautiful Italian furniture!"

Adri smiled. "Yes, Max said the bed was made up and everything."

Betty laughed. "Goodness me, yes, did that the day it was all moved in!"

Brad spoke now. "You are looking a little weary. All I want now is show and tell, and then I will go home."

Adri laughed. "Show and tell, huh? Max, would you please move the coverlet off my foot?"

Betty and Brad both moved closer to the back of the settee. Betty had seen a glimpse earlier but still gasped at the sight of the blue-colored and swollen foot. Light bruising showed above the instep and at the ankle area as well.

Adri told them, "This is show, and there will no telling by me, except to say—it will heal."

Betty reached into her pocket and asked Adri, "Here is a thick sock. Do you want it on now?"

Adri smiled and told Betty, "Give it to Max. He can be the bad guy when it hurts."

Max chuckled. "Now I know—bad guy, huh?"

Adri used her cheeky smile, and Max blinked, loving that it was directed at him.

Brad sighed. "I think I will embellish on the good side. If it hurts half as bad as it looks, that's too painful." He shuddered at the pain thought. Then he grinned. "I know you are in good hands, so I will say good night."

Adri smiled. "Good night, Brad. Thank you so much for your help."

"Anytime. Mrs. Betty, I will find my way out." Brad left, and no one spoke until they heard the front door close.

"I didn't want Brad to see me cry, so if you really want to put it on for me, that's okay," Adri explained to Betty.

Betty laughed softly and patted Adri's hand. "No, dear. I don't want to see you cry right now, so Max is elected. I'm going upstairs to put your things away if that's all right."

That brought grateful tears to Adri's eyes, and there was emotion in her voice. "Thank you, Betty."

Betty frowned at her and then patted her hand again, picked up the now warm ice pack, and left.

"Max, there is such a wonderful fondness between you and Betty. Now it seems the two of you are including m-me. Do you have family? Good family?"

Max decided to work on putting the sock on while she was distracted. He told her softly, "I had two wonderful parents and a sweet wonderful wife, but they are all gone now. Betty is my family, and her family is my extended family. There is one other family I still spend a lot of time with—the Wolcotts. John Wolcott is my best friend. I think I already told you that."

The sock was on, and Adri had only winched a little as he pulled it over the instep.

There was silence as Adri let that soak in. "You-you seem to be at peace about that. I mean about not having your own family."

"I am, but I have had a lot of years to adjust. God kind of had his hands full when my wife died. But time and keeping God in my life helped me to where I am today. There was a scripture verse that I clung to. Colossians 3:15, 'Let the peace of God rule in your hearts, to this you are called . . . and be thankful.' But you have to ask. You have to find the place in your heart that hurts and ask God to give you peace.

"I was a young teenager when I asked and received salvation, and when I shared that my past troubled me, the youth leader gave me that verse. I have it memorized. I just haven't applied it much, especially since college." Adri sighed. "I need to ask more."

Max agreed, "Yes, God supplies the peace when we are open to it. Karen, even in her suffering, knew the peace of God."

"That kind of leads into what I wanted to ask you about. Well, it changes the subject, sort of." Adri paused. "You have had a wife, so you know abo-about what love is be-between a man and a woman. I-I have had no examples in my life. I don't really ha-have a close married fe-female friend to-to ask." Adri ducked her head and was really blushing when she asked, "Tell me about that ki-kind of lo-love." Then she rushed to finish. "Do y-you have any idea what I-I am asking about?"

Max nodded, letting Adri know that he understood. He remained quiet for a long time, trying to form an answer. "Adri, it would be so much easier to answer you if you were more specific, but I think I understand why you are not. There are a lot of components to love. If a couple can start out as friends, that is wonderful. To be a friend, you need to get to know the other person. From being friends, it can easily move into love because the couple already likes each other. There are the wishes for the other person, like wanting them happy and not wanting to do anything that will hurt them physically or emotionally." Max looked closely at Adri's face. There was eager concentration. Max sent up a quick prayer. *God, give me the right words. This is really important.* "Adri, may I personalize my explanation? It would make it easier for me to help you understand."

Adri ducked her head and blushed and told Max shyly, "Okay."

Max leaned forward in his chair and spoke softly. "With my first love, my wife, we had been friends since grade school, and when we started dating, it didn't take us long to figure out that we loved each other and wanted to make our lives one. My second love, we weren't even really friends yet, but by the end of the first day, I was sure I already loved her. I had already seen so many different sides of her. As things moved along in our friendship, my love grew with each passing day. I wanted to be with her as much as possible. I hurt when she hurt. I wanted solid and wonderful things for her. I so enjoyed her carefree happiness with surprises and her work. I wanted to protect her but give her room to be herself." Max went silent and then added, "Now I want to take care of her when she is hurt or scared or confused and show her tenderness and gentleness and love in as many ways as I can think of. I want her to understand that God is foremost in my life, but she is the most precious earthly relationship I could ever desire. I want her to find true peace and contentment in her own relationship with God, and I want to help her anyway I can and anyway she will let me."

Max had watched Adri's face through all he said, and he knew the moment when she knew he was pledging his love to her in more ways than just saying I love you. When he stopped speaking, silent tears were running down her cheeks, but she was smiling. Their eyes were locked when Max got up from his chair and came to kneel by Adri.

With emotion in her voice, she told Max, "You . . . love . . . me!"

Max nodded. "Yes. I love you, sweet Adri! Is the idea of love a little clearer for you?" He asked as he gently used a tissue to wipe her cheeks.

"Oh, Max. I am overwhelmed! Yes, I think I understand what I have been feeling and just didn't know for sure if it was really love." Her tears started again, and Max pulled her gently to his shoulder.

"I didn't talk about the physical attraction because we have both recognized it for what it is. I do want to tell you, though, that the physical feelings, wants, and needs do grow as the love grows."

Adri trembled slightly, nodded, and told him, "I have found that out!"

"But not all physical attraction is love. It is sometimes just chemistry. It's important to label it correctly."

Adri nodded and pushed slightly away so she could see his face as she spoke. "I am not as good with words as you are, but you helped me to trust, and when I recognized just how much I really trusted you, I knew I loved you, even though I wasn't sure if I was right or not."

Max smiled. "I love you, Adri, and I am going to kiss you."

Adri gasped a little and said, "Yes, please."

Max brought one hand up to her neck, and Adri brought a hand up to Max's jaw. Max's lips tenderly descended to Adri's and caressed them gently. Time stood still.

As the kiss ended, Betty came into the library. "It's getting late . . . Oh my goodness."

Adri hid her blushing face in Max's shoulder, and Max looked up and grinned at Betty.

"Better than good!" Max teased in a low voice.

Max heard Adri's giggle and pulled away from her. "Okay?" he asked.

Adri nodded and leaned back against the pillows. She spoke to Betty. "You caught us! And yes, it is getting late."

Betty was still a little flustered but commented, "This is something important. Late doesn't matter." Then she smiled and approached.

Max saw the ice pack in Betty's hand, and he told Adri. "It's time to come back to earth. Betty has the ice pack. You need another dose of pills, and we, with Betty's help, should try to get you settled in bed." Max's gaze was so tender; Adri blushed again.

The mechanics of getting Adri settled into bed didn't take long. Adri took the pills first, hoping they would kick in before too much activity was required. Max carried her upstairs and placed her gently on the edge of the bed after Betty turned the covers down. Max made himself scarce while Betty helped Adri into her night shirt. Betty also helped her to the bathroom and in the bathroom while her nightly ritual was accomplished. By that time, Adri was in a lot of pain, and Betty called out for Max to carry Adri back to the bed from the bathroom door.

He set her gently down while Betty arranged pillows. Max carefully placed the ice pack on her foot, causing a jerk and a moan before her foot accepted the cold and weight of the pack. Adri took a couple of deep, cleansing breaths before seeming to relax.

Betty looked at Adri with deep concern. "Can I get you anything or do anything for you?"

Adri tried to smile, but it failed. "Betty, is it too much trouble to get me a cup of hot cocoa?"

Betty smiled. "No trouble at all! Max, would you like a cup too?"

Max smiled. "That sounds like a wonderful idea. Can you get it up the stairs?"

"No problem. Be back in about fifteen minutes," Betty said over her shoulder as she went out the door.

Adri sighed. "I wasn't sure if I could hold up much longer." Tears glistened in her eyes, and she told Max in a whisper. "It hurts so badly. A deep, pounding ache."

"Yes, sweetheart, there will be times, especially after having it down or moving, when it will do that." Max wanted to distract her, so he told her about his own experience. "About four years ago, I wasn't paying enough attention to what I was doing and smashed my left hand. Nothing was broken, but there was deep tissue bruising. The first seventy-two hours were the worst. I at least could get up and pace. You can't even do that. Now you know why I brought you home with me. I didn't want you to be alone in this."

Adri was distracted, and the tears had stopped. She asked, "Were you able to keep working when that happened?"

Max grinned. "I took the first few days off, and fortunately, I was working on research, so it didn't hold me up much."

Adri sighed. "Well, I will be laid up. I can hardly wait for the swelling to go down. I think it will hurt a little less then."

"Yes, the swelling does make it more painful in some ways. Have you experienced shooting pain up your leg yet?"

Adri shook her head. "Not since I've been on the pain meds. I did experience it several times before we got to the ER."

"Well, you probably don't want to hear this, but those shooting pains will probably happen again. But, sweetheart, when they do, I know a massage technique that will help a lot." Max smiled tenderly at her. "You just need to let me help you."

Adri blushed and said, "If you promise it will help, I'll let you."

Max chuckled, and that was what Betty heard as she got to the door. "Here's the hot cocoa. We should all sleep well tonight! Mine is waiting for me in the kitchen."

Adri smiled. "Thank you so much!"

Betty smiled and told Adri, "You can cry in front of me if you need to. What I said earlier about not wanting to see you cry was just for that one thing. Okay?"

Max had already handed Adri her cocoa, and Adri took a sip before she answered, "I guess I know that. I am just trying to be brave."

Betty patted her good foot and told her, "I love you, child, and I want to mother you, so don't cheat me."

Adri smiled. "Okay, I won't!"

Now Betty and Max both laughed. "If the two of you don't need anything else, I will go drink my cocoa and turn in."

Max gently removed the ice pack and handed it to Betty. "Please put this in the freezer, and good night, Betty."

Adri echoed, "Good night, Betty, and thank you so much for, well, for everything!"

Betty smiled. "You are welcome, and I hope you get a good rest."

Chapter 25

Adri slept soundly and restfully until five thirty in the morning. Then the throbbing in her foot woke her. Her voice was gravely and shook a little when she called out, "Max." She waited, cleared her throat, and called again. "Max."

"Coming, Adri." She heard the recliner shift, and Max was in the doorway. "What do you need, sweetheart?"

In spite of the pain, Adri could see that she had truly awakened Max. "I can't seem to reach my pills, and I really need an ice pack!"

Max nodded and moved into the room. "I did the ice pack about three, and it didn't even disturb you." While he was talking, he handed Adri the pills and the water. Then he took the water glass again when Adri finished with it. "I'll go get the ice pack right now. I can see you are hurting. Be right back."

Well, Max was right. I wish right now I could pace the floor or just shake my foot until it stops hurting. I can't. God, this is really painful. Please don't let it hurt so much!

Max was back, and while he put the ice pack on, he told Adri, "Betty said to tell you she will be up in thirty minutes to help you with your morning chores."

"Betty is up already? It's so early!" Adri asked in surprise.

Max laughed softly. "Betty loves baking in the early morning. She is making cinnamon rolls this morning."

"Cinnamon rolls? I don't think I have ever eaten homemade cinnamon rolls!"

Max grinned. "You'll really like these!" Max was glad to see the signs of pain leave Adri's face, and with sudden insight, he realized this was important. *She needs to be distracted when it hurts so much! I'll do what I can and ask Betty for help.*

Adri complained, "You are not very nice. Now my stomach is complaining, and it'll be at least an hour before I can quiet it!"

Max threw his head back and laughed, and Adri joined him in laughter. When they stopped laughing, Adri said, "Thank you, Max. The pain isn't intolerable now."

"Sweetheart, I was hurting too. I knew you were miserable. Now is there anything I can do for you right now?"

"Yes, could you prop me up with another pillow? My back is aching too."

Max picked up another pillow and moved to the head of the bed. With one arm, he gently shifted Adri's shoulders up, and with the other hand, he placed the pillow and then lowered her down. "How's that?"

Adri sighed. "Much better."

Max leaned closer and kissed her forehead. As he straightened, he asked, "Can I leave you for about ten minutes. I need to go clean up."

"Yes. I am comfortable for now." She smiled softly and told Max, "I'll miss you."

"Hmm. Just remember our kiss." Max grinned when Adri blushed.

Adri waved her hand. "Go!"

Max laughed softly as he left the room.

When Max returned, Adri could see that he had showered and changed, and as she took a breath, she realized that he smelled so good. She motioned to him to sit beside her. Her hand reached up to caress his jaw. "I really do like your beard."

Max captured her hand and moved it to his lips where he gently caressed her palm with a kiss. Adri's hand trembled slightly. "Max, I love so much about you. You have been so wonderful for me!"

Max kissed her palm again and then lowered their hands. "You, sweet Adri, have brought so much excitement, happiness, and joy to me."

Betty was approaching in the hall and called out, "Knock, knock."

Max continued to hold Adri's hand as he moved off the bed.

Betty came in smiling. "No kissing before breakfast."

Max's eyebrow arched. "Does it look like we are kissing?"

"Adri's cheeks are pink."

Max turned his head to look at her with such a tender expression in his eyes that Adri's cheeks gained even more color. Max winked at Adri and told Betty, "It doesn't take much this morning to bring the color to her cheeks. She is still thinking about the kiss last night."

Betty laughed. "Well, sweet girl, it is time to be more practical. First of all, you need to tell me what you want to wear today, and then we will get you fixed up and ready for breakfast."

After Adri told Betty what outer clothes she wanted, Max picked her up and nuzzled her neck, the whiskers tickling. Adri shivered at the contact, and Max grinned as he gently set her down. He told the ladies, "I will be in the library for the next thirty minutes and then back up here. Don't worry about it if it takes longer."

Betty shooed him out, and Adri just blushed.

Betty closed the bathroom door and asked, "Do you want a bath?"

Adri nodded. "I hope we can manage that at least. I know I can't shower today." Betty ran the bath water while Adri worked with her hair to put it up.

Even though Betty was shorter than Adri, she was strong and was able to help Adri as much as she needed. It took them forty minutes to complete the tasks, and Betty called out to Max when Adri made it to the bathroom door.

Max opened the bedroom door and noticed Adri was pale, and he went to her quickly and picked her up. "Are you hurting?"

"No, not too bad, but I am exhausted." Adri sighed.

Max smiled. "We will get you downstairs, and you can rest until breakfast is on the table."

"Okay. I am really looking forward to breakfast! I'm starved!"

Betty told Adri as they made their way downstairs. "After Max gets you comfortable, he needs to get the ice pack, and he can get you a cup of coffee if you want one."

"Oh yes, that would be wonderful!"

At the bottom of the stairs, Betty went toward the kitchen, and Max went with Adri into the library. As he gently lowered her to the settee, he asked, "Is your crew working today?"

"Yes, at least this morning there are scheduled deliveries. At some point, I will need my checkbook from the office so I can write their checks."

Max nodded and told her, "I'll get your coffee, and then we can discuss that and a few things I want to ask you about."

Adri rested, wondering why she was so worn out just trying to protect her foot. Her mind wondered. *I love this house. How am I going to leave in a week? I should be able to get around on my own by then. Probably if I had my crutches, I could start getting around mostly on my own by Sunday. I have to admit I like Max carrying me, but it may be just a little too much closeness right now. I am experiencing so many new feelings and wants and . . .* Adri shivered with remembered wants . . . *Maybe things are going too fast for me. Need to talk to Max about that.*

Adri's thoughts were interrupted when Max came back. He handed her a cup of coffee, set another cup down, then bent, and placed the ice pack on her foot.

Max settled into the chair nearby, holding his coffee, and smiled at Adri. "You are looking better already."

Adri nodded. "I am relaxed anyway."

"You looked like you were deep in thought when I came in."

Adri blushed, recalling her last thoughts. "I was. Max, everything about love is so new to me." Adri stopped. She didn't want to hurt Max.

Max saw the troubled look that crossed her face, and he assured her, "You can tell me what is troubling you."

Adri blinked and accused in a soft voice, "You are reading my mind again."

Max nodded. "As I get to know you better, your facial expressions tell me a lot."

"Oh. Well, I know I started it this morning when I invited you to sit on the bed but . . ." She huffed a breath out. "But maybe we are touching too much."

Max's face showed surprise, but then he smiled tenderly. "I think I understand. You need more tender care and less loving."

"Yes?" she said as a worried look crossed her face.

Max set his coffee cup down and leaned forward. "Your request does not upset me. Okay?" Adri gave him a small smile. "I admit that because you respond so wonderfully I forget that you are so new at this. So now I will keep that in mind and slow down. Is that what you need?"

Adri blushed but answered softly, "Yes, please."

Max grinned. "I did say slow down, not stop!"

Adri laughed softly. "Okay!"

Max sat back in his chair. They both sipped coffee for a bit. Max asked, "Have you thought about what else you would need from your house? Maybe your crew could bring things over."

"Betty already brought over more personal items than I will need for a week."

Max groaned inwardly. *I was afraid of that. She thinks she'll be back to her regular activities in a week. What can I say to help her understand how long it takes deep tissue bruising to heal?* He finally spoke. "Sweet Adri, I don't think you really understand your injury." Max got up and sat on the occasional table, nearer to Adri. "As is typical of doctors, the ER doctor did not tell how the healing will happen. I have hesitated to tell you what I went through with my situation. I don't want you fretting over it, but since it is your foot, you will need help longer than a week."

Adri went a little pale. "I guess you need to tell me all of it then."

Betty heard enough to know what Max was doing, but she came into the library anyway and spoke in a chipper voice. "No bad news before breakfast! Ice pack needs to come off, and breakfast is on the table!"

Adri protested. "But—"

Betty interrupted. "You don't need to lose your appetite. Besides, you already know the size of the kitchen, and I want your opinion about antique furniture that would enhance the storage and a little more work space in there. What better time for you to think about that than over food in the kitchen!"

Adri laughed now. "You are distracting me on purpose! You have had lots of opportunities to ask me about that!"

Betty nodded and looked at Max. "She caught me." Then Betty and Max laughed.

Betty turned to Adri. "Did it work?"

Adri laughed again and told her, "Yes, I am thinking about furniture now."

Max gave Adri a tender smile and picked her up to transport her. Betty grabbed the ice pack and a pillow to cushion the chair she would rest her foot on.

CHAPTER 26

During breakfast, Adri ate first. Then she described several pieces that would fill the need Betty had expressed, and she told Betty it could take a while to find that kind of thing because they were rare on the market. At seven forty-five, Max suggested they get Adri settled again in the library as Jocko would be there in thirty minutes.

After Max had Adri settled on the settee with the ice pack in place, he excused himself and assured Adri he would be right back.

Max returned with Adri's lap top in hand. "I thought you might want this at some point. You mentioned checking the Internet for the kitchen pieces you were talking about."

Adri gave Max a happy smile. "Thank you. I have a site marked, and I am going to check it right now."

Max was glad she was still distracted from the conversation that was started earlier. He wasn't looking forward to returning to that conversation but also realized that after Jocko had been here, she would need to face the reality. Another reason he brought her computer to her. She could look up on line about her injury.

Adri was busy on the Internet, and Max told her he was going to the kitchen to talk to Betty, and he would be back shortly.

Adri nodded, and after he was out of the room, she went to the search engine and typed in deep tissue bruising. She read several sites. Now she knew. She would be at Max's longer than a week.

Adri startled a little when the door chimes rang. She quickly pulled up the furniture site, then leaned back, and heard Max greet Jocko and then footsteps and the two men's voices in the hall. As they came into the library, Jocko greeted Adri.

"Good morning, Adri. You look comfortable, and I see you are already working." Now he was standing in her line of sight at the foot end of the settee.

Adri laughed. "Yes, these wonderful people around here keep asking about furniture."

Jocko sat down on the end of the occasional table and smiled. "Since you are so chipper, I guess you are not hurting too much."

Adri nodded. "Right now, I am fine. An hour and a half ago . . . well, we won't talk about that."

Adri nodded toward the folder. "Pick up that auction folder. Give me the check so I can sign it, and you look through and see if you understand everything. Oh, and you need to take my car. Max has the keys." Jocko looked surprised but was ready when Max tossed the keys to him.

Jocko turned his attention to the folder and studied the items closely. When he finished studying the last page, he looked up. "The only question I have right now—some items have a top bid number with a question mark. What does that mean?"

"You understand that the top bid number is the most I *want* to pay. There is a chance of some of those items going higher, and if I really want them, I will go higher. The question mark tells you I really want those items, and you have to use your discretion on that."

Jocko's face took on color. "That's the part that scares me."

Adri assured him, "Use your head. You know how I price. Calculate that a customer really wants it and whether or not they will pay close to that price. Does that help?"

"Yes, ma'am. That does help. I have gotten to know quite a few of your customers over the last year, and I think with that knowledge, I could guess the right overage if I need to." Jocko smiled. "Another question." He leaned over and pointed to a marking on a page. "Does this mean what I think it means?" Jocko tilted his head slightly in Max's direction.

Adri blushed just a little and nodded. The "M" on certain pages meant it was for Max, but Adri was sure Jocko understood her nod.

Jocko chuckled. "Last question. Should I check in with you and show you the paperwork this evening?"

"Call me. I would like to see the paperwork, but I'm uncertain how I'll be by then." Adri smiled at Jocko and told him, "I have a lot of confidence that today will go well for you!"

"Thank you." Jocko was very sincere in his thanks. "I'll be going then. Talk to you later."

He turned toward the door and called to Max who was sitting at his desk. "Later, Max. Have a good day!"

Max stood up and told Jocko, "You too!"

When Jocko latched the front door of the house, Adri asked, "What do you think, Max? Have I got a good assistant or what?"

"I believe he will do everything in his power to not let you down. That is built into his character, but your confidence expressed to him will give him extra incentive." Max was at the settee and bent over and kissed her cheek. "You did good!"

Adri laughed. "Yes, I did!" Then she sobered. "I looked on the Internet about deep tissue bruising. I am seriously laid up, aren't I?"

Max sat on the occasional table and reached for Adri's hand. He enveloped it in both of his, and he told her, "Yes, sweetheart. One week with it constantly up, and we really don't know how long before you will be able to put your full weight on it."

Adri nodded. "How long before you could use your hand the way you were used to?"

"It was eight weeks before I could use it without constant pain."

Tears came to Adri's eyes. "Oh, Max."

Adri blinked the tears away, and Max wondered if they were empathy for his past injury or despair for her present injury. He gently squeezed her hand and assured her. "We will get through this together. You have me and Betty here. You have Jocko and Gina and your crew for the business. We will all help you through it."

Adri nodded, and the tears appeared again. "I would be in a wilderness of uncertainty and loneliness if you hadn't rumbled into my life."

Max eyebrow went up. "Rumbled?"

The tears disappeared, and Adri smiled. "Yes. The first time I heard your wonderfully deep voice, it almost seemed to rumble in your chest." Adri blushed and continued shyly, "It sent shivers down my spine!"

A new light came into Max's eyes, and he grinned. "Interesting."

Adri wiggled her hand in his and asked, "Is that all you have to say?"

Max chuckled and told her, "I really wanted to kiss you for that, but I am trying to keep a promise."

Adri colored. "Okay."

Betty came in just then and chided Max. "It's time for the ice pack again and pills anytime. Max, you are off schedule."

Max grinned at Betty and told her, "It is a really good thing we have you to remind us." He gave Adri's hand a gentle squeeze as he let go and took the ice pack from Betty.

Betty had gotten the pill bottles from upstairs and was holding a fresh glass of ice water. She handed one and then the other to Adri.

"Now, Adri, what do I need to do for you today?"

Adri sighed. "Between what I read on the Internet about my injury and Max's persuasion, I guess I am here for quite a while. I will have my delivery crew bring over the rest of my things from my house, and I will need you to put them away for me."

Betty nodded. "Wise choice. I will be glad to get your room organized and everything put in its place. One problem though. There isn't enough wardrobe space."

Adri nodded. "I already thought of that. I'll tell Dan to bring another armoire over when they bring my clothes. Did you clean everything out of the chest of drawers?"

"Yes. If you're like me, you like to choose from those things every day." Betty laughed. "And no, Max, you can't ask what things. That is between us girls."

Max chuckled and shrugged.

Adri blushed because she knew Max knew what the "things" were.

Adri sighed again. "I guess I better call Dan and give him instructions. Oh, Max! You have to get down there before nine o'clock! What time is it?"

Max looked at his watch. "It is quarter till."

"You need to get there before they start unloading the dining room set. I want you to look at it, at least the furniture and decide if you would like it in your formal dining room. It's a gorgeous Spanish set that would go great in there if you like it!"

"I suppose it includes the urn that dropped on your foot?" Max asked in a dry voice.

Adri shuddered. "Tell them to leave the urns in the store room. Just go. You need to see it."

Max grinned. "I'm going! Call Dan." Then he chuckled as he left.

Betty sat down in a nearby chair and laughed.

"What's so funny?" Adri asked.

Betty was still laughing a little when she told Adri, "The two of you communicate like you have been doing it forever. Giving each other orders and all that."

Adri smiled. "You know what else? I have stopped stuttering!"

Betty thought for a moment and agreed, "Yes, you have. Why do think that is?"

Adri blushed and told her, "Max accepts me, appreciates me, and loves me. I feel secure now."

Betty smiled and nodded. "You need to call Dan."

CHAPTER 27

Betty stayed and kept Adri company. After Adri talked to Dan, she laid her head back and asked Betty, "How did you know I was coming here last night?"

"Max called me while you were in X-ray. Said he was bringing you home with him."

"Oh, that's right. I was alone then." Adri was quiet for a minute and then asked, "Betty, will you really be my mom for a little bit?"

"Oh, honey, of course!"

"My mother died when I was ten years old. Aunt Dixie finished raising me, but she was always *Aunt* Dixie. So through my teenage years and college, there were so many times I wanted a mom. There were teachers I was close too, but it was still different." Betty nodded. Adri continued. "I need to know if I really love Max, or if, since he is the first man I have let close enough, I just need him."

Betty's face was serious. "Tell me the thoughts, wishes, and emotional feelings you have for him."

Adri was quiet, thinking. Finally she thought she could voice her feelings.

"I am a mess because of my past, and men have always made me feel scared and belittled. From the moment I met Max, I felt I had worth as a person. When he seemed to intrude on my personal space, I believe he was truly sorry when he apologized, and I choose to forgive him instead of shutting him out. A first for me."

Adri took a deep breath and continued, "When I came to see this house, he accepted me as the happy, carefree person I became. I was so excited to see the whole house. I couldn't have been just the business lady, even if I had wanted to. Max accepted that side of me, almost like he had known that is who I am. He was the first man I wanted to surprise. I was sure he would enjoy the surprises and appreciate that I was willing to do that for him. By the end of Monday, I felt like he liked me, and I knew I liked him. When I shared my successes, he celebrated with me and spoke his approval."

Adri's voice trembled a little as she continued. "Then the negative things started happening. He was helpful and wonderful through them, but afterward, I began to wonder when he would grow tired of that and go away. Deep in my heart, I knew it would break me in two if he went away. First of all as my friend but also because I was sure I loved him, even though I had no examples to follow in love."

Tears came to Adri's eyes. "When I sent him away last Saturday night, I was so confused and scared that I was too much of a mess for him to keep caring, so I tried to put up my walls. But by Monday, I was so excited for the opportunity to see him. The walls crumbled, and I knew I had to keep on feeling what I was feeling and work on the things that were such a mess. Not just for me, but for Max too."

Adri used a tissue to mop her face and blow her nose. "Max is the first man I ever truly trusted, and I asked God for guidance in that trust. The trust grew, and as it did, well, I wanted to love Max, even though I wasn't sure I knew any real definitions of love between a man and a woman. What do you think, Betty? Do I really feel love, or is it dependence?"

Betty sat forward a little in her chair and told Adri, "For me as a woman, the trust truly had to come before the love. You might not have been sure about what you were—are feeling, but I would say that you are experiencing true love for Max, and as your relationship grows, you will know for sure. Did I answer your question?"

Adri was glowing and smiled softly. "Oh yes!"

Betty could see that Adri's doubts were gone. She got up and came to the settee and gave Adri a long, warm hug. Just as Betty straightened, they heard Max come in.

Adri took Betty's hand and told her, "Thank you so much for listening and helping me! I love you."

Betty smiled. "I love you, sweet girl, and I am honored you trusted me enough to talk to me."

Max came into the library, and his first observation was that Adri was glowing, and Betty had such a sweet, tender look on her face. He chose not to comment about that right now. Max told Adri,

"The truck will be here in a little bit," Max told Adri. "I am buying the dining room set of furniture only, and they decided they could load all your things and make one trip."

Adri smiled happily. "Good. So you got there in time?"

"Oh yes, I did! Dan had just finished talking to you when I arrived, so I was just barely in time." Then he teased, "Next time, give me a little more time so I don't have to arrive breathless!"

Adri giggled. "You are into good a shape. You don't even get breathless carrying me up the stairs!"

Max grinned and winked. "You are a pleasure to carry."

Max got serious. "Now, business. Do I need to carry a couple of chairs and you into the dining room so you can help set it up?"

Adri's face lit up, "Yes! I can work!"

Max chuckled softly. "I told you we would get through this together."

Adri nodded, and Max went to the kitchen to collect a couple of chairs. He came back and collected Adri and a pillow. They were near the dining room entrance when the door chimes rang. Max stopped where he was and called out, "Come in!"

Dan opened the door, stepped in, and grinned. "Just the lady I wanted to see! Your desk is at the back of the truck. You didn't say where that would go."

Adri blushed a little. "Max and I haven't decided yet. Just set it by the staircase out of the way for now."

Dan grinned even bigger and said, "Yes, ma'am." He turned and went out.

"I'm glad they are my friends. This would be really embarrassing otherwise," Adri told Max.

Max chuckled. "Me holding you is embarrassing?"

"No, me having to be carried is embarrassing!"

Max kissed her cheek and told her, "I'm glad you clarified that!"

Max continued into the dining room and got Adri comfortable. He glanced out the door and saw Brad and Dan carrying a small, delicate-looking desk with three drawers to the right and a flip up/down writing lid. It was compact and apparently sturdier than it looked. Denny followed with a dainty stool-type chair that apparently went with the desk.

Max squatted and asked Adri, "Where would you like your desk to go?"

Adri replied shyly, "In the library, but we would have to shift some things to put it where I would like it to go."

Max nodded. "Where would you like it to go?"

Adri was still a little shy and got a faraway look on her face. "My mother had it setting so she could look up and out a window while she sat at it. So every time I have taken it with me, I have placed it at a window." Then she looked at Max. He was already nodding. "I would like it at the window closest to your desk."

"That could work, but I'm not sure where the chair and table that are there would go. What do you think?"

Adri lost her shyness and was animated. "If the whole setting, settee, chairs, etcetera, was shifted to an angle and more toward mid room, it would work, and the furniture would all still be there. How does that sound?"

"Perfect! You will tell the guys how to shift it. Right?"

Adri giggled. "Yes, it needs to go right."

Max threw his head back and laughed. Adri was still giggling. That caught the attention of Brad who was walking by with a load of clothes. He grinned at Max and gave a thumbs-up.

Max stood up and told Adri, "Ice pack time. I'll be right back."

Adri nodded and continued to smile. Max was so much fun to pull puns on.

Max returned and placed the ice pack gently. Adri gritted her teeth until her foot adjusted to the cold. Max told her, "Looks like they are about ready to carry things in here."

Adri took a deep breath and replied, "Okay. Time for me to go to work!"

Max moved behind her to be out of the way, and all four guys came in carrying the table. Brad told them, "Sure am glad to move this just once. It's heavy!"

Kim told Max, "No returns on this." Kim grunted as he backed up a little more. "Max, you have to keep it forever."

Max chuckled. "You are safe. I really like this set."

As the guys set it down, Dan asked, "Right here?"

"Perfect! Now let's see if you get the rest of it right," Adri told them. Adri added under her breath so only Max could hear her. "Not left."

Max chuckled quietly and squeezed her shoulder gently.

It took all four men to carry in the china hutch, and as they came through the door, Adri directed, "Center on the far wall."

All four nodded. Next were the buffet and sideboard pieces, and Adri directed where those should go. The chairs were last, and Dan asked, "Now, where does your desk go? Brad and I will get that set while Denny and Kim get the chairs." Brad joined him, awaiting instructions.

"Just leave it where it is for the moment. It will go into the library, but we need to shift some things around first." Both nodded and headed for the library.

Max came around and announced, "Your transport, dear lady!" He grinned and picked her up.

CHAPTER 28

They arrived in the library, and Adri asked Max, "Can you hold me just a little longer? They can move the settee first."

Max smiled softly. "With pleasure!"

Adri blushed and whispered, "Behave yourself."

Adri turned her attention to the furniture. Dan and Brad seemed to read her mind after she told them how she wanted the furniture shifted, and when they thought they had it right, Dan asked, "Did we get it right?"

"Yes, exactly how I pictured it! Great job! Now the desk can go in front of the window!"

Max carried Adri to the settee and got her comfortable.

Denny was standing just inside the door with the stool in hand.

Dan motioned for Brad to stay where he was and joined Kim at the door. They went out and picked up the desk and carried it in. Kim and Dan went to set it down; Dan's hand slipped, and the front corner hit the floor with a thud, and the bottom drawer slide open. When Dan tried to close it, it seemed to be jammed. He got down on his knees and felt around the drawer and discovered a large manila envelope underneath. Dan pulled it out and turned to Adri with a grin.

"Trying to hide something?"

Adri had a startled look on her face. "I've never seen that!" Dan stood and brought it to her.

Adri took it and turned it over. Her face went pale at what she saw. Her full name was written across the front in her mother's beautiful script. Under her name, her mother had written: *My Darling Daughter.*

Max saw the color drain from her face, and he squatted down beside her. "Adri, what is it?"

Adri stared at the envelope for a moment longer. Then she looked at Max. She had trouble forming the words but finally said, "My mother put this there in the desk. She intended me to find it. I had no idea it was there." Adri looked down at the envelope again. Then she lightly traced the writing with a shaking finger.

Max noticed that the envelope was fairly thick. Adri's crew had gone quiet and was standing, waiting.

Adri's eyes filled with tears. "She's been gone over fifteen years. This must have been really important to her to hide it so well." Adri wiped her tears with the back of her hand. Then she looked up and realized her crew was waiting.

Adri tucked the envelope beside her, coughed a little and looked around the room, and realized Denny was still holding the stool. Adri smiled at him.

"You can set that right in front of the desk." Denny did as he was told.

Adri was a little distracted but finally remembered to ask Dan, "Did you remember to get the checkbook?"

Dan nodded. "I put it in the top of your desk so it would be secured."

"Thank you. I'll write your checks, and Max will take them to the office by noon. Thank you all for the extra help today. I'm sorry—do you think you will get finished by noon."

Dan and Brad looked at each other, and Brad answered, "Gina sold some odds and ends this morning for delivery yet today. We would guess we'll be done by two."

"So I will pay you till two, and you'll need to let me know if it goes past that."

They all said some form of farewell, but Denny needed to know, "Is my pretty lady going to be okay?"

Adri reassured him. "Sometimes we get surprises that are not always good, but yes, Denny, my foot will heal slowly, and the surprise in the envelope is still a mystery, but I will be okay! Thank you for asking."

Denny blushed and grinned. "See you soon, pretty lady!"

Adri smiled. "Bye."

They heard the crew close the front door and the truck started.

Adri turned to Max. "I want to look inside the envelope in a bit." Her hand trembled a little as she touched her forehead with her fingertips. "I need you with me when I open it. I think my life is about to change. It's just a feeling, and I have no idea how."

Max said quietly, "I'm here for you, Adri. Whatever you need."

Adri sighed. "I need some pills and the ice pack and the checkbook and my computer right now while I still have my head together."

Max smiled tenderly. "In that order, I think."

Betty came into the library and rattled the pill bottles and handed Max the ice pack. Max said with humor, "Betty to the rescue!"

Betty laughed. "Yes, and my white steed is out front."

Adri smiled and accepted the pill bottles.

Betty exclaimed, "Oh, but I forgot the water. Be right back."

Max positioned the ice pack, picked up Adri's computer off his desk where Brad had placed it and then went to Adri's desk, opened it, and pulled out the checkbook.

Betty returned with the water, and Adri took her pills. Max handed Adri the checkbook, which she tucked in beside her.

Adri sighed. "I need to take care of this business first. Is it almost lunchtime?"

Max smiled. "Are you hungry after all you ate at breakfast?"

Adri nodded. "Probably too much nervous energy used up all the calories."

Max chuckled, and Betty told her, "Lunch in an hour. Do you need a snack before then?"

"No, but if there is coffee, I would like a cup."

"I'll make fresh and bring it to you. Max, do you want a cup?" Betty was already at the library door.

Max nodded. "Yes, please." And Betty was gone.

Adri was punching buttons on her computer and told Max, "I won't look in the envelope until after lunch. Will Betty have time to at least sit and hear my explanation about Chester and Charles? I need to share that, and I want Betty to know."

Max gave her a gentle smile. "Are you set for a few minutes?"

Adri nodded. "Oh wait, I need my handbag too."

Max looked around and spotted the handbag on a chair across the way. He brought it to her and then told her, "I'll go talk to Betty. I'm sure she will take the time, but she may want to do a few more things before lunch. You know she loves you and is here for you."

Adri looked up at Max, and tears shimmered in her eyes. "I know. She was wonderful earlier and gave me motherly input when I asked her for it." Adri blinked the tears away.

Max bent and gently kissed her cheek. "I love you too. Be back in a bit."

Betty was about to the kitchen door to bring the coffee when Max came in. "Let's wait with the coffee right now. Adri wants to tell us, you and me, about Chester and Charles after lunch. I thought you should know in case you were planning something after lunch."

Betty had set the coffee cups on the table and turned to Max. "Why all of a sudden? Did something happen that I don't know about?"

Max nodded. "When the guys were moving Adri's desk into position in the library, a large envelope turned loose under the bottom drawer. I think I told you that Dixie thinks she would have all the information to discover her true identity. This envelope was put in the desk by her mother."

Betty gasped. "Oh, bless her heart! Has she opened it?"

"No. She wants to talk about the other first. She did tell me that she thinks her life is about to change."

"Oh my! Our sweet Adri!" Betty took a deep breath and told Max, "Our girl comes first. There is nothing to tend to after lunch that is anywhere near as important. You tell her I will be with her as much as she needs me!"

"I will. I'll take the coffee and keep her company in case she needs to talk about anything. I know she wants me to run the checks to the showroom when they are ready. Let us know when lunch is ready."

Betty nodded and waved Max out of the kitchen.

After lunch, Max got Adri comfortable on the settee, applying the ice pack after she was settled. Max and Betty each sat in chairs near the settee.

Adri took a deep breath. "Please be patient with me. Aunt Dixie knows most of this because she was around a lot, but I have never actually told anyone. After taking some psychology courses in college, I was able to recognize that what I went through the first ten years of my life was truly abuse. Mostly verbal abuse." Adri shifted and stared at her mother's desk and then looked at Max. "I was about five years old when it really started. My mother was my haven. She was a really good mother and loved me very much, but she was being abused as well, so she couldn't stop any of it."

Adri took another deep breath. "I was tall for my age, so Chester decided I was big enough to be his servant. He would order me around, demand I bring him things. Coordination at that age isn't that great, so when carrying things, I tripped a lot and dropped things. He was cruel in his criticism. He laughed or scolded constantly. Charles was two years older than I was and picked up Chester's attitude."

Adri went pale as she related. "I started hyperventilating when Charles, in his childish devilment, imitated Chester. Sometimes it was so bad I would actually pass out before my mother could rescue me."

Adri was silent for a bit, and then color came back to her cheeks. "My happiest childhood memories were when Chester would leave. I didn't know why he left, but when he did, he either took Charles with him or had him stay somewhere else. It was just me and my mother, and those were the growing times in our relationship. With the evil gone, we had fun, and we did everything together. When the evil would come back, it was usually a surprise. We never knew ahead of time when they would return."

Tears pooled in Adri's eyes. "If they arrived when Mother and I were in the middle of some fun project or as it was just finished, Chester always destroyed it. The first time it happened, in my childish anguish, I ran at him and attacked him. He grabbed me by my hair and jerked me back and slapped me hard enough to leave a bruise. He warned me to never touch him again." Tears were running down her face now.

Max came to her and used tissues to gently mop the flow. Adri glanced at Betty and saw she had tears as well. Max stayed by her side and held her hand.

Adri continued. "I was terrified of him after that, and Charles started picking on me. He would pull my hair so hard it would put me on the floor, and then he would sit on my stomach and hit me. He was sneaky about it, and my mother never could catch him at it. That was when Mother cut my hair real short, and of course there were repeated abusive comments about that." Adri sniffed and then took a tissue and blew her nose.

"That was when I started trying to hide. I found hiding places ahead of time. I would be constantly listening for the door, and the moment I heard it open, I took off for a hiding place. I was safe for about an hour. Then Chester would start roaring through the house. When that didn't bring me out, he would start hitting my mother. Wanting to protect her, I would come out of hiding. He always stopped when I would scream at him. He would turn to me with a horrible, ugly face and curse a blue streak. Then order me to do this or that. As time went by, everything escalated."

Shudders were coursing through Adri, and she had to stop. Max gathered her close in his arms and just soothed her until the shudders stopped. Adri asked, "Could I have some water, please?"

Betty was out of her chair and went to fetch a glass of water while Adri just rested in Max's arms.

After taking a drink, Adri handed the glass back to Betty. She didn't look at Max or Betty as she continued. "I am almost done. I was nine, and it was the beginning of the school year. They left, and Mother packed me up and took me to a girl's boarding school in Charleston. I was at the school a week before classes actually started. Mother explained that she needed to protect me from *them*, and even though I understood, I was so lonely and cried a lot. I have no idea how badly Mother was treated over that, but it must have been horrible. Nine months later, she was dead by her own hand."

Adri took a few cleansing breaths. "That same day, Aunt Dixie already had Mother's desk in her pickup when she came to the school and packed me up and took me home with her. I only saw Chester and Charles briefly at the memorial service a week later. That was when Aunt Dixie became my protection. I felt safe with her. During college and after I started my business, my biggest fear was that they would come back. I was sure that if they ever did, they would try to ruin the rest of my life." Adri pointed at the desk. "Now you know why my mother would hide something so well that it would stay hidden for seventeen years."

Max nodded. "I also understand your need for distance from men. Oh, Adri, you have had so much to overcome! I am even more humbled that you allowed me to become your best friend."

Adri touched Max's cheek and noticed the tenderness in his expression. "Now you know why I said you are so good *for* me. I needed a new sample, and God gave me you!"

Max smiled softly. "I am so glad you shared. I can pick out ways you have already overcome some of it and not just with me. But I want you to understand that if I can and if I need too, I am willing to help with anything else. I love you and want you whole."

Betty spoke for the first time. "Adri, honey, I will step in as Mom any time you need me. This was so much more damaging to you than I could have ever dreamed. Promise me you will talk to me when things are uncertain."

There was emotion in her voice when she answered Betty. "I know I can count on both of you, and I couldn't ask for a better mom now!"

CHAPTER 29

Adri asked for help to the ladies' room. When Max brought her back, she asked about sitting up on the settee and propping her foot up. Max didn't have a foot stool in the library, and Adri suggested they use the chair that went with her desk. Max and Betty, between them got her situated, including a fresh ice pack, so she was comfortable.

Adri looked at them both and told them, "I don't know what kind of surprises are in store for me next. I know this is taking a chunk out of your day, Betty, but can you stay a little longer?"

Betty smiled. "I've already decided it is left over for dinner, and the dishes are in there doing themselves, so, honey, I have all the time you need."

Tears came to Adri's eyes, but she quickly blinked them away. "Thank you!"

Betty went and sat in a chair, and Max sat next to Adri on the settee. He picked up the envelope and laid it gently on Adri's lap.

Adri looked at the envelope and studied her mother's handwriting. *I need to open it.*

Adri broke the seal and unfastened the metal clasp.

Max told her softly, "Adri, Betty and I are praying."

She gave him a weak smile and said, "Me too."

She picked up the envelope and gently shook the contents out onto her lap. The top page had large block letters at the top. *READ THIS FIRST.*

There was one page of a handwritten letter. It was dated two weeks before her mother died. Adri looked at Max. "Well, here goes." She sighed and began reading silently.

> *My Dearest Adri,*
>
> *First, I want to tell you that I love you very much, and I pray that you will find this when the time is right in your life, and you can deal with it in a wonderful way.*
>
> *This is really good news, and I wish I could stay to tell you in person.*

After reading that much, Adri said quietly, "I think I will read it out loud." Adri went back to the top and read in a calm voice.

> *My Dearest Adri,*
>
> *First, I want to tell you that I love you very much, and I pray that you will find this when the time is right in your life, and you can deal with it in a wonderful way.*
>
> *This is really good news, and I wish I could stay to tell you in person.*
>
> *I am writing this to you so you can know who you really are. Chester Winfield is not your biological father, and Charles Winfield is not your biological brother. They truly are no relation to you. I married Chester when I was four months pregnant with you. Charles is Chester's son from his first marriage. If I had known what kind of man Charles really was, I would have made a lot of different choices.*
>
> *You, my dearly loved daughter, have a much nobler heritage.*

Adri gasped. Then she turned to Max. "I am not a Winfield!"

> *Your biological father was Farran Baldwin Wolcott III.*

At this point, Betty and Max were very startled, and Betty gasped.

> *I say* was *because he died one month after you were conceived. Farran and I were planning to be married. It was not to be.*
>
> *You will find enclosed your correct birth certificate and your father's family history. There are many loving family members, and they are a happy people. You can choose to learn to know them. They would be glad to know that you are their family.*
>
> *If you wish to have someone to introduce you to the Wolcott family, contact Abbott and Elizabeth Winfield (no relation to Chester). These wonderful people were our best friends. When we knew them, they had an adorable baby boy named Adriaan Maxwell Winfield, and they called him Max.*
>
> *My darling daughter, I will forever love you. I regret many of my choices that led to your hard life. I know that God has forgiven me, and I pray that someday you will forgive me.*
>
> *Your loving Mother*
> *Margaret Agnes Davies*

Max reached over and put his hand on Adri's shoulder. He said gently, "Oh, Adri. Sweetheart, I don't know what to say."

There was stress in her voice when she said, "I guess by your reactions, these are the Wolcotts you know so well?"

"Yes.'

Adri's voice held pain when she said, "Why? Why didn't I grow up there? Why did my mother do this to me?" Quiet tears were streaming down her face.

Max cleared his throat. "Adri, there may be an explanation among the other things. She may have had a good reason."

Adri shook her head. "There can't be a reason good enough."

Adri felt numb. Nothing made sense right now. Her heart hurt so much right now.

Betty came and sat down on the other side of Adri. She reached over and took her hand and told her, "Honey, this is just the beginning of what she has to tell you. You can't stop now. When you find out more, it might not hurt so badly."

Betty moved the letter aside. "Here is you birth certificate. You were born June 10, 1982, in Dallas, Texas," she told Adri.

Adri jerked alert. "I have always celebrated my birthday on June 1. And Dallas? I thought I was born in West Virginia! Is my real name on there?"

Betty nodded. "Yes, but it's different than we thought. Adri truly is your first name. There are two middle names, Anne Margaret and then Wolcott. And your father is Farran Baldwin Wolcott III."

While Betty was keeping Adri busy, several things started clicking into place for Max. *That's why Grandmother was so upset about Adri's accident! She knows Adri is her flesh and blood. But that raises questions. First of all, were they ashamed that Margaret was with child before the wedding and ran her off? Why didn't they take Adri in when her mother died? Are the Wolcotts not the people I thought I knew? Oh, Adri, please get more information. I can't believe there is a simple explanation!*

Adri took the birth certificate and studied it. Betty commented, "Two middle names are a little unusual, but not unheard of. Did your mother always call you Adri?"

"Yes," Adri spoke slowly. "She always said that Adrianne was too big a name for someone so small and dainty."

Betty glanced down and saw the note on the next bundle of papers. They appeared to be pages torn from a journal. Betty read the note out loud. *"These pages may answer your questions. I am so sorry."*

Adri gently picked up the bundle and sighed. "Well, maybe I need to read these." Adri looked up. "I think I would like to be alone right now."

Max accepted that. "I will be at my desk if you need anything."

Betty asked, "Are you sure?"

Adri nodded. "My mother thought this was important for me to have. I am passed the shock but have a lot of questions, and reading the journal pages seems awfully personal."

Betty nodded. "If you need me, tell Max to come get me. I'll be in the kitchen."

Adri's face was a little pale when she nodded and then bent her head to the task of reading what her mother had written so many years ago.

CHAPTER 30

When Adri got to the last page of the journal, she felt a lot of sympathy for her nineteen-year-old mother. She had lost the love of her life, had a much desired but troublesome pregnancy to deal with and a new horror to face at the age of twenty when her daughter was born. The woman who had written these journal pages was not the person Adri remembered as her mother.

Adri sifted through the remaining items on her lap. There was a stapled packet of newspaper clippings, a small bundle of letters, and a few pages of family history printed from a computer. The last thing that had been in the envelope was her mother's Bible. Adri remembered crying when Aunt Dixie hadn't been able to find it for Adri after the memorial service. This was one thing Adri was really glad her mother had saved for her.

She sighed and called out, "Max, I need to talk. Will you go get Betty?"

Max came back with Betty and Adri told them, "This is all too new. I can't personalize it right now." She paused and then started the story in a sad voice. "My mother went through a lot. If she hadn't been so emotionally exhausted, she wouldn't have made so many major mistakes. It may be a while before I am ready to forgive her."

Max nodded. "Forgiveness might take some time."

Adri sighed. "In a way, I wish she hadn't left this for me—but she did, so I need to work it through." She looked down at the page and then looked at Max. "Farran and Mother were at the Wolcott Country Estate for a week so Mother could get to know the family. They were engaged to be married. Midweek, Farran went horseback riding with his brother, his closest friend, Connor. Farran had an accident and died instantly. Mother was going to tell him that morning, after his ride, that they were going to have a baby. The family rallied around her and comforted her. She planned to stay and raise their baby in this loving family. She hadn't told anyone in the family that she was carrying Farran's child yet."

Adri chewed her bottom lip and then continued. "Six weeks after Farran's death, Connor was comforting Mother, and she told him about the baby. A few days later, he told her he was in love with her and would raise the child as his own. Connor and his wife had a one-year-old son and a baby on the way.

Mother told him he was just feeling guilty that he didn't really love her. She writes that she was afraid Connor would mess up his marriage if she stayed. She left that night and disappeared. When the Wolcott family almost found her, she accepted Chester Winfield's marriage proposal and married him immediately. She was hidden again for a while."

Adri shook her head, as if to clear it, and continued. "After the baby was born, there were new problems. Chester was hoping for a boy. The baby was about a month old when Connor showed up. Chester wouldn't let him in the house and threatened him if he ever came back. Then Chester threatened Mother, telling her he would kill the baby if she ever contacted the Wolcotts or told the baby who she really was.

"With Chester holding that over her, Mother started planning that someday somehow her daughter would know who she was." Adri's shoulders sagged, and she cleared her throat. "Twenty-seven years later, I know." She stared straight ahead.

Adri sighed. "If Connor hadn't messed things up, my life would have been so different. I wonder if he just thought he loved my mother. Once she was out of reach, did his affection turn back to his wife?"

Max nodded. "I can answer that question. They just celebrated their thirtieth wedding anniversary by renewing their vows. They have five children. Their eldest son, John, was my best friend in school. Still is. He and I both married our high school sweethearts."

Adri gave a weak smile. "Well, Mother did the right thing for them anyway."

Max nodded. "Yes."

"Mother did write on a later page that she should have sought comfort from other members of the family rather than Connor. They were drawn together by their deep grief. She also wrote that news of the baby should have been told to Farran's parents instead of Connor. Her hindsight was 20/20."

Betty was sympathetic. "That poor girl! She needed time to make the right choices, but that wasn't a luxury she had."

Adri straightened her back in a stretch. "I think it's time for the ice pack, and I guess I need to recline again. My knee aches."

Max and Betty stood at the same time. "I'll get the ice pack," Betty told them. "Max, help her get comfortable again."

When Betty returned, she asked Adri, "Do you need me right now? I need to be working on dinner if you only need Max's company."

Max cleared his throat. "Betty—only?"

Betty laughed. "I think that came out wrong, but you get the drift."

Adri smiled. "I'm good for now. Thank you, Betty."

Betty smiled tenderly. "You are welcome, hon."

Once Adri was comfortable, she mused, "I met my grandmother. I think she knew who I was. Max, will you tell me about the Wolcott family, since you know them so well?"

"You, I think, are named after your grandmother. Her name is spelled as one name, not two. She is a joy to be around. Farran the second has been gone about five years now. He had heart trouble. They had five boys and one girl. There are eight grandsons and ten granddaughters, eleven counting you. There are a total of twelve great-grandchildren and counting. I never knew my own grandparents, so both of them treated me like a grandson. I was an only child, so I was at Grandparents' house or Connor and Abby's house a lot while growing up."

Adri could hear the fondness, the love in Max's voice. She could tell that he cares a great deal about these people.

Adri had anger in her voice. "Connor really messed things up for me! Is he the impulsive type?"

Max thought a minute. "No, he is actually a very deliberate type. I wonder if it was his grief and guilt talking. At some point, he must have realized that his actions, indirectly, not only cheated your mother out of happiness but also a child. If he used to be impulsive, losing his brother may have cured him of that. The only way to know for sure would be to ask him."

Adri looked down at her hands and twined them together. "I need to talk to Connor Wolcott. I need to understand why—what—oh, I just need to understand." She looked up at Max. "I want to go through the rest of what is here." She held up the envelope. "Then he needs to help me understand."

Max nodded. "No problem. I can call him and ask him to come see you. When do you want to do that?"

"The sooner, the better. If he can come, Sunday afternoon."

"Okay. I can call him now and get that settled." Max felt his pocket. "I must have left my phone upstairs when I cleaned up this morning. You okay for a bit?"

"Yes. I'm comfortable and have everything I need."

Max smiled. "Be back shortly."

Max trotted upstairs and went into his bedroom. Yes, his phone was on his chest of drawers. Max and Connor spoke from time to time, so his number was programmed in. He pushed buttons and waited. He sat down on the love seat by the fireplace.

Connor answered the phone. Max greeted him. "This is Max. You are just the man I wanted to talk to."

"Hi, Max. Haven't spoken to you in a while. What's happening?"

"Well, for one thing, I moved out of the city. I am now residing in a wonderful colonial house that dates back to the early 1800s. It is somewhat in the country, and I am home!"

"Well, it's about time! What took you so long?"

Max laughed and then said seriously, "I believe it was God's timing."

"No kidding? How do you figure?"

"This is the reason I really called. Are you alone, and do you have time?"

"Yes to both. What's going on?"

"My next-door neighbor is Adri Anne Margaret Winfield-Wolcott."

Max heard a sharp intake of breath and a chair squeaking. "How do you know she is a Wolcott?"

"Because she knows."

Connor groaned, "Oh dear god!"

Max sat straighter on the loveseat and asked, "Connor, what is going on? You sound like it is the end of the world!"

There was silence. "Come on, Connor. Why are you so shook, and why haven't you—the most loving family in the world—contacted her and taken her in?"

"It's a long story." Connor sighed.

"Yeah? Don't you think you need to start talking?" There was still silence. Max told him, "She is in your family tree on the Internet, so it is not exactly a secret."

Connor groaned. When he spoke, there was anger in his voice. "I told that child not to do that." His tone sounded defeated now. "My granddaughter is into genealogy. It is common knowledge in the family that Adri exists, but it was supposed to *stay* family knowledge. It had to be Jennifer who put the information there."

Max waited for Connor to continue. When he didn't, Max told him, "Adri wants to talk to you on Sunday afternoon, so if you don't want to answer my questions, you need to get prepared to answer hers. She at least has the common sense to want to talk to only you for now, instead of asking some really embarrassing questions in front of the whole family."

Connor's voice was defeated. "She knows that much?"

"Yes, she does. Her mother left her a letter and journal pages that explain a lot of what happened the months before birth and while she was an infant. You probably know what I'm talking about."

"Yes," Connor said quietly.

"I think she wants to hear your side. Are you prepared to tell her?"

"Max, I don't have a side. She probably has the accurate information. But things have just gotten really complicated." Connor sounded defeated.

Max was angry now. "Connor, I am invested in this woman. You are going to pull it together, and you are going to tell me and her why your family has not come forward and claimed her when you must know that she is very alone."

"Two words, Max. Two words. Chester Winfield," Connor responded with anger.

"What? He's in California, and no one has heard from him in seven years!"

Connor's voice was low. "I know. And he stays there because we pay him to." There was anger again as he added, "The biggest mistake I made in connection with Adri was going to Chester's house to try to claim her as an infant. It didn't seem that big a problem when I did it, but after Margaret died, he resurrected his threats and demanded money. We have been paying him for seventeen years to not harm Adrianne."

"Connor! That's blackmail! Why haven't you had him arrested?"

His voice held defeat again. "I believe him when he says he has friends. If he is arrested, his friends will show up and, his words, take care of things."

"Your brother Conrad is an attorney. He can't do anything?"

"He doesn't know. My mother and I are the only two that know the whole story, the whole sorry mess. My doing, I admit, but Mother is terrified for Adrianne. She cries over this a lot. I can't get past how big a fool I was twenty-seven years ago. We keep a close watch on her."

"How do you do that?"

"I'll answer that, but first tell me, how invested are you in Adrianne?"

Max answered softly, "I am courting her and intend to one day make her my wife."

"How long have you known her?"

"Almost two weeks."

Conner tried to laugh, but it came out more of a bark. "It never did take you long to decide important things." He sighed. "Have you met Jocko?"

"Yes. Jocko has been someone I have known for a long time. You know that. He was one of Adri's delivery crew but is her assistant in the business now."

"He reports to us how she is doing. How's her foot, by the way?"

"Seriously damaged and looking at a long recovery. You, I assume, also know that she has moved into my house for the time being?"

"Yes. Mother and I were both relieved to know you are looking after her."

"Connor, are you coming on Sunday?"

"Yes. I just hope word hasn't gotten to Chester that she is at your house."

"What do you plan to tell her?"

"I'll answer her questions, and that may mean telling her about Chester too. I am assuming you will be at her side when we talk."

"Yes, I will be. By the way, do you know where in California Chester currently lives? Is it still San Diego?"

"No, he—they are in San Bernardino."

"What time will you be here on Sunday?"

"About one thirty if that works for both of you."

"It will. You obviously know where I live, so we will see you Sunday."

"I know you are, but I'll say it anyway. Take good care of our sweet Adri and thank you, Max. See you Sunday."

The connection ended.

CHAPTER 31

After Max left, Adri shuffled through the pile. Adri read her mother's letter again. She studied the birth certificate. She picked up the newspaper clippings. These were news articles about Wolcott marriages, births, sports achievements, and celebrations, all dated before her mother died.

When she finished with the clippings, she decided not to look at the letters right now but picked up the Family History pages. She studied the family tree, recognizing names that she had seen in the clippings. The last entry on the family tree was January of the year her mother had died. Connor's children were all listed. The other three uncles were named Conrad, Devin, and Elliott. The aunt's name was Diane (Wolcott) Shever, married to Dominique Shever.

Adri laid the papers down. She knew Dom and Diane Shever. They had been really good customers of hers when she first started her business. She had refinished a couple of family pieces for them too. And they had sent their friends to her.

The ice pack was getting uncomfortable on her foot, so she reached down and removed it. Finally, the swelling seemed to be going down some.

Adri picked up the Family History pages and read about the first settlers and the remarkable generations since. They were all achievers and successful people. The family was large and into many walks of life. When she finished reading, she was impressed.

She picked up the packet of letters. She studied the top envelope. It was addressed to her mother, Margaret Winfield, and had no return address. Adri removed the ribbon that tied them together. The bottom envelope had the word *copy* written on it in her mother's handwriting.

I don't have a good feeling about these. I really don't want to read them. Maybe I should just read the copy that Mother probably wrote.

Adri carefully opened the envelope and pulled out the single sheet of paper. She unfolded it and spent a long time just looking at it. There were obvious signs of teardrops. There were words or even whole sentences scribbled out. Adri realized that her mother had suffered a lot while trying to write this. It was addressed to Connor.

Finally, she read what was on the paper.

> *Connor,*
>
> *You have to stop writing. So far Chester doesn't know about your letters.*
> *HE CAN'T FIND OUT.*
> *My baby girl is in danger if he does. Were his threats not clear?*
> *HE WILL KILL ADRI IF YOU KEEP DOING THIS. SO STOP!*
>
> *I should have made you see, sense, and stayed, but I didn't, so LEAVE US ALONE.*
>
> *Margaret*

Adri was very still for a very long time. She suddenly realized that tears were running down her face, and she knew her heart had completely softened toward her mother. She forgave her.

Max didn't immediately go back down to Adri. He had one more phone call to make. He looked up the number in his phone and dialed. When a female voice answered, "Doc's Investigations, " Max asked, "Is Doc in? This is Max Winfield."

"One moment please."

Doc came on the line. "Hey, Max. You need another interview?"

Max laughed. "No, but I have some work for you."

"Name it, man. I'll get right on it."

"I believe these people live in San Bernardino. Names are Chester E. Winfield and Charles S. Winfield. I need them found and checked out. Financial situation, health, and lifestyle."

"That's just a hop from here in Riverside. How soon you need this?"

"As soon as possible."

"Max, my man, you got it. I'll get on it right now. Cover this one myself."

"Thanks, Doc. This could be real important."

"All my jobs are. Get back to you ASAP."

The connection ended.

Max looked as his watch. He had left Adri alone for almost an hour. He jumped up and went quickly down the stairs. When he got to the library, he saw the tears running down her face and went to her, squatting beside her.

"Adri?" His voice was soft but deeper than usual as the concern threaded through it.

"Oh, Max! My mother was so terrified and so alone. I've forgiven her. I survived, and I have not had to live with the terror. I didn't know until today that my life was at stake. She did what she had to do."

Max smiled gently. "I am so glad you have been able to work that through." Max pulled out his handkerchief and gently wiped away the tears.

Adri held up the small stack of letters. "I haven't looked at these, but I think they were from Connor. I'll read them tomorrow." She laid them gently on her lap. "Were you able to talk to Connor? Will he come?"

"Yes, sweetheart, he will be here at one thirty Sunday afternoon. He has promised to answer your questions." Max stood and picked up the ice pack. "I'm sorry I was gone so long. I didn't expect to be. And you need a fresh ice pack."

Adri smiled. "That's okay. I have discovered that the Wolcott family members are achievers, builders, movers, and shakers. It seems my biological father had made his first million before he was twenty-four. So even though I seem to be the physical image of my mother, I must have the Wolcott ability for business."

"Oh yeah? Does that mean you are working on your second million?"

Adri laughed. "No, but my business is doing well! Even better right now, since I am working on a whole house."

"Touché!" Max sat in the chair and asked. "Have you been through everything except the letters?"

"Yes. I wish I had some pictures to go with the names, and of course, I don't have anything past 1993. I know the family has grown. You said there were great-grandchildren."

Max gestured toward Adri's laptop that was setting on the occasional table. "Use the computer. There is much more out there. You just need to know where to look. In fact, I can take you to the family Web site, and there is an updated family tree that I can print off for you."

"Oh, please do, Max. I want to look at it!"

Max gave her computer to her and was smiling, big.

Adri looked up. "What?"

"You seem to be excited. Does that mean you may want to meet your family?"

"Well, think about it. I have never felt like I really belonged. I've been like a fish out of water, and I am ready to be in the pond."

"First things first. I'll get a fresh ice pack, then I'll get you set up on the web page and you can enjoy the pictures while I print off the family tree."

Adri was connected to the Internet and fidgeting, waiting for Max to get back. *I am excited! I have relatives, and from all reports, they are wonderful. How blessed am I? When this first hit me, it was a shock, and I was disappointed that I have missed the 'family circle', but that is the past. I have a grandmother! And uncles and aunts and cousins. Wow!*

Max came back and placed the ice pack. Then he took Adri's computer and typed in the web address, bookmarked it, and entered the password.

"The password to this Web site is 'Adrianne', Grandmother's name."

He moved the computer back to Adri's lap. "Enjoy the pictures for a minute. I'll print off the family tree." Max went to his computer and pulled up the Wolcott information. Max wanted to double-check what he was sure he saw earlier. He found that Farran III and Margaret (Davies) Wolcott were listed like they had been married, their birth and death dates listed. Adri Anne Margaret was listed with the correct date of birth. Max printed the pages and stapled them together.

When he brought them to Adri, he told her, "Connor has an overzealous granddaughter. You will find your name, spelled the way it is on your birth certificate, on these pages with the correct birth date."

"Really?" Max nodded. He sat down on the occasional table.

"The Wolcotts knew my true birth date? How?"

"I don't know, Adri. Maybe another question to ask Connor."

The two of them spent a quiet, relaxing time looking at pictures and matching names to faces. The two most recent celebrations were posted with a lot of pictures. Adri was excited to see these people. Suddenly, she said, "Max, you're in these pictures!"

"Yes. They have been like family to me nearly all my life. Especially close since I lost my parents, then my wife, Karen. They are wonderful Christian people. I was at Grandmother's birthday party and the anniversary celebration."

Adri paged down and stopped at the next picture. "Connor and his wife, Abby. They look really happy. I'm glad. Marriage is supposed to be permanent."

Max responded softy, "Their marriage is very solid from what I can tell."

Adri looked up. "Was your marriage solid?"

Max nodded. "We didn't have a lot of time together, and we were still in the newly married attitude when Karen was diagnosed with cervical cancer. We traveled a little while she still could and then the last four months of her life. We loved at a deeper level as I took care of her to the end."

Adri said softly, "That must have been very hard for you. Losing the love of your life."

"It was. Grandmother and Abby and John and his wife, Carol, were my main support. I'm not sure I could have gotten through it without them."

"What was Karen like?"

Max sat back in his chair and smiled. "She was a take-charge person in most areas of her life, but she couldn't keep track of things, like car keys or mail or the hamburger she had just bought at the store. The problem was she was thinking and planning ahead and didn't keep track of the mundane things. She loved children and volunteered at a church program that gave mothers a break, and she was looking forward to us having children. That didn't—couldn't happen. We were married two years, five months, and three days." Max sighed and then smiled again. "God decided he needed her more than I did. I was angry about that for a while, but I would have married her again even knowing what would happen."

Adri thought for a moment. Then she said softly, "You are a wonderful man. Your heartache and your trust in God mesh and have made you the man you are today. I pray my life experiences will turn out as well."

Max smiled, picked up her hand, and told her, "You have already come a long way. You are more at peace now than you were earlier this afternoon, and you have accepted caring and loving from me and Betty with more grace than I expected. Your past experiences have formed you, and with every new day, you will be able to see just exactly who you are becoming."

Adri nodded and then ducked her head, and her head came up with the beautiful, soft blush in her cheeks. "Until you came into my life, Mr. Adriaan Maxwell Winfield, I thought I knew who I was and wanted to be. I'm not happy with that person anymore. You and God have a lot to answer for!"

Max smiled gently. "I'm glad you included God because I believe he brought me here."

"I do too."

Betty came in and announced that dinner was ready.

Adri laughed. "Finally. My stomach has been complaining for an hour! I don't know what has gotten into me. Meal time was always a regular chore, and I kept the schedule, but I was never hungry like I have been today."

Betty beamed, "You like my cooking—has to be that!"

Max grinned. "It's all the energy you are putting into loving me!"

Adri laughed. "Yes to both!"

In spite of the many different turns the day had taken for Adri, it was a happy group that went to eat.

CHAPTER 32

"Max, I have a question." Adri laughed softly. "I seem to have a lot of questions!"

Max had just settled her on the settee after dinner, and he had seated himself comfortably in a chair.

"What's your question?"

Adri blushed. "I am really enjoying being here with you and Betty even if it is because I need help." She hesitated. "I don't think I will ever go back to my house." Adri stopped and looked down at her hands.

Since Adri was looking down, she didn't see Max's total look of surprise and hope. Max hadn't heard the question yet, but his heart was beating double time, and he felt intense anticipation at what the question might be.

Adri looked up, and her eyes met Max's. "I don't want my house setting empty, so I wondered what you would think about me offering it to Jocko and Gina? They could be resident overseers of everything there."

Max cleared his throat. "I need to make sure I understand what you really want." Max cleared his throat again. "Are you saying that you will stay here, permanently?"

Adri blushed and smiled softly. "I think you are willing to give me time to truly get it together, but I feel right in saying that you don't ever want me to leave, and I don't want to."

Max was at her side in an instant. "My sweet Adri!" He gathered her into his arms and kissed her gently and told her, "I have already told several people that I intend to marry you. I just hadn't told you."

Adri blushed again. "Now you have. I wouldn't want it any other way, but I do still need some time."

"Yes, sweetheart. I know that and have no intention of rushing you. You have a whole new family to discover and some burdens to release. I am here at your side, however long it takes."

Max lowered his head and asked softly, "May I kiss you again in celebration?"

Adri blushed softy. "Yes, and then you will answer my question!"

Max gave her a very tender smile and a tender, deeper kiss. Adri participated, sighing softly when the kiss ended.

Max moved back, releasing Adri back onto the pillows. He took both her hands and squeezed gently. "I think your idea is a really good one. Resident keepers are very practical. Would you be truly comfortable with that?"

Adri laughed softly. "Oh yes! It would be so much better than having someone there that I don't already know and love."

Max's eyebrow went up. "Love?"

Adri nodded. There were tears in her eyes when she responded, "Yes. Since you pledged your love and I was able to confirm with Betty this morning that my heart was right on target toward you, I have discovered that the important people in my life have held a piece of my heart." She blinked the tears away. "I was just never willing to admit it before."

"Oh, Adri, that is a huge step forward because I know you are talking about your crew too. It feels wonderful, doesn't it?"

Adri's face lit up and she smiled. "Yes, very wonderful! Oh, Max, I am learning so much so quickly right now. And I really like most of it!"

Max was going to respond, but Adri's phone rang. Max released her hands. Adri had to shift slightly to get her phone out of her pocket. She opened her phone and told Max, "It's Jocko." She answered. "Hello, Jocko!"

"I would say you are in terrific shape! You sound so cheerful!" Jocko told her.

Adri laughed. "Yes, I am doing very well. Where are you?"

"I'm here at the showroom. Just got back. Wanted to check in and see if I could come on over." Jocko grunted at the end of his sentence.

Adri asked, "Are you moving something?"

Jocko laughed. "Yeah, I bought a crib for Josh at the auction, and I am unloading the pieces out of the back of your car and into the showroom. We don't have room for it right now."

"Oh my! You mean you took it apart just so you could bring it now?"

Adri was pretty sure there was embarrassment in his voice when he answered, "Yeah. I just couldn't leave it there."

Adri laughed happily. "That is so sweet! When you get that accomplished, you come on over. I want to know how your day was!"

Jocko grunted again. "These pieces are kinda heavy one-handed. I'll be there shortly!"

"Okay. Oh! Since you are at the showroom, I need you to bring something with you. There is a red-striped cushioned foot stool there somewhere. I need that to put my foot up on."

"I'll find it," Jocko told her.

"See you soon."

Adri turned to Max. "Jocko bought a crib for Josh at the auction and brought it back with him." Adri laughed happily. "I can hardly wait to tell him he can put it back together at their new place!"

Max chuckled. "Do you think you might have to help him reassemble it?"

Adri tilted her head. "As sharp as he is, I think he'll get it back together. But if he needs me, I'll help."

Max nodded. "What I wanted to tell you when we were interrupted, the little bit that you are learning that you don't like, I am here to help. Just remember that!"

Adri was very serious when she answered, "Most of what I am learning is a result of your patience and guidance and Betty's quiet leadership as a woman and the wonderful relationship you share with Betty. I was impressed with that the first day we met!"

Max smiled tenderly. "You just can't stop surprising me, can you?"

Adri nodded with her cheeky smile as the door chimes rang. Max went quickly into the hall. Soon he was back with Betty and Jocko.

Betty had the ice pack, pill bottles, and ice water.

Jocko with the foot stool Adri wanted.

Jocko smiled and told Adri, "Take care of you first." Max indicated for Jocko to set the stool at the other end of the settee.

When that was accomplished, Jocko moved closer and handed the auction folder to her. Adri just laid it on her lap and asked Jocko, "So how did it go? Sit down and tell me."

Jocko flushed a little and had a puzzled look on his face. "You're different." Adri nodded.

Jocko took a deep breath and asked, "Can I have the folder back?"

Adri smiled and handed the folder to him. Jocko sat down in the chair across from Adri, and after opening the folder, he related, sometimes with excitement, other times with deliberately picking his words and sometimes showing slight disappointment. The final result was that he had gotten everything Adri had sent him to get and only going over on two items and not too much over.

Adri had listened and nodded but just let him talk. When he finished, Adri smiled a happy smile and told Jocko, "I am very pleased with your successful day. Did you enjoy it?"

Jocko colored again and laughed. "Actually, yes, I did. It was interesting to talk to others at the auction, and I learned some new things. I did enjoy it!"

"How are you getting home this evening?"

"I was going to call Gina when we are done here."

"You don't need to do that. Take the company car home."

Jocko looked confused. Adri smiled. "My car."

Jocko's face lit up. "Oh! You have never called it that before."

Adri laughed. "I know, but I have never had such a hardworking assistant before either!"

Jocko smiled. "You are different. What's going on?"

Adri glanced over at Max who winked at her and gave a slight nod. She looked back at Jocko and told him, "I found out today that I was not born a Winfield but am a part of the wonderful Wolcott family that you grew up with and love like family."

The statement had the desired effect. Jocko had a totally amazed look on his face. "You are Farran the third's child. Have to be! I know all the others! This is great! Wow!"

"There is more."

Jocko jumped up. "More? Isn't that enough?" He walked toward the door and then came back. He sat down again. "Okay, what else?"

Adri laughed happily. "Good news for you and Gina and Josh. I won't be living in my house anymore, and I want the three of you to move in there and be resident overseers of the place."

Jocko went pale and then red in the face. "This is too much! Adri, where are you going to live once you are back on your feet?" His voice faded on the last word.

For the first time since Jocko had been in the room, Max spoke. "Right here."

Jocko looked from Adri to Max and back to Adri. His expression was a question mark.

Max leaned forward in his chair and told Jocko, "Adri will probably go through an extended healing time, and she needs readily available care. Betty and I can do that for her. When she is back on her feet, we perhaps will be ready to announce a more permanent status."

Adri giggled at Max's explanation.

Jocko whispered, "You're getting married?"

Adri put her index finger to her lips. "Shush! Don't tell anyone!" Then she laughed.

Jocko slumped back in his chair. He rubbed his face. "Am I dreaming? Ever since I walked in, it has seemed like a dream."

Adri was serious now. "You don't accept surprises as wonderfully as Max does. You are not dreaming. Unless you have found a place to live . . ." Jocko shook his head no. "I truly do want the three of you there in my house. It is certainly big enough for you—master's bedroom with full bath, living room, kitchen, two more bathrooms and three bedrooms, and a room that could be playroom, den, and office. Lots of closet and pantry space. Are you sold yet?"

Jocko had emotion in his voice when he answered, "Yes, if you are sure."

Adri smiled. "Jocko, you have been special since you came to work for me. One of the changes in me is that I want to tell people that are special to me, and I want to show them. My house is your new home, and since you, especially, and

Gina will be carrying the load in the business for an extended spell, whatever furniture you want, you just need to pick it out and move it in."

"Thank you! Oh, Adri, you have been a terrific boss, and I am really enjoying this different you! So, Ms. Wolcott . . ." Jocko grinned at the look of surprise on her face "Are you through with me for the time being? I would really like to go home to my family and share these wonderful surprises!"

After the surprise of hearing the name, tears came to Adri's eyes. Max noticed and came to her. Adri was trying to blink the tears away and told Max, "Happy tears. I didn't know it would sound so good!"

Max smiled gently. "It's still very new."

Adri nodded, took the tissue from Max, and dabbed her eyes. Then she looked at Jocko who was looking very serious. Adri smiled. "Yes, you need to go and be with your sweet family. Saturday's are only a half day, unless there is something special going on. Tomorrow's schedule is clear. Have a good evening, Jocko."

Jocko grinned. "I think I am still in shock, but I can hardly wait to share with Gina. Thank you so much, Adri. We love you."

Adri nodded. "Drive carefully."

Max got up and told Adri, "I'll walk him out." Adri nodded again.

Max stepped out on the veranda with Jocko and told him, "I spoke with Connor this afternoon and know that you have been reporting to the Wolcotts. I don't mind if you share what you have learned." Max grinned. "I personally couldn't be happier."

Jocko grinned. "You didn't contradict what I said about her being Farran's child, so I guessed right."

"That is correct. How did you know?"

"I've known for some time, maybe five years, that there was another family member and that people were reporting back to Mrs. Wolcott on how this person was doing. They still talk about Farran, and I've picked up tidbits. It pretty much clicked into place when I started working for Adri, and I volunteered to keep them updated, and they were so grateful. Adri's parents' engagement photo is in the family room, and she looks a lot like her mother. I have no idea about the reasons, but I really enjoy that Adri can get to know her family!"

Max nodded. "You need to be on your way. Give my love to Grandmother."

Jocko nodded. "Good night, Max."

CHAPTER 33

Adri's night was restless. She would wake up from a sound sleep with her foot throbbing, and even though she took the pain pill if it was time, she couldn't go back to sleep without waking Max and asking for the ice pack. The first time Max went for the ice pack, he came back and found tears running down her face, and she was rocking the upper half of her body. After he placed the ice pack, he gently held her and rocked with her, uttering soothing words and phrases until the tears stopped, and she fell asleep.

The second time the pain woke her, she didn't hesitate but called out for Max immediately. He came in, picked up the warm ice pack. "I'll be right back, sweetheart."

It seemed a long time to Adri. The tears were running down her cheeks when Max returned.

"I'm sorry it hurts so badly." Max sat on the edge of the bed and picked up her hand, which was clenched in a fist. He gently rubbed the knuckles.

"Max, it didn't hurt this bad before." She sobbed the question. "Why does it hurt so badly now?"

"This won't make it feel any better, but the reason is that bruising involves nerves, and the larger the area, the more nerves involved. The nerves are regenerating now, and you feel more pain."

"Talk about something to distract me."

Max nodded. "Your Aunt Dixie was special to you for what, eleven years. Are you still close to her?"

Adri's tears stopped. She made a face. "There's a long explanation for that question."

"Umm. I'm listening."

Adri's foot jerked with a sharp pain. Then she was still.

"Aunt Dixie kept things from me. A lot of things. And some resentment grew over the secrets that were kept. Aunt Dixie and I are pleasant with each other, but that is all."

Max could see that Adri wasn't noticing the pain in her foot now, but he was questioning his notion that talking about her aunt would be a good thing. "What kinds of things?"

Adri sighed. "Mother's suicide made front page headlines. I read one newspaper notice that talked about her being an oil empire heiress after her memorial service. Even at ten years of age, I understood the reality. Chester had been living off my mother's money. I assumed he still was after Mother's death because Aunt Dixie never told me any different. When I turned twenty-one, I learned the truth. Chester got nothing of her wealth. It was all mine." A shudder went through Adri, and she moaned from the pain that shudder caused in her foot.

"So the resentment was that you thought Chester was living high?"

Adri got a startled look. Then she thought for a minute. "No. Aunt Dixie, just by her attitude made me believe that her and I both needed to work hard for what we had, when in reality, she could have used the proceeds off of two high-producing oil wells right away and supported us both." Adri stopped and thought for a moment. "Saying that out loud, it sounds selfish and petty."

"How old was your aunt when you went to live with her?"

"She was thirty-two." Adri thought for a moment. "She had been restoring antiques for twelve years already in her own business." There was another pause. "I guess if I had been her, I would have kept working as usual. Max, she did the right thing. I owe her an apology."

Max smiled softly. "Is that all you feel resentment about?"

Adri was quiet. When she spoke, it was with sadness. "I think she had to know that I wasn't a Winfield. Why didn't she ever tell me that?"

"This is new, since yesterday." Adri nodded. "What reason would she have to tell you that during your growing up years, especially if she couldn't tell you who you really are?"

Adri thought about that. "You don't think she knew? She was a really good friend to Mother." There was silence again. "You are right. She still doesn't know, probably. Max, I need to call her! Maybe she could come see me here so that we can get back to a close relationship. I love her and really miss her!"

Max was grinning. "Sounds like a good plan to me!" Adri yawned. "Do you want to try to sleep some more?"

Adri nodded. "Yes, it's way too early to stay awake."

Max chuckled softly, leaned in and kissed her cheek, and then left to try to get some more sleep himself.

Max answered the door chimes at 10:00 a.m. Dixie was right on time. Max greeted her with a big smile, and Dixie told him in a soft voice, "You, I think, are responsible for this!"

Max just tilted his head. "I am really pleased to meet you!" He softened his voice. "I haven't told Adri we talked."

Dixie nodded. "So where is my girl?"

"In the library. This way." Max led her to the library.

Dixie was as tall as Adri, but with the big-boned structure, she looked larger. Her face wore no makeup but was nice-looking, even with a few age wrinkles that were starting to appear. Her grey hair was pulled back in a bun. Max appreciated that she seemed to have aged well.

Dixie saw Adri sitting on the settee, and there was pure joy in her voice when she greeted her.

"Adri, my girl!"

Adri turned her head, and happy tears shimmered in her eyes, and there was a big smile on her lips. "Aunt Dixie! Come sit with me!"

Dixie moved quickly around the end of the settee and just stood, looking at Adri. Adri opened her arms, and Dixie bent to give a quick hug. She sat down beside Adri and told her, "You are looking really good!"

A few tears escaped Adri's eyes and responded, "You too! It has been too long, and I know it's my fault. I am so sorry!"

Dixie nodded. "So how are you really doing with your injury?"

Adri knew Dixie probably wouldn't say she forgave her unless pushed, so Adri accepted the nod to mean the hurt was all behind them. Adri smiled and told Dixie, "The damaged nerves are waking up, and I am more miserable today than I was yesterday, but Max and Betty are really taking good care of me!"

Max had moved to a chair and sat down. Now Dixie gave him a good hard look and then nodded her head again.

"I believe Max is looking after you all the way around."

Adri blushed. "Yes, he is a wonderful listener and gives good solid advice. He is good to and for me."

Dixie's face softened. "You always could read between the lines with me." She laughed. "And that gift probably works really well with your customers!"

Adri and Max both laughed, and Adri nodded. "Very well. Max wants me to fill all the rooms in this house with antique furniture. Business is good otherwise too. I, just a week ago, hired an assistant and a part-time showroom sales lady. That is a very good thing since I am laid up now."

Dixie smiled. "I hear a lot of trust in your voice. You are finally willing to trust others. That has been a hard road for you."

Adri agreed, "God sent a godly man into my life, and when I discovered he wouldn't let me down, I started paying attention to the other people in my life and realized that they are all trustworthy. Including you. Early this morning, I realized that I had trusted you so much more than I ever admitted to myself. I discovered I was keeping us apart over something selfish and pitiful and knew I needed you back in my life."

There was a little moisture in Dixie's eyes when she reached out and gently squeezed Adri's hand. She turned to Max. "Thank you, Max. I needed this girl back, and you helped bring her back to me."

Max smiled and leaned forward. "I just asked the right questions. Adri did the rest. She just keeps proving how much courage she has in facing the hard parts of the past. She's come a long way in healing."

Adri was blushing. Dixie looked at her and laughed softly. "You still blush so easily!"

Adri nodded. "Aunt Dixie, I have more things that I want you to know."

Dixie sat back comfortably. "So, girl, tell me all."

"Well, Mother's desk"—Adri waved her hand toward the piece of furniture—"gave up some secrets yesterday."

Dixie's face lit up. "What?"

Adri was very serious when she told her, "There was this." She pulled the envelope from beside her. "It was taped to the underside of the bottom drawer." Adri held it so Dixie could read the front.

Dixie's hand covered her mouth for a moment. "It's from your mother!"

Adri nodded.

Dixie continued, "You know you are not a Winfield. Who are you really?" Dixie's eyes searched Adri's face.

Adri smiled softly. "I am the illegitimate daughter of Farran Baldwin Wolcott the third."

Dixie's eyes darted from the envelope to Adri to Max and back to Adri.

"Do you know who they are, the Wolcotts?" Adri asked softly.

Dixie nodded slowly.

"If you are like I was yesterday, the biggest question is *why?*"

Dixie nodded.

Adri told Dixie what her mother's letter and journal pages had in them and the information she had gleaned from Connor Wolcott's letters and her mother's desperate note to Connor. She pulled out the birth certificate and showed it to Dixie.

After Dixie had absorbed all that Adri said, Dixie said, "I still don't understand why they didn't come get you when your mother died."

"I question that myself," Adri agreed. "I don't have an answer yet but hope too tomorrow afternoon. Connor is coming here to answer my questions."

Max got up and came and squatted by Adri. He took her hand and told her, "I've been looking for an opportunity to tell you." Adri nodded. Max continued, "When I spoke to Connor yesterday, he told me that Chester had come to them, with gangster types, and blackmailed them, telling them that your life was worthless unless they paid him to let you live. And the condition was that they still could not be in touch with you."

Adri gasped, and Dixie exclaimed, "NO!"

There was a long silence. Dixie spoke with bitterness. "He couldn't let his threats die with Margaret. Of course not. She didn't leave him her millions." Dixie was red in the face and got up and pretty much stomped across the room. "I could kill him! No, I could hang him by his thumbs in the richest part of town so he could see the rich live but not participate. No, I could bury him alive so he would eventually smoother to death thinking about all his evil deeds. No, I-I could—"

"Aunt Dixie, please," Adri interrupted her. She spoke in a quiet, pleading voice.

Dixie stopped when she looked at Adri and saw the tears running down her cheeks. Dixie rushed back to Adri. "Oh, honey, oh, my sweet girl! I am so sorry!"

Adri started gasping for air. Max immediately went to his knees and leaned in and took control of Adri, telling her to breathe slowly. Dixie sat back and watched as Max continued to give instructions. It took a while, just as it had the last time she had felt threatened by Chester. When Adri was breathing normally and started to tremble, Max picked her up from the settee, holding her close. He took her place on the settee.

Adri turned her face into Max's shoulder and cried softly, releasing the hurt that went so deep. When she stopped crying, he asked gently, "Can you talk about it?"

"He couldn't let go. His evil is still with me. From what you said, I still can't be a Wolcott."

Max touched her cheek gently. "I have a friend of mine looking into Chester's situation in California. I am really hoping to hear from my friend before today is over. I will find a way to cut all ties, and you and the rest of the Wolcott's will be free of him. I have prayed about this a lot, and I know God will provide a way."

Adri raised herself enough to look into Max's eyes. What she saw confirmed her hope. "Oh please, Max. Please, God, let it be over with."

"Amen," Dixie said quietly.

CHAPTER 34

"It's time for some more pills and the ice pack." Adri sighed.

"Knock, knock." Betty came in.

"Come in, Betty. Adri just said she needed you!" Max called over his shoulder.

Betty was in the front of the settee and had a confused look on her face. Adri smiled shyly.

"Aunt Dixie, I would like you to meet Betty Ozlow, the sweet lady that is helping to take care of me. Betty, this is my Aunt Dixie Winfield. I was her responsibility for half my growing-up years."

The ladies greeted each other. "Adri needed me, and this was handy," Max gave the explanation.

Betty smiled. "Are you going to need help getting up from there?"

Max chuckled. "No, ma'am." He scooted forward a little and stood, not even jostling Adri. "Do you need to recline again?" Max asked Adri.

Adri nodded. "I'm sorry, Aunt Dixie. We need the whole settee."

Dixie jumped up. "Of course, sweet girl. It's all yours."

As soon as Adri was settled, with pills taken and ice pack placed, Max's phone rang. Max laughed. "Perfect timing." He looked at the number. "Excuse me, ladies. I need to take this call." Max strode quickly toward the library door. "Hey, Doc." Max stepped out of the library and circled to the back side of the stair case.

"Max, my man. Depending on why you wanted to know, it's either good news or bad news. I'm guessing good."

"Okay. So what is it?"

Doc laughed. "Always wanting to get to the point. Charles, the son died from a drug overdose three days ago. The old man didn't take the death well. He drank himself into oblivion and then had a major stroke and not expected to live. Still hospitalized."

"No kidding!"

"So, is it good news?"

"Yes, in the sense that they can't cause any more trouble. No, because I figure their destination is down and not up."

"Are they relatives of yours?"

"Four and five generations removed. How'd you find out so fast?"

"Looked up their address and went to visit. The only person there was the old man's sweetie. She had their last thousand dollars in her pocket and wasn't giving it to anyone, and she was fixin' to leave. Tomorrow would have been too late. I would have had to work harder for my paycheck."

"You checked all this out?"

"Oh yeah. The son will be buried by the county, and the old man is hospitalized and failing according to a sweet young nurse. They apparently had no bank account, and the neighbors talked about high living to start with but just month-to-month existence for the last five years or so. Neither worked, so no one knew their source of income."

Max asked quietly, "In all the people you talked to, was there any indication he would have had some connections to a rougher element?"

"You askin' about bad guys? Yeah. They were around off and on until he couldn't afford them anymore. About three years ago. I checked that out too. They dropped him like hot potatoes when the money could barely support his drinking and carousing and Charles's drug habit."

Max swallowed and said, "Okay, Doc. I've heard all I want. You'll send the documents and your bill?"

"Of course!"

"I have a new address. Got a pen?"

Max gave the address. "Thanks, Doc. Glad you could help with this. Take it easy."

"Hold on, Max," Doc interrupted. "Just got a note. Chester just passed away. It may take a few days longer, but I'll package it all up—death certificates and so on."

Max took a deep breath. "This information will be very important to some people I care about. Thanks, Doc."

"Hang in, Max. Glad I could help. Bye."

The connection ended.

Max stood still for a moment. He needed his brain to settle around this news. *Thank you, God! You have answered in a way I never dreamed yet perfect! Thank You!* He pulled in a deep breath and then exhaled slowly. He turned back toward the library.

After Max left, Betty asked Dixie and Adri if they would like to have something to drink.

Dixie asked, "Is hot tea with lemon too much trouble?"

Betty smiled. "Not at all. Adri, what would you like?"

"A cup of coffee, please."

Betty nodded. "I'll be back shortly."

"How do you feel about being a Wolcott? Do you even know any of them?" Dixie asked Adri in her usual blunt way.

Adri smiled. "I have reviewed family history and discovered that when I opened my business, the only sister to my father, well, her and her husband asked me to find furnishings for the house they had just purchased. It is big, like this one, and for about eight months, we spent a lot of time together to find those furnishings. I really enjoyed that. My guess is they knew who I was, but of course I didn't know who they were, that they were my family. Then just a few days ago, I met Mrs. Wolcott, my grandmother."

Adri blushed. "Oh course, I still have the habit of answering your last question first!"

Aunt Dixie laughed. "I noticed, and obviously I am still in the habit of asking too many questions at one time!"

They laughed together and then Adri spoke, "My assistant called me Ms. Wolcott last night after he found out that is my true heritage."

"Why would you tell your assistant right after finding out?" Dixie interrupted.

Adri nodded. "It was simple. Jocko, my assistant, grew up on the Wolcott Estate. Before he came to work for me in his current capacity, he was the groundskeeper for four places, so I have actually gained quite a bit of information about the Wolcotts from him. Anyway, when he called me Ms. Wolcott, it felt so right. I was sure inside me that is truly who I am!"

Dixie nodded. "I remember you crying over not being able to figure out who you really were. Those teenage years were rough for both of us. I knew you weren't a Winfield, but I did not know who you really were, so telling you, I think would have just made things worse."

"I had a brief angry thought toward you because I figure you had to know Mother was already pregnant when she married Chester. Max reasoned that you probably didn't know my heritage, and what would be the point back then to know the truth? That made sense."

Betty came in with the hot tea and coffee and carefully handed it around.

Max came in too and took the coffee cup meant for him.

"Do you have time for a cup of coffee with us?" Max asked Betty.

Betty smiled. "I'll go get it from the kitchen table."

"Adri likes being a Wolcott already," Dixie commented.

Max nodded. "She read the family history and was impressed with all she found out. I'm not surprised. They are impressive people but very ordinary too."

Betty was back and perched on the third chair in the grouping, completing the circle.

Max spoke quietly, "The phone call was from my friend, a private detective in California."

Max had their full attention. He looked at Adri. "Sweetheart, Chester and Charles are completely out of the picture as of today." Max saw the pure relief roll over Adri's face. Max knew she would completely take his word for that, even if he didn't say anymore. That was how much she trusted him. "My friend, Doc, talked to people and verified everything before he called me. The rest is a little shocking, so brace yourselves." Max paused, took a deep, cleansing breath and then a sip of coffee. "Charles died of a drug overdose three days ago. Chester drank until he collapsed and then had a massive stroke. He died this morning."

There was silence.

"God's timing is always perfect," Dixie said softly.

Max nodded. He was still watching Adri. Her eyes had widened at the news, and now she blinked and connected with Max's gaze.

Adri cleared her throat and said softly, "I was through with them seventeen years ago, even though they still haunted me. Finally, now they are through with me." Tears came to her eyes. "I am finally free!" It was a joyful statement. "Max, you have to call Connor and Grandmother! They need to know!"

Max smiled tenderly. "Yes, sweet Adri, they need to know."

Betty stood up and came to Adri. "I know we are not supposed to rejoice over people dying without salvation, but I am very glad they can no longer trouble you, honey. We rejoice your freedom with you!" Betty bent and kissed her cheek.

Adri smiled. "Thank you, Betty!" Betty gathered up the empty cups and went to finish up lunch.

Dixie sighed. "Adri, honey, have you really worked through all the bad experiences? Are you really free?"

"Aunt Dixie, since I left your home, I have been so fearful that they would one day show up on my doorstep. I was so sure they would try to ruin the rest of my life. Now I know that, at least, can't happen. So in that sense, I am free." Adri paused. "Max has been so supportive of me that I have found that I can communicate with men that are good, and I can stand up to men that are antagonists. I have found a new me. I won't say I am completely over the bad, but I don't think I will let myself be put down anymore."

Max said softly, "If there are still shadows to deal with as time goes on, she knows I am here for her."

Dixie nodded. "I have had fears of them coming back too. I recognize that the news Max gave us has released a tension in me that I have carried around for years." She stopped and then said slowly, "I have a real hard time giving out praise, so the two of you need to listen well. You probably won't hear it again." She turned to Max. "You seem to be a perfect fit for my sweet girl, and I count on you to take care of her." She turned to Adri. "I see a different person in you, Adri. You have confidence and trust and an even sweeter and more caring way of being yourself. I am proud of you both!"

Dixie had a little extra color in her face, and she stood up and announced, "I need the ladies' room. Max, will you point the way."

Max nodded, stood, and walked with Dixie out into the hall and pointed out the spot she needed to go.

After Dixie left, Adri was glowing with the words Dixie had found the courage to utter. She also smiled tenderly. Knowing Aunt Dixie as well as she did, this was truly a rare and special occurrence.

Max came in and told Adri softly, "I feel like I just received a blessing."

Adri nodded. "Treasure it."

Max laughed softly. "I am. When Dixie comes back, I will go make some phone calls."

Adri smiled. "Say hi to Grandmother for me."

"How did you know I needed to call Grandmother too?"

"Well, you said Chester went 'to them', and I assumed it would be Connor and the Grandparents that he threatened."

"Yes, you are right. According to Connor, the rest of the family have only must know details and really don't know the whole story," Max assured her.

"I am so glad. Maybe the rest of the family still has tender thoughts toward my mother."

CHAPTER 35

Dixie came back and heard Adri's wish. She smiled and told Adri. "If you are talking about the Wolcotts, yes, they do."

Adri was startled. "How do you know that?"

Dixie smiled. "I have done restorations for three of your father's siblings, and they have, or their wives, have talked about your mother to me. Always in a wishing and tender tone."

"Has it been recently or over the years?" Adri wanted to know.

Dixie laughed. "Both. Just finished a piece for Diane, and she was real chatty about you too!"

Max smiled. "I'll leave you ladies for a bit. Sounds like there is more to share."

Dixie nodded, and Adri smiled.

Adri's first question was "So you don't just *know of* the Wolcotts, you actually know some of them."

Dixie nodded. "That's why I wondered about them not taking you in. They are good Christian people and generous and kind. I am really glad that it was Chester's fault and not theirs that kept them from coming and getting you." Dixie stopped talking and her face went red. "That beast makes me so angry! He was evil incarnate!"

Adri shivered at Dixie's anger, and that disturbed her foot, and she sat up and grabbed her shin because the pain was sharp. Dixie realized what happened. "Oh, honey! I'm so sorry!" She came over and stood by the settee. "Is there anything I can do?"

Adri was a little breathless from the pain, but she reclined back and took her Aunt's hand. "No, Aunt Dixie. I just need to be still, and Max has discovered that talking to distract me is the best way for me to get away from the pain."

Dixie nodded. "Let me tell you about Conrad and Della Wolcott . . ." For the next fifteen minutes, Dixie talked not only about the Wolcotts that she had done work for but also talked about the furniture she had worked on. She had just finished when Max came in.

Max had his phone and told Adri with a smile, "Sweetheart, Grandmother would like to talk to you."

Adri blushed and smiled. "Okay." She took the phone from Max and spoke into it shyly, "Hello, Grandmother!"

Mrs. Wolcott said softly, "I have waited so long to hear you say that! Adri, are you really as excited as Max says you are? I mean to know you are a part of our family?"

Adri was still a little shy, but there was enthusiasm in her voice. "Oh yes! Jocko called me Ms. Wolcott last night, and it sounded so right!"

"Adri, you have been a part of my heart since the day I knew you were conceived, and now I plan to really get to know you. I am so pleased that you wish to truly be a Wolcott."

There was emotion in Adri's voice when she responded, "Oh, Grandmother! I really want to get to know you and all the family!"

Mrs. Wolcott had a slight tremor also when she replied, "Max will help us get together. He promised." There was a pause. "I understand you have your Aunt Dixie with you, and lunch is ready, so for right now, I will tell you I love you, and we will talk soon."

"Yes. Okay, talk to you soon."

"God bless you, child. Good-bye."

When lunch was over, Dixie said she needed to go now but promised to come back soon. Adri stayed in the kitchen with Betty, while Max walked Dixie out.

Dixie told Max, "That girl really loves you, and she is absolutely growing by leaps and bounds because of it. She is working past her hang ups. Something that really concerned me over the years."

Max smiled. "Not all because of me. She is stretching to give God a real place in her life again. From what she has said, that relationship has been estranged for quite a while."

Dixie nodded. "I know." Dixie turned to Max before getting in her pickup. "My turn. I am proud to call you cousin. It is wonderful to find a member of the Winfield family with true standards and sincere caring." Dixie reached out and gave Max a quick hug and then told him, "See you soon!"

Max smiled again. "With pleasure, Dixie."

As Dixie's pickup pulled away, Max turned and went back in the house and to Adri.

Adri smiled. "It was so good to see Aunt Dixie again! But I am so tired." She sighed.

Betty came over and gave her a hug. "It's no wonder! You have been on an emotional roller coaster for the past twenty-four hours, and your body is working on healing. I would say you need a nice long rest."

Adri nodded. "Max, I think I want to go upstairs if that's okay. I think I need a nap too."

Max grinned. "Your wish is my command. The timing is good as I have a few errands to run, and Betty can keep the pills and ice packs on schedule."

"Okay. I would like to take my mother's Bible with me," Adri requested.

Betty smiled. "I'll get it from the library. Max can get you up the stairs."

When Adri was settled comfortably on the bed and everything situated for her, Max leaned over and brushed her lips gently with his and told her, "Rest well. I'll see you later."

Adri was already feeling drowsy and smiled softly and nodded.

Betty laid the Bible beside Adri. Betty and Max left.

Adri woke slowly. The ice pack was cold, so Betty must have been in recently. Adri checked the time. She had slept almost two hours, and it was time for pills. She found them and a fresh glass of water on the bedside table and took care of that. She picked up her mother's Bible and opened it to the ownership page. She read how Margaret had filled it out. Then she just started paging through, reading marked verses. Then she was surprised to find a small handwritten note. It was her mother's writing. It was on a small notebook-size paper, dated and seemingly a note to herself about a marked scripture. Adri kept paging and found more notes. She left the notes referring to scripture where she found them.

But there were other notes, notes referring to Farran and her joy in their relationship. These notes she pulled out. Adri was thrilled. It was like finding a treasure. By the time she had leafed through the whole Bible, she had found at least two-dozen notes about Margaret's joy in Farran and his love. The last note she found was dated the day of Farran's memorial service. Margaret had written: *My darling, my life, there is new life growing in me. I never had the chance to tell you. Our child will be loved and will know who he/she is. The Wolcott name will continue, and this child will be our shining star. I can only go on because of this child. I will remember you always. I will love you always.*

Adri cried, the tears a silent memorial to her father and her mother. She now knew who her father was, at least in relationship to the love he and her mother had shared. She realized that many of the feelings her mother so eloquently penned in relation to her father were many of the same feelings Adri felt for Max.

Finally, she tucked the gathered notes back into the Bible and laid it gently back down on the bed beside her. Adri closed her eyes and just let her mind drift over what she had discovered. Then she thought about Max and the joy she found in those thoughts had her smiling.

This was how Max found her when he came in with a fresh ice pack.

"Are you awake?" he said softly.

Adri's eyes popped open. "Oh yes! Max, I love you!"

Max's smile was tender. "And I love you, sweetheart!"

Adri laughed happily. "Come sit. I want to share something with you."

Max grinned, replaced the ice pack, then sat on the edge of the bed, and told Adri, "You must have rested really well! You are glowing!"

Adri smiled shyly. "Yes, the nap was good, but what I found in my mother's Bible is the reason I am glowing! I finally have the words." Adri stopped.

Max's eyebrow went up. "The words for what?" he asked softly.

Adri blushed. "The words to tell you how I love you. My mother left notes in her Bible about how she loved my father. The notes were wonderful, and I can so relate to what she wrote about her love for him."

Max reached up and softly caressed Adri's cheek. "I would love to hear the words."

Adri grasped his hand with both of hers and rested their hands near her heart. She blushed and began in a whisper. "I love that you have seen me as a person of value from the first moment we met. I love you for your tender and caring ways. I want to be a whole person who is ready to become a part of you and be one with you. I want to enrich your life with my gifts. Gifts of joy of life and energy in being there for you. Gifts of making you laugh and giving you surprises that you enjoy. Max, I love your wisdom and your very presence. I need you, but most of all, I love you."

Max's eyes were lit with a beautiful tenderness, and his smile was gentle.

"Adri, that is wonderful!" Max searched her face and saw the eagerness, the waiting. He leaned in and kissed her with a tender and searching kiss, and Adri responded with enthusiasm and searching of her own. Max ended the kiss gently, sighed, and told Adri, "You are very tempting, and I could do that again, but to honor you, I will resist." Max laughed softly. "You are really catching onto the many components of love, and it is wonderful!"

Adri was blushing furiously. "Yes, I think I am. Thank you, Max."

Max laughed softly again. "You are most welcome, and thank you, sweetheart!"

"Now would you like to go downstairs? I have some surprises for you!"

Adri laughed. "Yes, please! I can hardly wait for your surprises!"

Max untangled the bedding and removed the ice pack. When he picked her up, he held her especially close and whispered, "My sweet Adri."

Adri hugged his neck tighter and rested her head closer as Max turned and carried her out of the room.

When they arrived in the library, Adri told Max, "I would like to sit up with the footstool."

Max nodded and set her down in the right place and got her settled. He kissed her cheek and told her, "You just wait right here." He moved around the settee and went to the far side of his desk. "Close your eyes," he told Adri.

Adri smiled and did as she was told. She heard Max come back, and his voice was at her level when he said, "These are for you."

Adri opened her eyes and saw Max on one knee, holding a bouquet of red roses. Tears came to Adri's eyes.

"Max, they are beautiful!" Adri leaned forward and smelled the closest rose. "Oh, Max, thank you! I have never gotten flowers, and I will remember this forever!"

Max laughed tenderly. "There is more." He moved the flowers to his right and set them on the occasional table. He reached into his shirt pocket and held out a beautiful diamond ring. "Adri, we have professed our love to each other in very special ways. I would be honored to place this ring on your finger as a pledge to cherish you all our lives. Adri, will you consent to marry me?"

Tears of joy were trailing down her cheeks, but her voice was steady and clear.

"Yes, Max, I will honor you by wearing your ring and . . ." After a brief pause, Adri said with excitement and joy, "Yes, I will marry you! Oh, Max, I love you!"

Max picked up her left hand and placed the ring on her ring finger while saying, "My sweet Adri, I love you!" Then he pulled her hand to his heart and leaned in and kissed her with promise, the most passionate kiss yet.

When Max pulled back, Adri was blushing and laughed happily. "Max, I have to heal before I can walk down the aisle!"

Max laughed too. "Yes, I know, but I hope I have just given you incentive to heal."

They laughed happily, and Max moved up on the settee and sat close, putting his arm around Adri. "I will tell you again that I will not rush you. When you really feel you are ready, you just need to tell me that it is time to plan our wedding."

Adri nodded and snuggled in Max's embrace. "I know. I've known since yesterday that I am forever yours and believe with all my heart that you are forever mine."

"Yes, my love, forever." Max kissed her again, this time slowly and softly.

CHAPTER 36

On Sunday morning, Max invited Adri to watch a church service with him on his computer in the library. It was the early service of the church he and Betty had attended in the city.

Max had a hard time keeping his eyes on the computer screen. Adri had dressed up this morning. She was wearing a shimmery white blouse with ruffles at the neck and down the front to her waistline. Her skirt was the prettiest shiny midnight blue he has ever seen with splashes of flower prints all over it. Her hair was pulled up in a barrette in a lose style that still let her hair nicely frame her face. She was beautiful.

Fortunately, her attention was captured by the church service unfolding on the screen and didn't notice his distraction.

When the sermon started, Max did his best to concentrate. The sermon title had certainly caught his attention. "Life is hard. God is good." The pastor talked about the ridicule Noah had to endure. He talked about the trial of faith Abraham had been through with his son Isaac. He talked about how Isaac entreated God for children when his wife was barren. He talked about the load of guilt Jacob carried for stealing his brother's birthright until he asked forgiveness of his brother, Esau. He talked about the exile of Joseph when his brothers sold him into slavery. Then he talked about all the blessings these people received when they sought and obeyed God.

Max wondered if they could have heard a more appropriate sermon for what was going on in Adri's life. Max looked at Adri. She was softly wiping tears from her face. When she noticed he was looking at her, she whispered, "God really got me today. I was already headed that direction, but I understand even more how important and necessary it is that I deal with all of it."

Max nodded. "I was holding bad feelings against Connor and most of the Wolcotts. I had something to work through too."

Adri asked, "Because of what—because of me and what we know?"

"Yes."

Adri's eyes teared up again. "Oh, Max. I'm sorry."

Max shook his head as he reached and stroked her cheek with the back of his finger.

"Don't you be sorry. You have shared things that should not have happened to you. You have the courage to work it through, and I am glad—glad that you have touched me deeply enough to open my eyes to how cruel some people can be. I have worked through most of it already, and God will use it for his good. Please. Don't be sorry!"

Adri nodded. "You said just the right thing at the right time. Again." She smiled. "How can you be so tuned in to me, to what is the right thing to say?"

Max picked up her hand and gently kissed her fingers. He smiled tenderly. "God must be giving me wisdom. I prayed for that when I barely knew you, and I continue to pray for his wisdom."

Adri nodded. Max studied her face. "You look like you want to say something."

Adri sighed. "I am a little nervous about meeting Connor."

"Ahh. Can you tell me why?"

"Max, if everything my mother wrote is accurate, he is another man who messed up my life. How do I even begin to understand and forgive? After reading his letters, I thought I would be able to listen to him and forgive him. I really hope I can, but I don't understand his foolishness. Maybe what he has to say will help me understand?" Adri felt agitated. She sighed. "Can you tell I am nervous? Why does all the hurt keep haunting me? I can't seem to understand why it's all inside me when I thought God was taking care of it? Especially knowing *they* are gone."

Max pulled her to him, his arms circling her with tenderness. "Sweetheart, it takes time and work. For me, I had to choose to let God take my pain after Karen died. Some people seem to be able to say it and get rid of it. I had to turn it over to God, sometimes on a moment-by-moment basis."

"Why do I keep calling it back? I just can't seem to let go of the past." Adri sighed again.

"You have the past right in front of you right now. Your mother's communication opened it all up again. You are taking steps, but the past will be in front of you for a while. Just because your head is making sense of it, it doesn't mean that your heart has healed."

Adri nodded against his shoulder. She pulled back. "Max, how do you know so much?"

He considered the question carefully. "I do have some experience, and I research and write about things like this. It's a gift from God."

"In so many ways, I feel like I stopped maturing as a teenager. Maybe it's because I kept hiding from the hurt instead of dealing with it."

"Sweetheart, you are not hiding from it now. You are dealing with it. Maybe not as fast as you think you should, but God is working, and his timing is so important."

Adri smile. "You and Aunt Dixie have that in common. She used that phrase a lot when I was growing up. Oh, Max, I am so glad she is truly back in my life!"

Max nodded. "She is really happy about that too! She called me this morning while you were dressing and thanked me again. Of course, she was checking on you too, and I told her we are engaged. She wants to give you away at the wedding!"

Adri laughed happily. "Okay! I will let her! There is nothing traditional about her, and it fits!"

Max chuckled quietly. "I like the idea too! It's time to take care of you again. Do you want to just recline on the settee?"

"Yes, please! I want to enjoy my roses, and I want to look at Wolcott pictures again on the computer. That is the easy part of all this. Having family, real family!"

Max grinned as he picked Adri up. "And just think you haven't even met them yet!"

Max got Adri comfortable, handed her computer to her, and went to get a glass of water and the ice pack. When he came back, he placed the ice pack and asked Adri, "Is it hurting less today? You only woke me once last night."

Adri made a face and then smiled. "The ache is constant now, and it is at a tolerable level but always there. At times I want to stretch it or twist it, but I have already found out that does not help!"

"No, that causes sharp pain," Max agreed.

"Enough about that. I need you to help me match up families. Yes, I've seen all the names on the family history, but I would like to fit the children and grandchildren with the older generation in the pictures."

Max laughed. "We have only just begun to search the family Web site. We will pull up the annual family portraits, and you'll have your matches."

Max sat on the occasional table, reached over, and punched a couple of keys, and a whole new world of pictures opened up for Adri. Adri and Max were completely absorbed in this project, and they were both a little startled when Betty came in and announced that lunch was ready.

Connor Wolcott arrived right on time. Max had settled Adri on the settee with the foot stool under her foot. She waited. Her heart was pounding double time as Max went to answer the door chimes.

Connor greeted Max with a handshake and a smile. "Thank you again, Max, for all you have done and are doing in this situation. I am here and glad to be if I can help Adri in any way."

Max nodded and greeted Connor. "Adri is in the library. She is nervous but really wants to hear you out in answering her questions."

Connor nodded. "It will not be easy, but at least there isn't the extra stress of the evil of Chester. It was such a relief to get your phone call yesterday."

As they talked, they were walking toward the library.

Max told Connor, "Adri has dealt with everything connected to Chester and Charles, so this meeting will deal with the Wolcotts."

Connor just nodded

When they got to the seating area, Max introduced them. "Adri, this is Connor Wolcott. Connor, I am pleased to introduce Adri Wolcott, my fiancé."

Adri smiled slightly and nodded.

Connor grinned. "Fiancé? Since when?"

Max told him. "I proposed last night, and she graciously consented to become my wife when she feels she is truly ready."

Connor nodded. "That's good to know. Adri, I am here for you and will tell you anything you want to know."

Max indicated that Connor sit in the chair across from the settee. Max sat beside Adri and placed his arm along the back behind Adri.

Adri nodded again, and her cheeks took on a light blush as she spoke. "Please. Tell me about Farran—my father's accident. I don't know what happened."

Connor nodded. "We had gone riding. One of our favorite things was racing. I challenged Farran before we got to the open meadow. We were still riding through the trees." Connor stopped and covered his eyes for a moment. "Farran had just looked back to where I was and didn't turn forward soon enough. A large tree branch hit him in the face and broke his neck."

There was silence until Connor added, "I challenged too soon, and Farran died because of it."

Adri nodded. "You took the blame for that, didn't you?"

Connor sighed, "Yes. At that time, I felt I was guilty of killing my brother and best friend. After the shock was past, the family rallied around me and worked on helping me to see it differently. It took several years to get my heart to accept that I wasn't guilty."

Adri let that soak in before she asked, "What really happened between you and my mother the night she left?"

Connor took a deep breath, exhaled slowly. "I said too much. Margaret had told me, three days before, how she was glad she was carrying Farran's child, but she felt ashamed to bring this kind of disgrace to the Wolcott family. I assured her that we would consider her always as a noble lady, and we would never view her as dishonorable. We would always see her as Farran's bride. She still expressed shame."

He stopped and hung his head. His voice was a little muffled as he continued. "The night she left, I told her that I would always honor my vows to my wife and children, but that I loved her and would raise her child as my own. She would always be the baby's mother, but I would be honored to fill the father figure."

Connor looked up then, and there was real pain in his voice. "I think she would have stayed if I hadn't told her I loved her. She was so fragile, emotionally, and I think that frightened her. If I had just not said that one thing, but I couldn't take it back. The next morning, my parents and I began a frantic search for Margaret. We couldn't find her."

Adri's voice was a little chocked when she asked. "Did you really love her, or was it the guilt talking?"

Connor sighed. "I was a mess of emotion and grief, and Margaret's pain was so deep I thought I loved her. Turns out, her leaving made me realize that I had said that out of regret and guilt and deep empathy for her. I cared for her, but I truly loved my wife."

Adri's eyes blurred as tears filled her eyes. She turned her face away from Connor and into Max's shoulder.

There was stress in Connor's voice as he spoke. "I'm so sorry, Adri!"

CHAPTER 37

Adri took a deep breath, and the tears were gone when she turned back to Connor.

"My mother emphasized what a wonderful family the Wolcotts are. Max confirmed that. I have acquired a lot of information about the Wolcotts over the last few days. There is an attorney of some reputation and other powerful positions among family members. Why were the Wolcotts not able to stop Chester in his threats and in the blackmail? Especially when he moved away. There had to be a way."

Connor's face lost more color, and the stress showed around his mouth. "We finally paid him a larger sum to send him to California, and we thought we might be able to come get you then. We had plans in place until two rough-looking characters showed up at a family celebration and terrified the entire family with continued threats. He didn't intend for you to ever come to us." Connor straightened his shoulders and told Adri, "As for stopping him, my father was pretty sick around that time seven years ago, and Mother was under a lot of stress and was convinced that if we involved the power vendors in the family, that Chester, in his evil, would do something that would be irreversible. She really was terrified for you and talked me out of just putting a private detective on Chester to find out about his actual influence on the bad element." Connor cleared his throat. "Mother can be very persuasive."

Adri had a faraway look when she said, "As their children, we try to listen and try to do as they ask. I remember that from my own mother." Her vision focused again, and she turned to Max. "Remember I would hide when Chester came back. My mother begged me to stay hidden, but when she was being hurt—I couldn't."

Max touched her check. "Yes, you said you needed to protect her. It shouldn't have been that way, but I understand why you felt the way you did."

Adri shook her head to shake away those memories. She turned to Connor. "Your letters to my mother after I was born really caused her a lot of stress. Didn't you realize how harmful they could be?"

Connor's face registered surprise. "She kept those letters?"

Adri nodded. Connor got up and began pacing. "I was still in rescue mode. We had found out what kind of person Chester was and wanted Margaret and you back home where you belonged. We thought that Chester was only threatening us. When Margaret wrote me a desperate note telling me to stop— that was when we found out the horror she was living with as well." Connor's voice broke with emotion when he added, "I should have known Chester would use his threats with her too."

Connor sat down and leaned forward in his chair. "Adri, we want you to know that we prayed for Margaret and you always. We wanted to do more, but we really were frightened for your life." He stood and said, "I need some fresh air. I'll walk around your house, if that's okay."

Max nodded. "Be my guest."

Connor looked at Adri. "I'll be back, and I will tell you anything else you want to know."

Adri nodded, and Connor left the room.

"How are you doing with all this?" Max asked.

Adri thought for a moment and sighed. "I don't think I was surprised at his account of Farran's death. I suspected he blamed himself for that." She thought for a moment, and a shiver of horror ran through her. "I didn't know my life was in danger. Max, did the Wolcotts really keep a watchful eye on me and keep me safe all these years?"

Max smiled gently. "I believe they did. I believe they knew where you were all the time. Connor will tell you how, if you ask him."

"You spent so much time with them. Did you ever hear of me?"

Max sighed. "I have been trying to remember. Since Grandmother's name is Adrianne and my name is Adriaan, I really can't say. If I heard anything about you, I don't recall being curious or gaining any information that would have clued me in. Connor told me you were well known in the family, but I wasn't included." Max paused. "That stung a little. I felt so much a part of the family, yet I don't believe I knew anything about you."

"They are only human, Max."

Max smiled gently. "I said something about that to you once."

Adri nodded. "It's a good thing you did. As the information settles into my heart, I am finding I can allow for their human mistakes." She looked down and twined her fingers together and then added, "I am not as upset about new information generally like I thought I would be."

Connor was standing in the doorway of the library, and he cleared his throat. Max and Adri looked up. Adri smiled a true smile where her right brow elevated slightly.

"Please, come in." Her voice was warm and welcoming.

Connor paused. Adri was beautiful in her own way when she smiled like that. He had thought she was the exact image of her mother, but now he realized, this was truly her own beauty. He smiled in return and came toward them.

"Am I not a monster anymore?"

Max smiled, and Adri continued to smile as she replied softly, "You were never a monster. A very human and caring person but not a monster."

Connor sobered. "I made a lot of mistakes."

Adri nodded. "Human mistakes. I will admit that some of what happened, to my way of thinking, falls under the heading of foolishness. I do wonder. Would Chester have known to come to you to blackmail if you hadn't come to his house to try to claim me?"

Connor frowned. "I don't know. It never occurred to me. I would have thought that Margaret would have told him since she was marrying him."

Adri shook her head. "I don't think so. In her journal pages, she mentioned that you had almost found her, and she quickly accepted Chester's marriage proposal. She married him to stay hidden from your family."

Connor covered his face with his hands and groaned. He shook his head and let his hands fall. "I guess that falls on me too. I should have never gone to his house."

Adri glanced at Max. She wasn't sure she should ask the next question. He seemed to realize she may need his approval and just slightly nodded his head.

"Connor, all those years ago, were you an impulsive person?" Adri asked.

Connor looked a little confused, but he answered, "No. I have always been very deliberate and think things through." He paused like he was thinking and then continued slowly. "Farran's death did mess me up. The family says I was different. They never named it." Connor stopped again. He sighed. "You ask that question because of a lot of the other things we have talked about."

Adri nodded.

Max spoke quietly. "Connor, I am aware that grief changes some people. Do you think maybe your grief over Farran perhaps had you scrambling to fix things that you believed you caused?"

"I will admit to being frantic and hopeless. I recognized that in me the moment Farran fell to the ground. Since the guilt hung on so long . . . Yes, my actions were more impulsive than deliberate then. I'm sorry."

There were tears shimmering in Adri's eyes when she told Connor, "You made a lot of wrong choices, but so did my mother. I was able to forgive her, and I do forgive you. You had no intention of messing things up." The tears trickled slowly down Adri's cheeks. "I'm sorry my questions have brought new sorrow to you."

Connor's expression softened, and he told Adri, "No, child, you don't need to apologize. I understand your need to know, and I came here today to help you, regardless of the cost to me. I know I can't make up for all the lost years, but right now, I am interested in as fresh and clean a start with you as is possible." His voice softened. "Adri, I would still like to be your father figure. I would like to do that for you and for your father."

Adri's tears came faster. With emotion in her voice, she said quietly, "It just hurts so badly right now. I hurt for all of us."

Max shifted and gently pulled her to him. "Sweetheart, I hurt too. Life isn't easy, and sometimes it is really unfair, but God will carry us when we need him to. Give your hurt to him."

Adri nodded, and Max supplied the tissues. After a minute, Adri had herself pulled together. She told Max, "I need a break. Betty needs to help."

Max nodded. "I'll go tell Betty and then come get you."

"Okay." Adri turned to Connor. "I need a short break, and then I hope we can get on to more pleasant questions."

Connor smiled gently. "You take your time. I am here for you today."

Adri nodded as Max came back, lifted her, and carried her out of the room.

CHAPTER 38

Max settled her reclining on the settee and placed the ice pack. Adri asked Connor, "Please, could you move to the chair one over so I can still see you?"

Connor stood up and moved as asked. "Yes, of course."

"Thank you. Betty is bringing coffee for all of us."

Connor nodded. Just then, Betty came in with the tray of coffee. Max took it from her and served Adri and then Connor and took his own coffee before he sat to the right of Connor.

Adri sipped her coffee and then asked, "On the Wolcott Family Tree that Max printed out for me, my name and birth date are correct according to my real birth certificate. I have always celebrated my birthday on the first of June, and I did not know that the Anne in my name is actually the first of two middle names. How could you get it right on the family tree when I didn't even know?"

Connor sat forward in his chair and held his coffee cup with both hands. He smiled. "I didn't know it was there until Max told me the other day when he called. I have a granddaughter, Jennifer, who is really into genealogy. I called her and asked her to explain." Connor chuckled. "She had never heard her grandpa so unhappy, so she was pretty quick with her answer. She had apparently been searching the Internet for your birth certificate and didn't have any luck. One day, she was doodling and decided the name Adrianne could be two names. So she did the search that way and had a hit in Texas. From there, it was easy, she said. She knew it was a family secret, but she just could not keep the new information to herself, so she posted."

Adri smiled. "That is John and Carol's eldest. What is she, about twelve?"

Connor looked surprised and answered, "Almost twelve. She is a wiz on the computer and has been doing the genealogy for almost two years already."

"Sounds like another history buff in the family," Adri told both of them.

Max chuckled, and Connor smiled.

Adri was shy when she asked the next question. "Max tells me you have kept track of me all these years. Will you tell me about that?"

Connor smiled big now. "You had assigned guardian angels everywhere. Do you remember Mrs. Addison in junior high?" Adri nodded. "All we asked of our angels was to try to be close enough to you so they would know what was going on with you. Mrs. Addison told us when you were in the hospital with a burst appendix, how your grades were, if you were dealing okay with the bumps in your life. That kind of thing."

Adri sighed. "Do you know that Mrs. Addison was my only visitor in the hospital, and she came every day! It meant so much to me."

"She cared about you, not just to help us out."

Adri nodded. She thought for a moment. "Jonesy. She was my angel in high school."

Connor chuckled. "Yes. Virginia Jones. We still stay in touch, telling her about you."

Adri had a weary expression now. "Did you pay these people to do this?"

Connor smiled broadly. "Not a penny. Your grandmother had her sources, and when she found out who might help us out, she would invite them over, feed them, and ask if they would be willing to be your angel. You would have to know your grandmother to understand how well it worked."

Adri took a deep breath and asked, "Who was it in college?"

"Your roommate, Cindy. While you were working on your place down the hill, it was Amanda, your yard lady."

"No kidding! I was paying her according to her contracted estimate, and I wondered why she spent so much time at my place."

Connor smiled gently. "You have a lot of people who care about you."

Tears came to Adri's eyes. "I still kept to myself a lot, but they always seemed to be there at the right time." Adri wiped her eyes. "I guess when I opened for business, it was Dom and Diane."

"Yes. They were thrilled to get to know you and were disappointed when their house was full, but their friends kept coming, at least a dozen different ones before you hired Jocko."

Adri sat up straight, and her face lit up. "Jocko is my angel now?"

Connor and Max both chuckled. Connor nodded. "Your grandmother was concerned about that. It was the first man we recruited. But the only people around you on a consistent basis were men."

Connor chuckled again. "Jocko actually came to us after he made Dan's acquaintance. After his first few days of working for you, he already thought the world of you and was glad to tell us about you."

Adri blushed and smiled. "It is wonderful to hear a different perspective about the people that played such important roles in my life. I stay in touch with all those angels with a letter and Christmas card every year."

Max said gently, "You told me and Betty that you didn't have anyone, and I know that was true right now, but you have certainly had a lot of some ones."

Adri laughed happily. "I am blessed."

Everyone had finished their coffee. Max got up and gathered up the cups and placed them on the tray. After he was seated again, Adri asked, "This is a question that I'm asking out of curiosity. Did the money you and Grandmother paid Chester put a strain on things for you? You don't have to answer if you choose not to."

Connor shifted forward in his chair and answered, "Your father had made a lot of money and invested well before he died. My occupation is financial management, and I took over the needs of his estate. My parents agreed that using Farran's money was how we needed to take care of you. So in a sense, your father took care of you in the financial arrangement we had with Chester. The original investments are still in place, and it was interest money that made the payments."

Adri was stunned. She couldn't form any words to respond.

Connor continued gently, "Your father's estate belongs to you, and you can claim it anytime you want to."

Adri's eyes widened with a startled expression on her face. She looked at Max and then at Connor and asked in a whisper.

"I am inheriting from my father?"

Connor smiled. "Farran had already made a will before he died, leaving it all to your mother, and on her death, it was to go to any offspring. That is you, sweet Adri. It wasn't the family that made that choice. It was Farran."

"It's almost like he knew about me!" Adri whispered, almost to herself.

Connor nodded. "The will was finalized right before he and your mother came to visit that week. We somehow felt that he must have had an instinct anyway."

Adri took a deep breath and let it out slowly. "This is very much unexpected." Adri shook her head a little. Max saw a troubled look crossed her face. She shook her head again, and the troubled look was gone. "Uncle Connor, I will have to let that soak in!"

Connor's face flushed a little, and he blinked quickly. "Does the 'uncle' mean you have mostly forgiven me?"

A tear trickled slowly down one cheek. "Yes, Uncle Connor. I already told you I have forgiven you. I may still have a few things to work on, but God kind of set me up for this, so I choose to follow my heart."

Connor couldn't blink the tears away this time. "Oh, my sweet Adri girl. Thank you." He stood and came to her, leaned in, and kissed Adri's cheek.

Max came and stood behind the settee and tucked his handkerchief into Adri's hand as Connor reached into his own pocket.

Adri said softly, "My questions have run out, and I need some rest."

Connor nodded. "I am available and will be here for you. Whatever you need. You or Max can just call. Our time of separation is over."

Max cleared his throat and told Connor. "I have your number."

Connor blew his nose and then answered, "Yes. Now Abby is waiting to hear about this afternoon. I need to go home." Connor turned back to Adri. "You and I will get to know each other. I've loved you like my own daughter all these years, and I like you already, but I really want to know you."

Adri mopped some new tears and told him, joy in her voice, "I have a family now! I want to know all of you! Uncle Connor, I need a hug."

Connor bent and hugged Adri, her arms going around his neck. Connor held her close and then finally straightened. He had to clear his throat before he asked, "Max, will you walk me out?" Max nodded. Connor turned back to Adri. "I'll only keep him a minute, and I will call you soon. I love you, Adri."

Adri nodded. "Please call soon."

Max walked Connor out to the veranda. Connor asked, "You know her. Is Adri okay?"

Max tilted his head and asked, "Why are you asking? Adri is a very open person right now. Claiming the Wolcott name has given her a lot of confidence."

Connor shook his head. "She seemed to withdraw in some way when I told her about her inheritance."

Max nodded. "I noticed that too. Something is troubling her about that, but she didn't say what. It will come out in time. Connor, don't be too concerned about that. Just go home and share with Abby and the family. Adri means it when she says she wants to be part of the family."

Connor nodded. "Thank you, Max, for everything."

They shook hands, and Max told him, "You have a good evening."

CHAPTER 39

Max went back to the library and was surprised to see Adri in tears. He went to her and asked gently, "Adri, sweetheart, what is it?"

"Oh, Max. It's the same thing all over again!" Adri's voice was heavy with emotion, and the tears came faster.

Max knelt by the settee and gathered Adri close. The tears turned to sobs. Adri's hands had gathered some of Max's shirt into her fists. She clung to him and cried. Max just held her and stroked her hair gently.

Max's thoughts were racing. *It has to be the inheritance. She was good with everything else. How can it be the same thing all over again? Wait. Dixie said Adri asked a lot of questions about her inheritance from her mother. There must have been something unanswered. What could it be? God, she is crying like she is deeply hurt. What about an inheritance could hurt her this bad? Unless . . . unless she has their money but doesn't have them! Oh god! How do I help her with this? Does she blame you? Does she feel she is being punished with their leftovers? God, give me wisdom here!*

Adri's sobs had stopped, and her hold on his shirt loosened. Adri's voice was flat when she asked, "Please, Max, I need a cold cloth and a glass of ice water."

Max laid her gently back against the pillows. "I'll be right back, sweetheart," he promised.

Max stood and went for what Adri asked for. He prayed the whole time he was gone. When he got back, he handed the glass of water to Adri. When she finished with it, he took it and set it down, and then he knelt and began bathing Adri's face gently with the cold cloth. Adri had closed her eyes and just rested as Max ministered to her.

When he stopped, Adri opened her eyes and noticed the wrinkles in Max's shirt. "I'm sorry. I messed up your shirt." There still wasn't much emotion in her voice.

Max knew she needed to talk but wondered if she was just too tired, so he asked. "Do you need to rest or nap right now?"

Adri gave a slight nod. "Yes, I think so."

Max kissed her forehead gently and told her, "I am going to quote a scripture verse to you. 'Remember ye not the former things, neither consider the things of old. Behold, I will do a new thing; now it shall spring forth: shall ye not know it? I will even make a way in the wilderness and rivers in the desert.'" Then Max told her, "I will be at my desk. You rest."

It was about thirty minutes later, Adri spoke. "Max, where is that scripture in the Bible?"

Max answered softly, "Isaiah43:18 and 19."

Adri asked another question. "When is dinner? I smell something really good!"

Max was there standing by the settee. "Fifteen minutes or so. Are you feeling a little better?"

Adri reached for Max's hand. "Yes. I need to talk about it after dinner. But your verses really have me thinking," Adri sighed. "The pain was very real in my heart!"

Max sat down on the occasional table. "I knew you were really hurting, and when you can tell me, maybe the healing can start. I so wanted to take your hurt on myself, but when it is that personal, I was helpless. All I could do is hold you."

"It is enough for now. Thank you, Max."

Max smiled gently. "I love you."

Adri blushed and smiled in return. "I know."

Max asked, "Do I need to get Betty to help you before dinner is on the table?"

"I think you can just take me there. I will manage on my own this time."

"Are you sure? It's almost time for pills again and the ice pack."

"Please, my love, let me try."

Max sighed. "Okay. Are you ready?"

When Max had her situated at the table with her foot up and the ice pack on, Adri's comment was "I am so glad to have it up again. Sure is a good thing I have so many other things occupying me now, or I would go crazy." Adri tried to get a smile. "You realize I am a doer, not a sit stiller!"

It worked. Betty and Max both laughed as Betty set the casserole dish down on the table.

Max nodded. "I really wonder how long we will be able to keep you with your foot up. I am guessing I will be taking you to the showroom soon."

Adri's eyes were laughing, but her face remained serious. "Very soon!"

Max smiled tenderly. "We will pray and get this meal eaten for now."

Adri nodded, and they all bowed their heads while Max said the prayer.

Adri decided to get the nighttime chores done and settled into bed. Her body was weary, and the bed seemed to be really appealing.

After that was accomplished, Adri invited Max to pull up the chair from the corner.

"We are going to talk. Hand me the tissue box in case I need it."

Max did as he was asked and got comfortable in the chair. "I am ready to share what is troubling you."

Adri nodded. "On my twenty-first birthday, Aunt Dixie sat me down and presented me with my inheritance from my mother. Everything that she had inherited from her parents was put into a trust that was to be available to me that day. Aunt Dixie had all the paperwork, bank statements, and so on. She also had a separate folder of bank statements showing how much money had accumulated off my mother's two oil wells. Max, I became very rich that day. Mother's inheritance is still untouched. I was able to do everything to start my business from the oil well money, and I did not scrimp on anything that I decided to do."

Adri had told all this in a matter-of-fact tone of voice. "And I still didn't use it all. But it has been accumulating again because I make a good living off my business and don't need the money."

Max said softly, "I understand that kind of shock would leave you overwhelmed. When you were crying earlier, I sensed it was deep hurt."

Tears came to Adri's eyes but briefly. Adri nodded. "That hurt was over my mother choosing to leave me. She chose to take her life and leave *me* alone. She made sure I was financially cared for, but I felt I wasn't important enough for her to stay with me."

Max nodded. "I think I hear you saying that the deep hurt was again over your father taking care of you but not being in your life."

"That is exactly why I was crying and why I said it was the same thing all over again. I have his money, but I never had him. But now I can put that in the same envelope with the hurt over Mother, and I can seal it and give it to God."

"You say that like maybe you're done with all that hurt," Max stated softly.

Adri nodded her head. "Having discovered what she had to live with beyond what I already knew and knowing my father made one bad choice with no coming back. Then the verse you quoted, 'Remember ye not the former things, neither consider the things of old.' And there is Jeremiah 29:11, 'For I know the thoughts that I think toward you, saith the Lord, thoughts of peace, and not of evil, to give you an expected end.' Max, God is telling me that he was always in charge of my life, always taking care of me. If I truly believe that, and I really do now, then regardless of the choices of others, God never left me alone and brought me to here, to today, and verse 19 is coming true right now. 'Behold, I will do a new thing; now it shall spring forth, shall ye not know it?' He is allowing several new things in my life that are to be celebrated. The hurt is truly in God's hands now." Adri finished with such a sweet smile.

Max cleared his throat, but there was still emotion when he told Adri, "This is a really big discovery and a big step for you. I am so thankful God has opened up your heart to his very real presence."

Hearing the emotion in Max's voice, she knew how deeply it touched him, and tears shimmered in her eyes now. Adri took a deep breath, blinked the tears away, and continued. "Now comes the last part of Isaiah 43:19. 'I will even make a way in the wilderness and rivers in the desert.' I think I have a couple of uncles who can help me set things up, but I need ideas."

Max thought for a moment before he asked, "A way to use the money that is yours but don't know what to do with?"

Adri laughed softly. "You track with me so well. It still startles me a little."

Max smiled. "I love you so much, and I try really hard to get it right!"

Adri reached out her hand, and Max enveloped it in both of his.

"Max, we need to pray about how God wants to use the money 'to make a way in the wilderness and rivers in the desert!' I was thinking of donating to already existing foundations and/or creating new foundations. But every bit of that thinking is very limited. I haven't peeked into the outside world much, but I know I want to help others who are or have suffered abuse. A hint of the direction I am thinking."

Max nodded. "My thinking is in the direction of abuse victims and maybe victims of violence. We need to search the Internet for what is already out there."

Adri smiled. "And I should probably warn Uncle Connor about all this. I realize he has worked hard over the years to keep the estate intact in the event I was to claim it, but depending what all is involved, he may have to sell things. That may be hard for him."

Max looked at Adri for a long moment, and then he told her, "Sweetheart, in your own sweet way, you are concerned about his feelings. This is new for you, isn't it?"

Adri blushed. "Yes. I am so blessed and want to share, but I really don't want to offend or hurt my new family. They are very important to me!"

Max smiled. "When you get to know them, you will discover generous and giving people. I am actually looking forward to your talk with Connor. He may surprise you."

"I am so glad you know my family! That is something else that makes you special to me!"

Max smiled tenderly, "Thank you, sweetheart!" He stood and bent and kissed Adri soundly. When he moved back, she was blushing and smiling.

Adri told him, "I am ready to start planning our wedding. We can set the date, but it needs to be at least ten weeks. I don't want to limp down the aisle!"

Max grinned. "I checked the calendar earlier, and that would be the week after your birthday!"

Adri laughed happily. "That works for me!"

EPILOGUE

Adri's foot was slow in healing. It was three weeks before she could handle leaving her foot down for more than an hour at a time. At six weeks, she suffered the pain to at least hobble to the bathroom in her bedroom. At eight and a half weeks, she discarded the crutches for a cane; and finally on her birthday, she limped just a little, and the limp disappeared by the wedding day.

Adri and Max were busy. Once the foot would tolerate being down enough for Adri to use crutches, she spent some time in her showroom, especially when Jocko went to auctions.

Max took her to different Wolcott homes as the invitations came in. Grandmother decided that Adri should meet smaller groups first and that the wedding would be the large celebration with everyone there.

Grandmother and Aunt Dixie helped with the wedding plans, and it was decided that the wedding would take place on the Wolcott Estate in the beautiful garden. Beautiful because Jocko's father, then Jocko, and now his brother, Simon, worked so hard to keep it beautiful.

They spent more time at Max's friend, John's house, or invited his family over for a meal. John's wife, Carol, and Adri clicked right away; and their daughter, Jennifer, became Adri's shadow and buddy. Adri chose Carol, John's wife, to be her matron of honor, and John would be the best man. Jennifer would be the junior bridesmaid, and her brother, Dillon, would be the junior groomsman.

The auctions Jocko attended continued to garner furniture for Max's home, and by the middle of May, most rooms were furnished and decorated to Adri's satisfaction.

Adri and Max grew closer as they spent time in Bible reading each day and spent the majority of the days in each other's company. Adri still went to Betty about "Mom" things, and their relationship became very solid.

Adri wasted no time in going to her uncle Connor and talking about foundations. Adri told him that she would like for him to take over her trust as well, and Connor felt honored that Adri would trust him to do that. Connor assured her that he thought she had some really good ideas in wanting to use her millions to help people and agreed that after the honeymoon, they would sit down and get serious about arranging things. Connor also suggested that her uncle Conrad needed to be in on setting things up, as that was one of his specialties.

Her uncle Connor also persuaded Adri to let her father's estate pay for the wedding, reminding her that fathers did that for their daughters.

The night before the wedding, Adri stayed at Grandmother's home. Grandmother told Adri that she had the same zest for life that her father had, but she complimented Adri on enjoying a slower pace than her father.

The wedding day dawned bright and clear and only mild humidity. Adri and Grandmother had a quiet breakfast enjoying each other's company.

The ceremony would begin at 10:30 a.m. Max would dress at John and Carol's before coming over. Aunt Dixie arrived so she and Grandmother could help Adri into her dress. Her dress was her mother's. The one she intended to wear in three short weeks from the anniversary of her father's memorial service. But as her mother wrote—it was not to be. Grandmother had saved the dress, and Adri was thrilled! As she slipped into the beautiful gown, she felt her mother was smiling down on her.

Adri and Aunt Dixie waited inside the double French doors of the library while guests found chairs arranged on the lawn. Carol and Jennifer arrived and joined them. They all watched as Max in his black tuxedo, and his groomsmen and the pastor took their spots. On the appropriate music, the ladies moved out of the house. When it was their turn, Aunt Dixie took Adri's hand, and together they moved toward the fountain where the ceremony would take place.

As they approached, Max locked his tender gaze with Adri's, and Adri had the sensation of floating the last few steps. When the music stopped, the pastor asked solemnly, "Who gives this woman to this man?"

Aunt Dixie said, "I do with joy!" Instead of stepping forward to join Max and Adri's hands, she stood still and released Adri's hand.

Then Adri heard rustlings behind her, and she turned her head to look. Aunt Dixie turned her by the shoulders, so she was fully facing the guests. The entire Wolcott family was standing, as was Jocko and Gina, Dan, Brad, Kim, Denny, Amanda, Cindy, Virginia Jones, Catherine Addison, and Betty, of course.

Uncle Connor gave the signal, and the standing crowd gave a joyful "we do!"

Then they all sat. Immediately tears sprang to Adri's eyes, and she was laughing happily. Aunt Dixie was prepared and handed Adri a handkerchief. When Adri was in control again, Aunt Dixie turned her back to Max, took their hands and joined their hands, and went to sit in her chair.

The pastor continued with the ceremony. Adri was aware that she said the right things at the right times, but she was still dazed by the wonderful surprise of every last one of the special people in her life enthusiastically and joyfully giving her into Max's care.

Then the pastor told Max, "You may kiss your bride."

Max bent close to her ear and whispered, "I love you." Then he kissed her soundly.

The pastor asked them to turn to the guests, and he pronounced, "I present to you Mr. and Mrs. Max Winfield." There was applause and wolf whistles as the music started. Max bent and swung Adri into his arms and carried her to the veranda.

Adri held his face and kissed him. She asked, "Did you know they were going to do that?"

Max of course knew what she was talking about and told her. "No, I did not! But I loved it and know that they all love us both!"

Adri nodded. "Oh, Max! God is wonderful! This family is wonderful! Life is wonderful!"

Max grinned. "Amen!"

Printed in the United States
By Bookmasters